"Young
readers will happily
fall in line."
—**Kirkus Reviews**

"Frolicsome
and breathlessly
paced."
—**Booklist**

"Eye-grabbing black-and-pink graphics."
—**Publishers Weekly**

"The whole package is fresh and
funny and even philosophical when
it comes to values that third-
graders understand."
—**San Francisco
Chronicle**

Be sure to read **all** the **BABYMOUSE** books:

#1 BABYMOUSE: Queen of the World!
#2 BABYMOUSE: Our Hero
#3 BABYMOUSE: Beach Babe
#4 BABYMOUSE: Rock Star
#5 BABYMOUSE: Heartbreaker
#6 CAMP BABYMOUSE

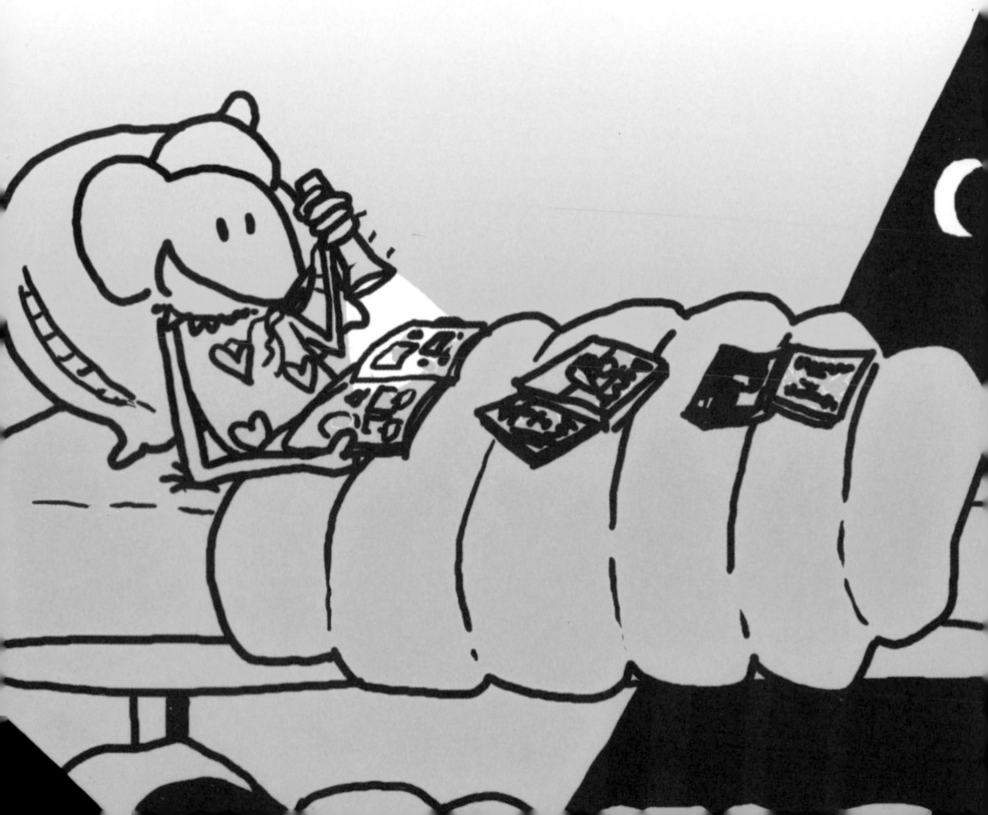

BY JENNIFER L. HOLM & MATTHEW HOLM

RANDOM HOUSE  NEW YORK

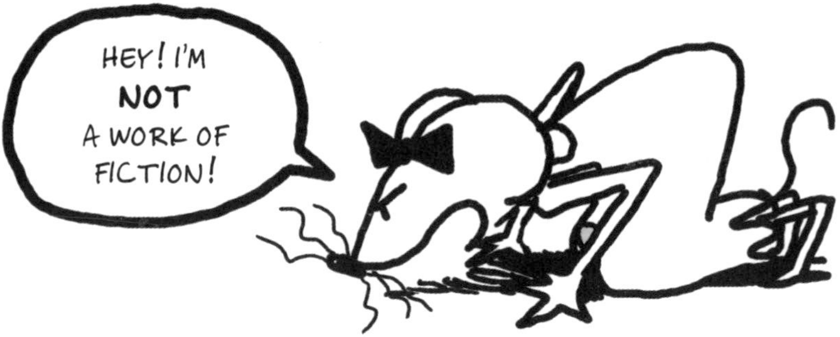
HEY! I'M **NOT** A WORK OF FICTION!

This is a work of fiction. Names, characters, places, and incidents either are the product of the author's imagination or are used fictitiously. Any resemblance to actual persons, living or dead, events, or locales is entirely coincidental.

Published in the United States by Random House Children's Books, a division of Random House, Inc., New York.

www.randomhouse.com/kids
www.babymouse.com

Educators and librarians, for a variety of teaching tools, visit us at www.randomhouse.com/teachers

Library of Congress Cataloging-in-Publication Data
Holm, Jennifer L.
Babymouse : Camp Babymouse / Jennifer L. Holm and Matthew Holm.
p. cm.
ISBN: 978-0-375-83988-7 (trade) — ISBN: 978-0-375-93988-4 (lib. bdg.)
1. Graphic novels. I. Holm, Matthew. II. Title. III. Title: Camp Babymouse.
PN6727.H592B26 2007 741.5—dc22 2006050391

PRINTED IN MALAYSIA 10 9 8 7 6 5 4 3 2 1 First Edition

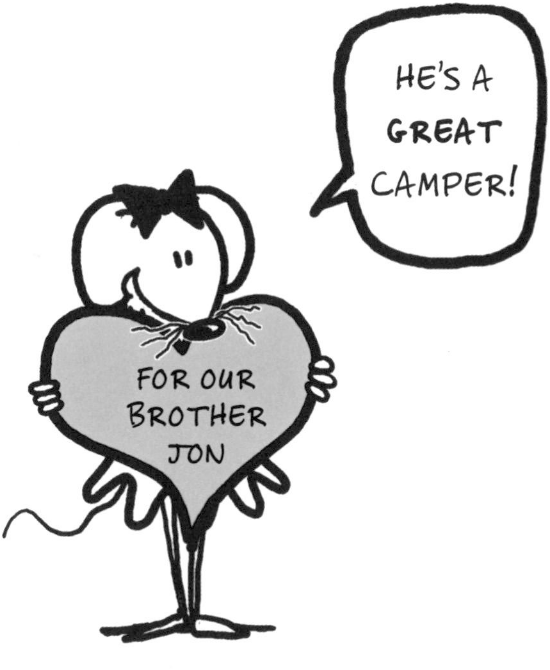
HE'S A **GREAT** CAMPER!
FOR OUR BROTHER JON

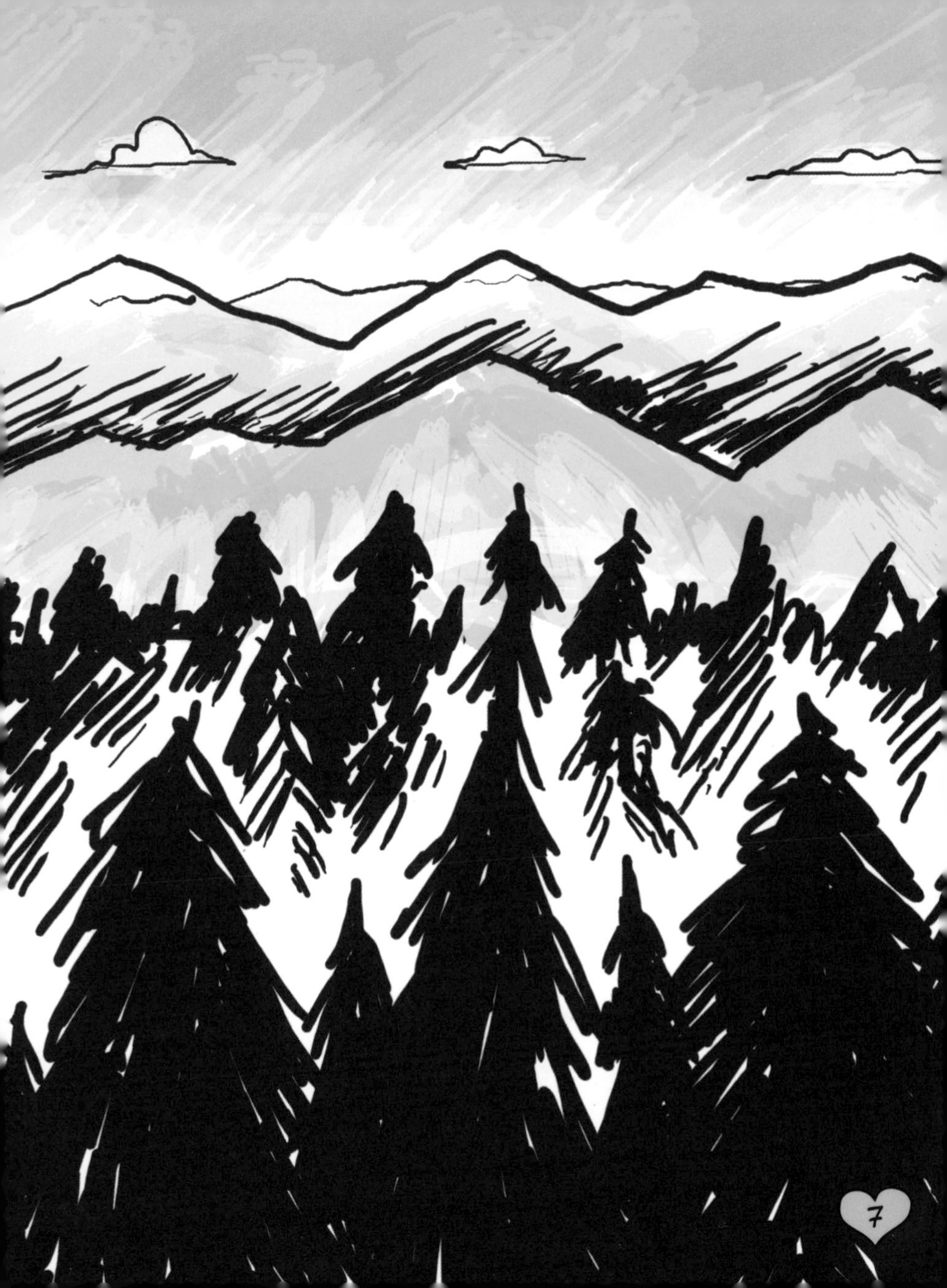

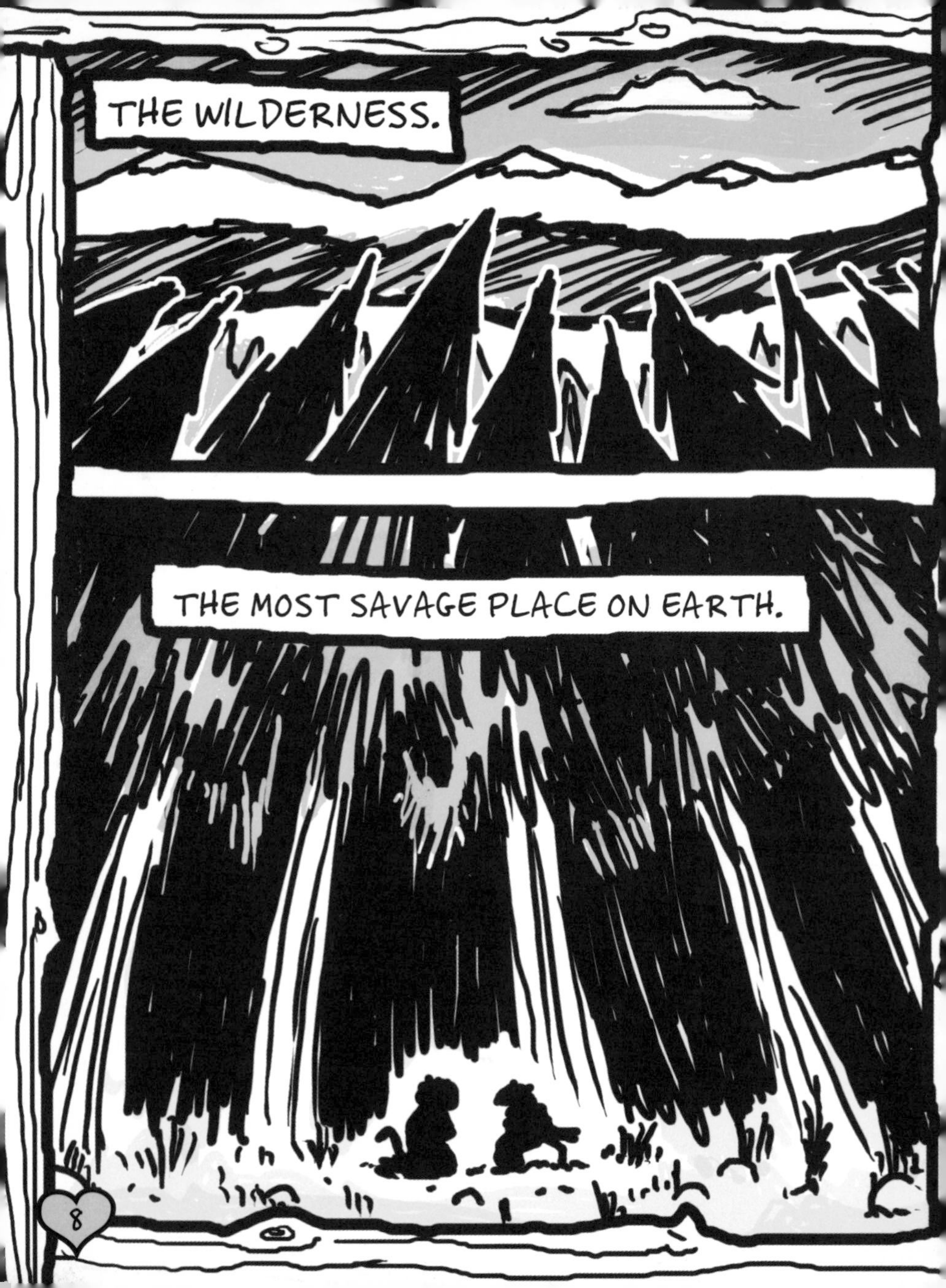
THE WILDERNESS.
THE MOST SAVAGE PLACE ON EARTH.

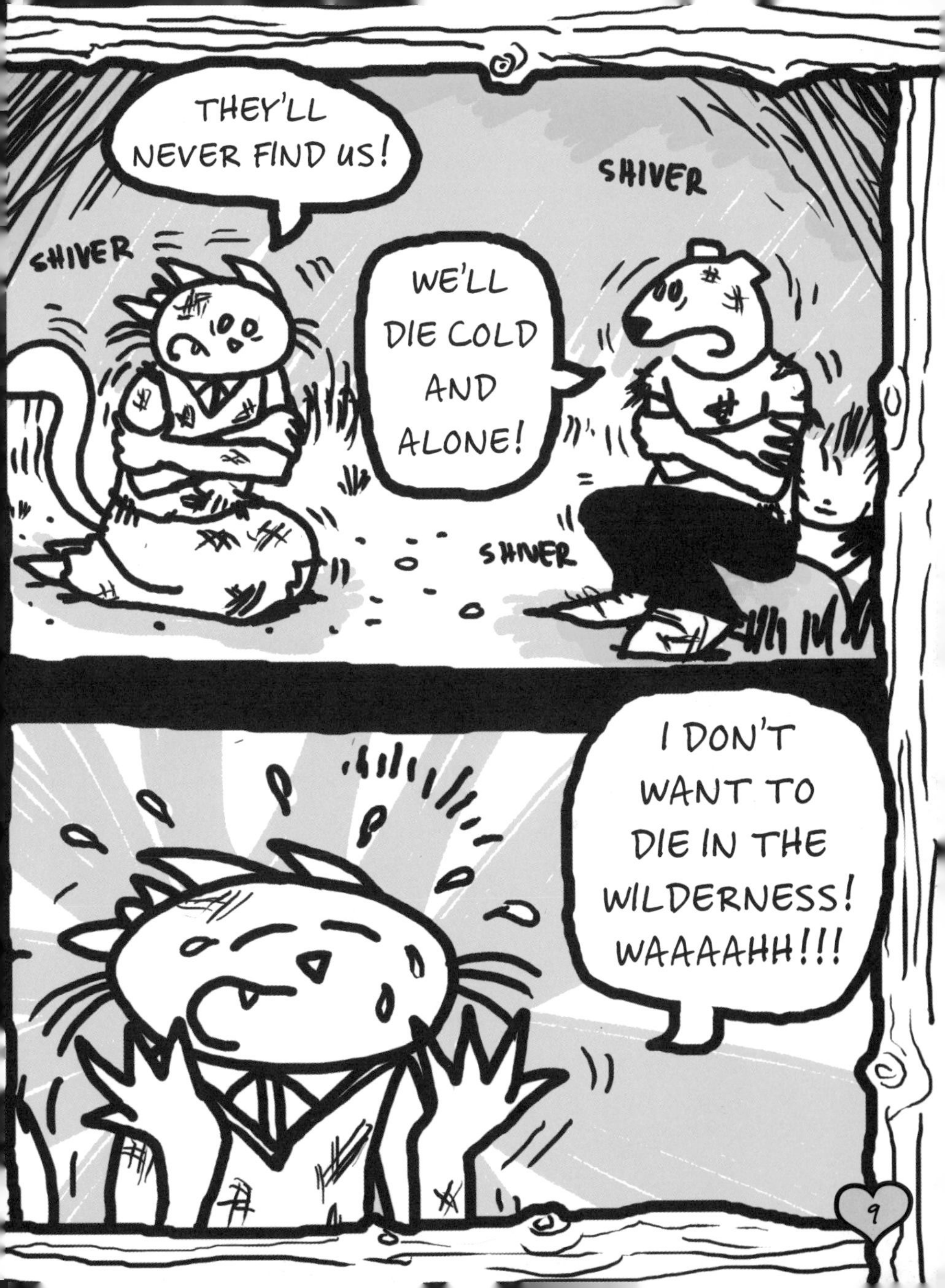
THEY'LL NEVER FIND US!
SHIVER
SHIVER
WE'LL DIE COLD AND ALONE!
SHIVER
I DON'T WANT TO DIE IN THE WILDERNESS! WAAAAHH!!!

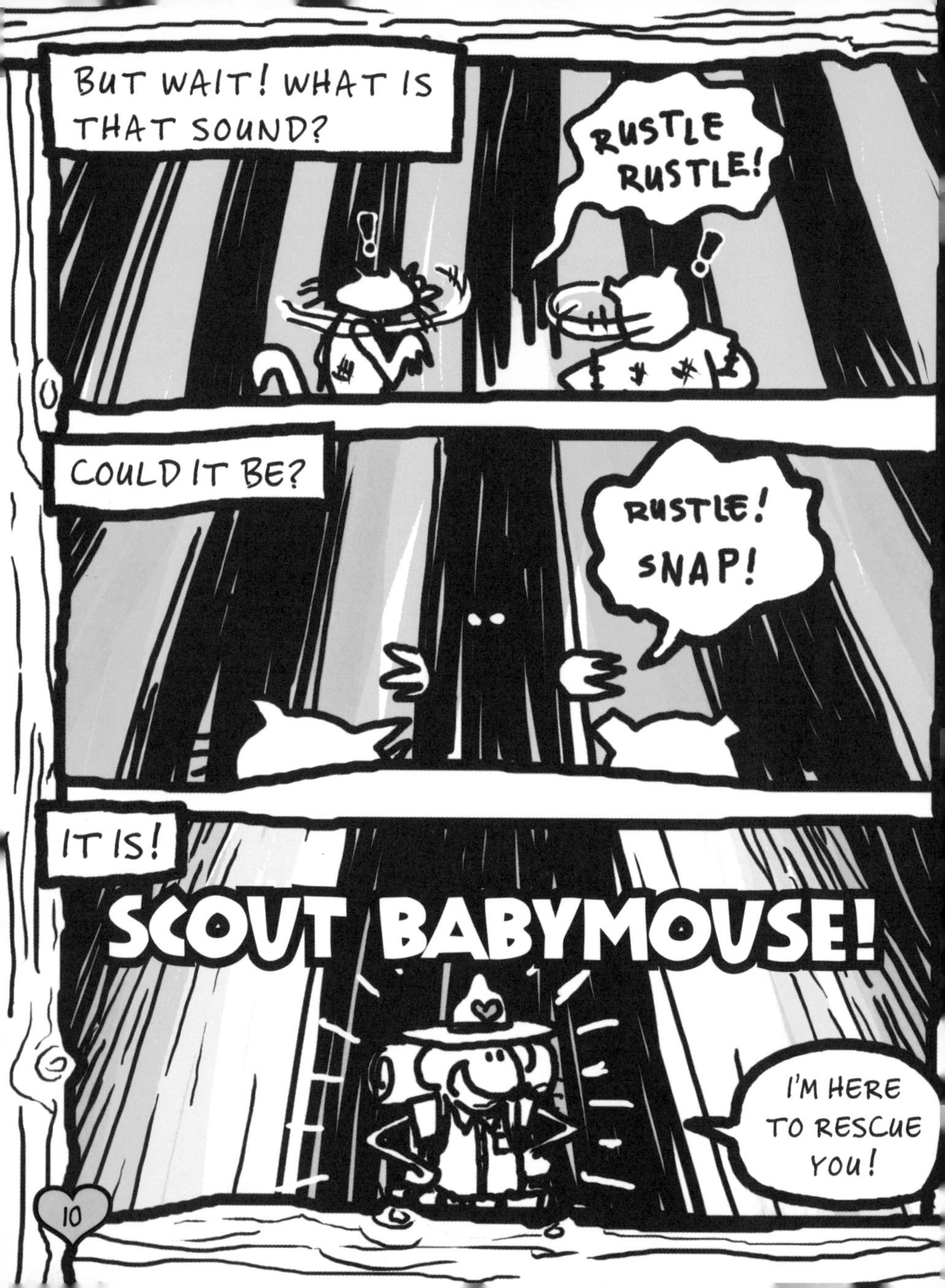
BUT WAIT! WHAT IS THAT SOUND?
RUSTLE RUSTLE!
COULD IT BE?
RUSTLE! SNAP!
IT IS!
SCOUT BABYMOUSE!
I'M HERE TO RESCUE YOU!

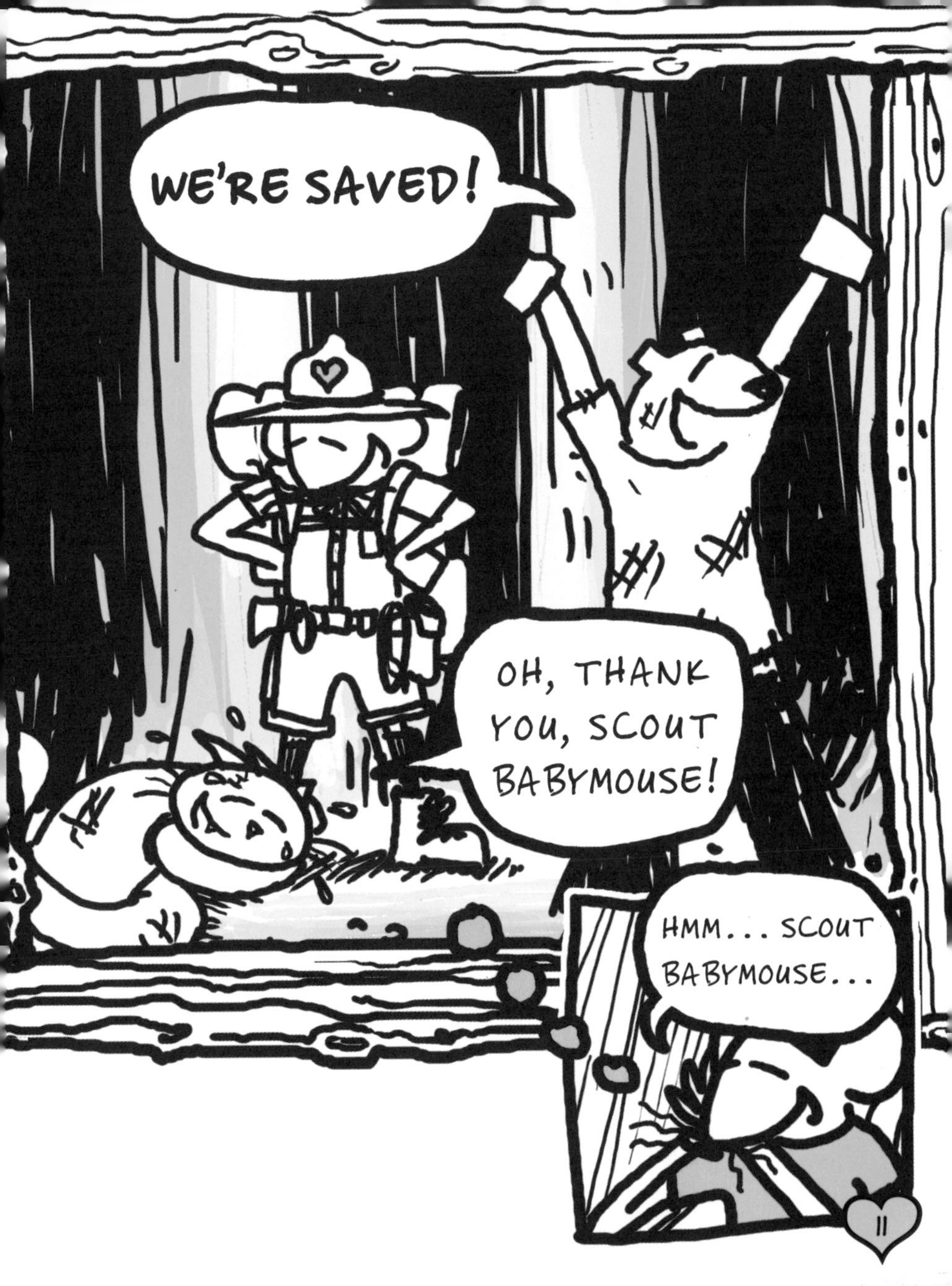
WE'RE SAVED!
OH, THANK YOU, SCOUT BABYMOUSE!
HMM... SCOUT BABYMOUSE...

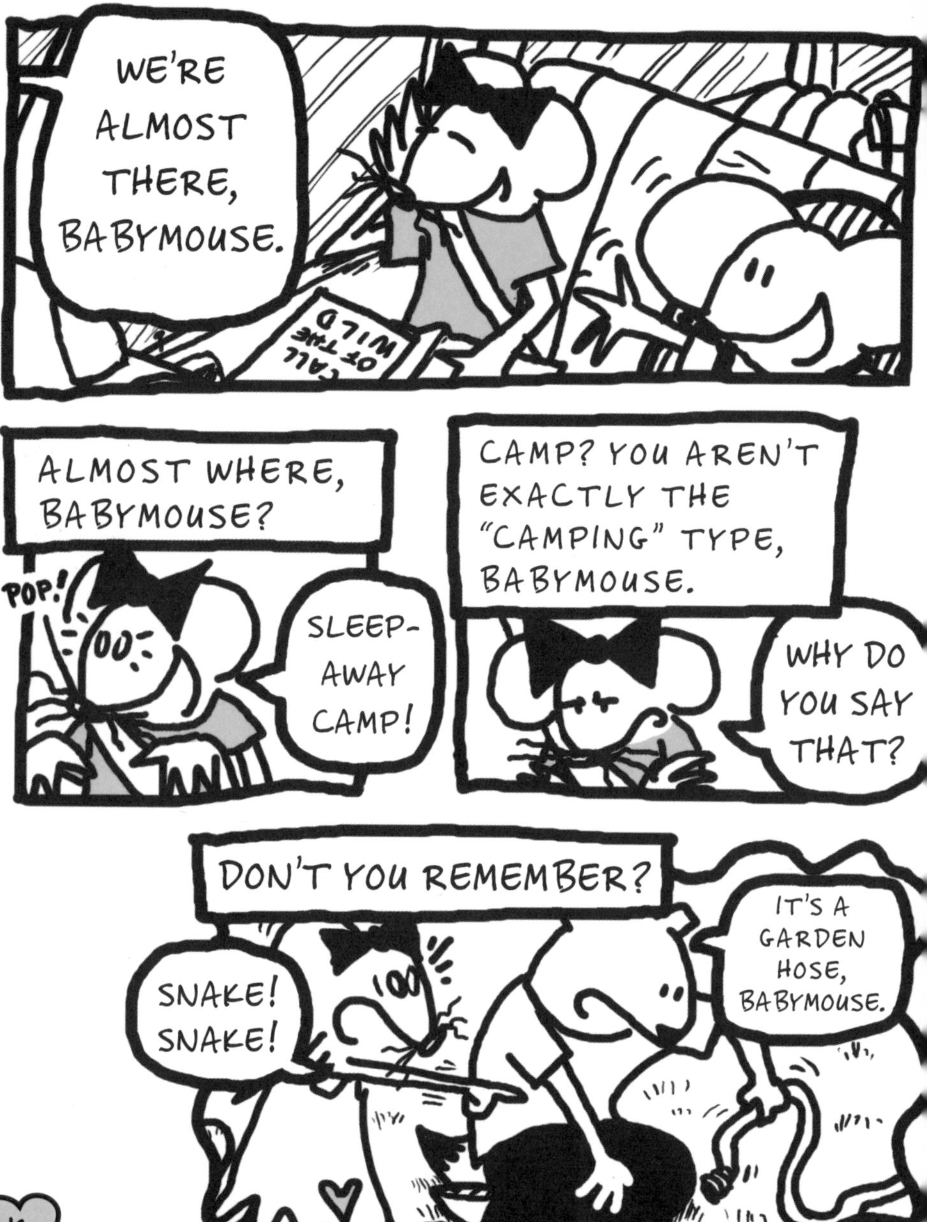
WE'RE ALMOST THERE, BABYMOUSE.
CALL OF THE WILD
ALMOST WHERE, BABYMOUSE?
POP!
SLEEP-AWAY CAMP!
CAMP? YOU AREN'T EXACTLY THE "CAMPING" TYPE, BABYMOUSE.
WHY DO YOU SAY THAT?
DON'T YOU REMEMBER?
SNAKE! SNAKE!
IT'S A GARDEN HOSE, BABYMOUSE.

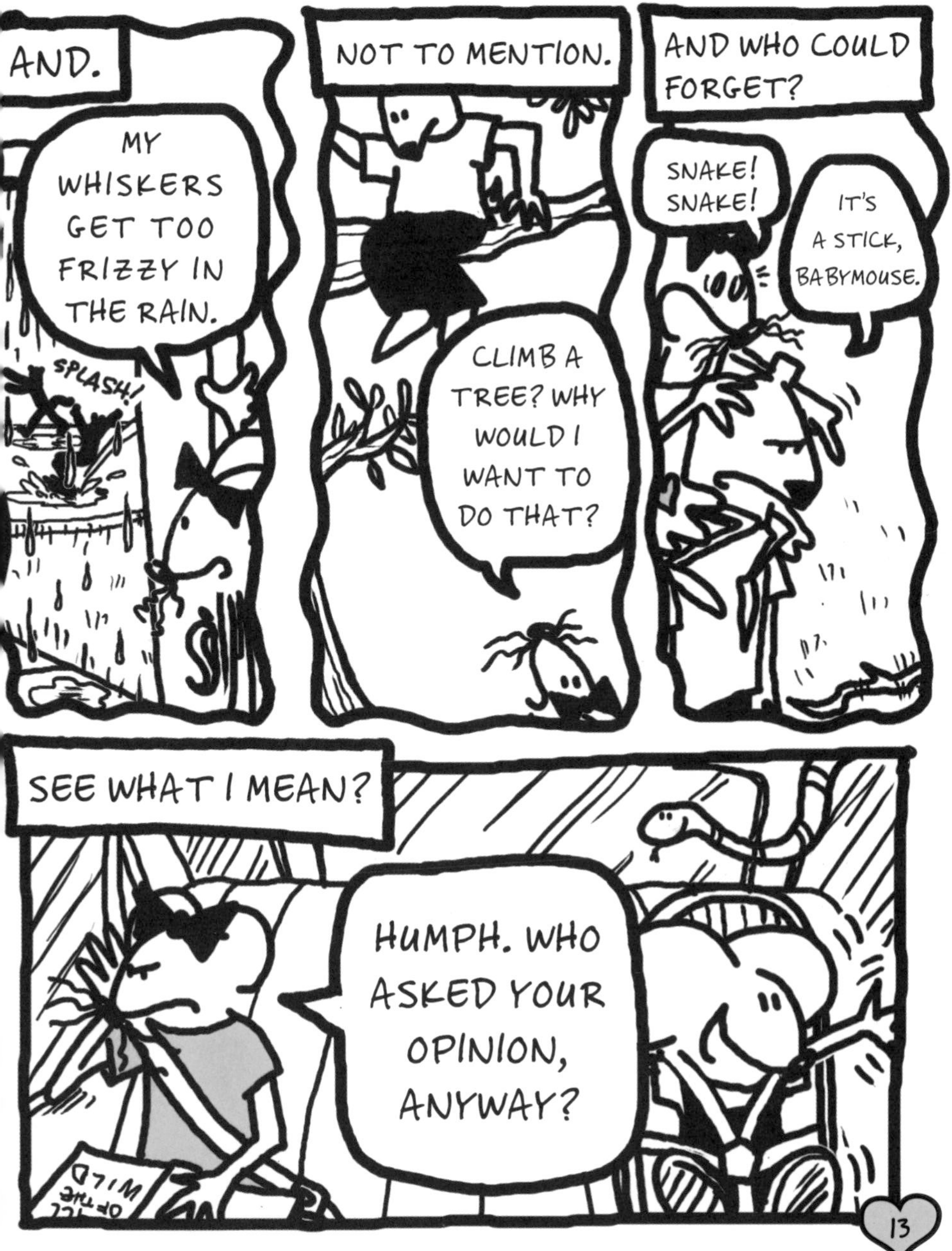
AND.
MY WHISKERS GET TOO FRIZZY IN THE RAIN.
SPLASH!
NOT TO MENTION.
CLIMB A TREE? WHY WOULD I WANT TO DO THAT?
AND WHO COULD FORGET?
SNAKE! SNAKE!
IT'S A STICK, BABYMOUSE.
SEE WHAT I MEAN?
HUMPH. WHO ASKED YOUR OPINION, ANYWAY?

BABYMOUSE!
BABYMOUSE!
CAMP WILD
WHISKERS
"WHERE GIRLS GO
TO GET LOST!"
YAY!

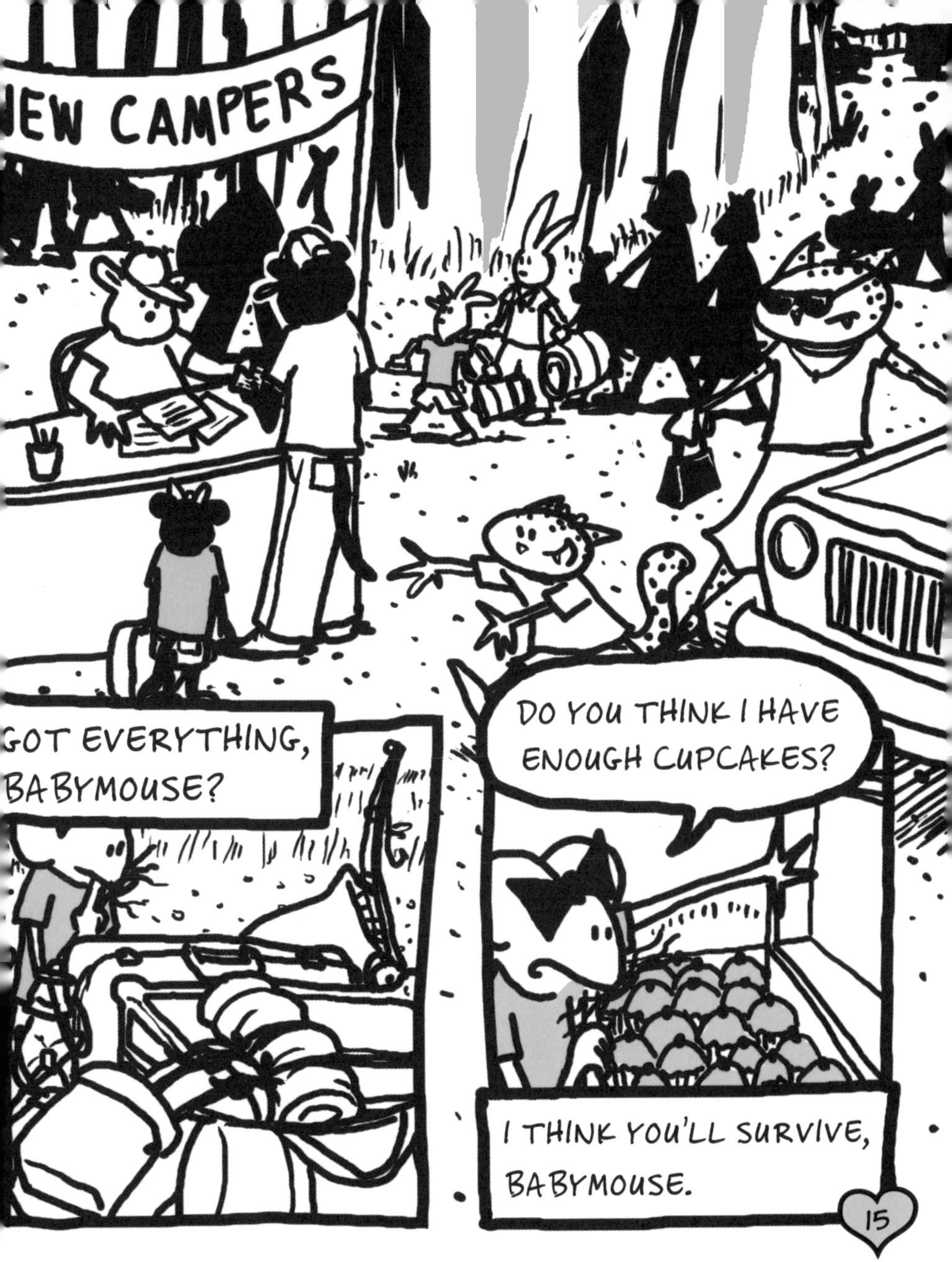

EW CAMPERS
GOT EVERYTHING, BABYMOUSE?
DO YOU THINK I HAVE ENOUGH CUPCAKES?
I THINK YOU'LL SURVIVE, BABYMOUSE.

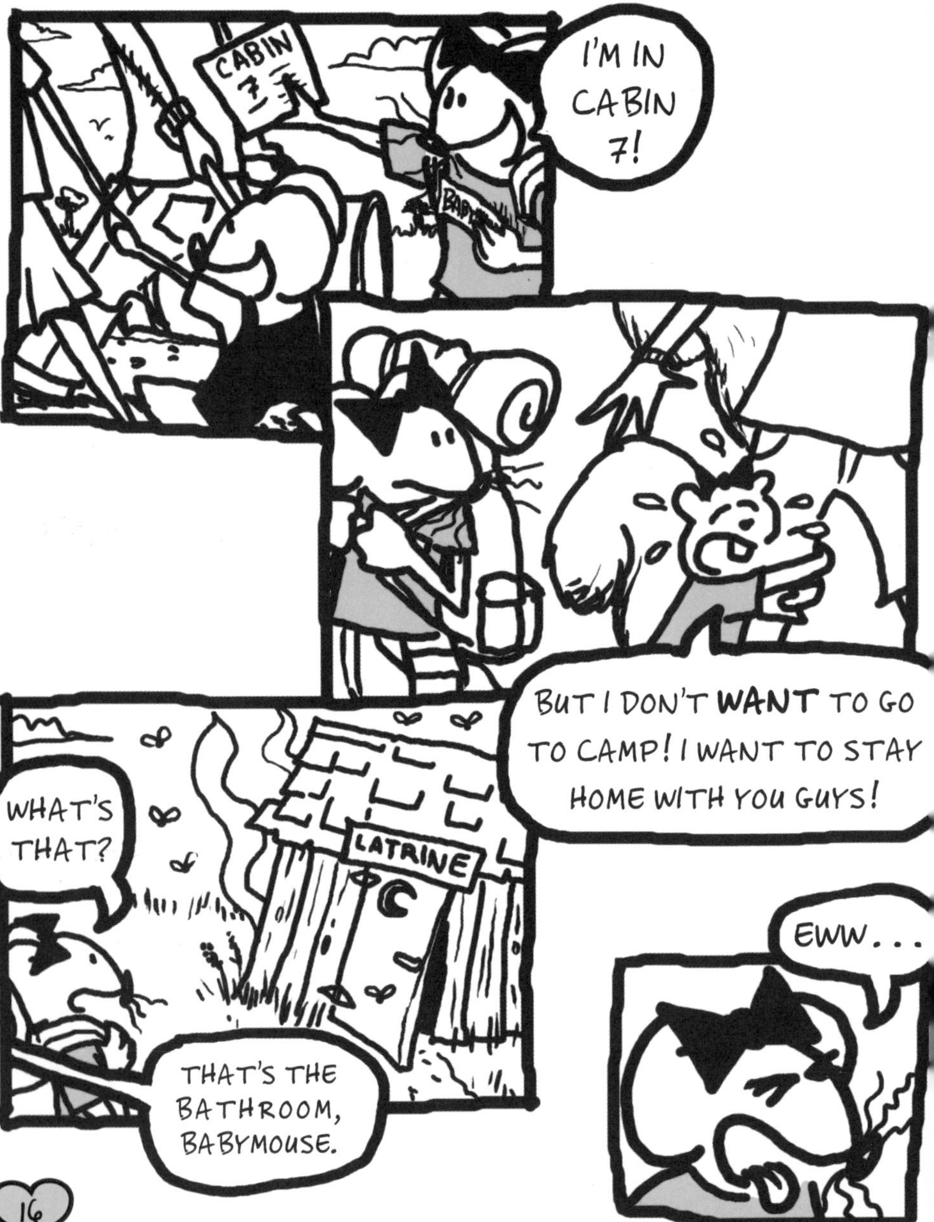
CABIN 7
I'M IN CABIN 7!
BUT I DON'T **WANT** TO GO TO CAMP! I WANT TO STAY HOME WITH YOU GUYS!
WHAT'S THAT?
LATRINE
THAT'S THE BATHROOM, BABYMOUSE.
EWW...

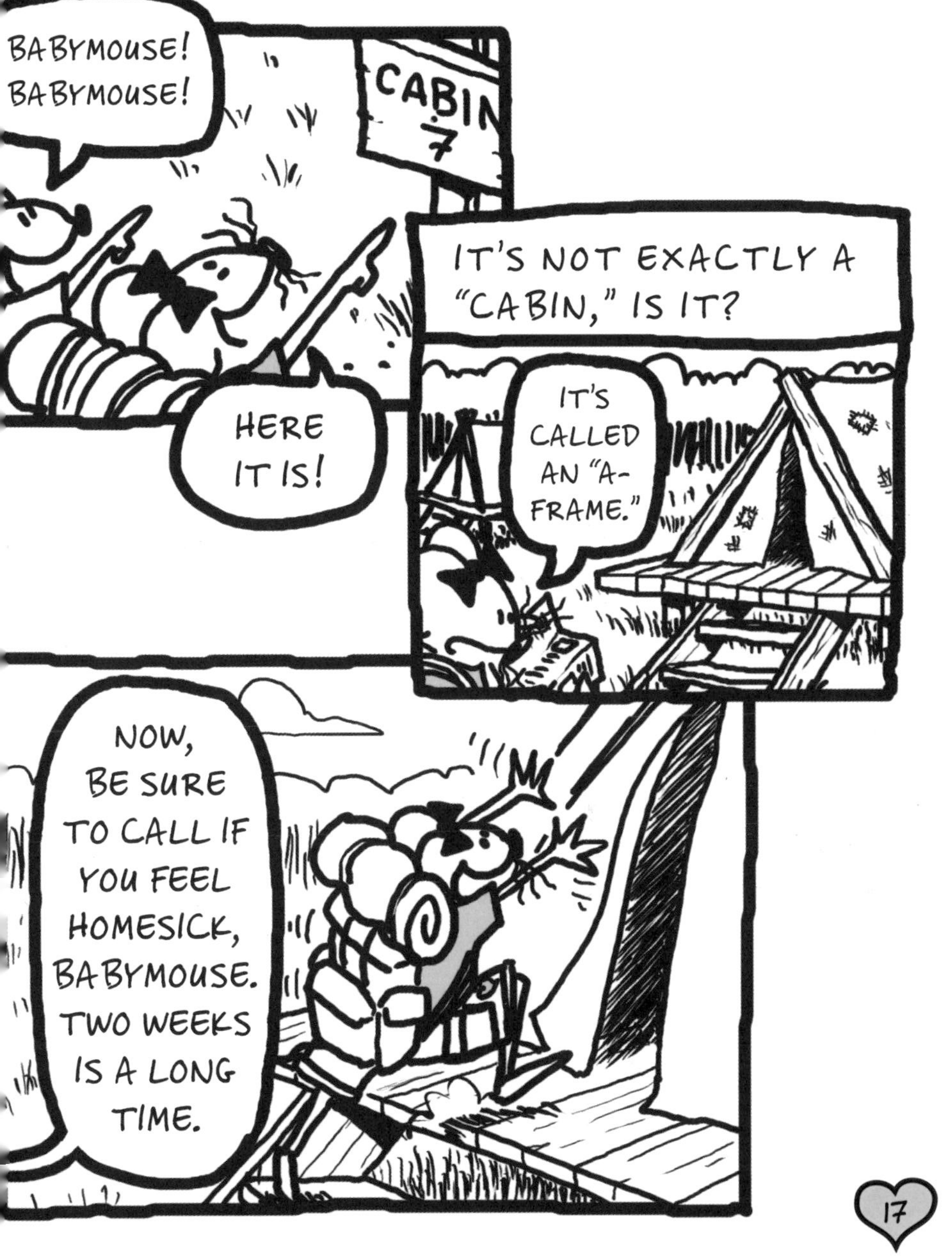
BABYMOUSE! BABYMOUSE!
CABIN 7
HERE IT IS!
IT'S NOT EXACTLY A "CABIN," IS IT?
IT'S CALLED AN "A-FRAME."
NOW, BE SURE TO CALL IF YOU FEEL HOMESICK, BABYMOUSE. TWO WEEKS IS A LONG TIME.

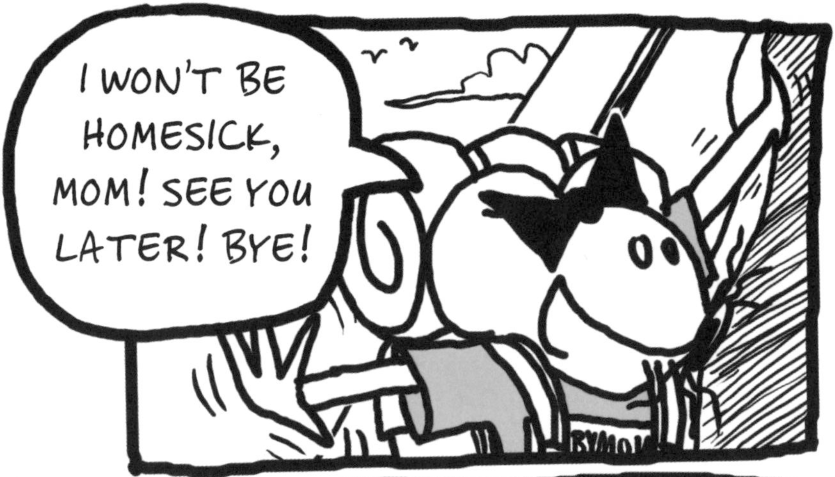
I WON'T BE HOMESICK, MOM! SEE YOU LATER! BYE!
BYMOU

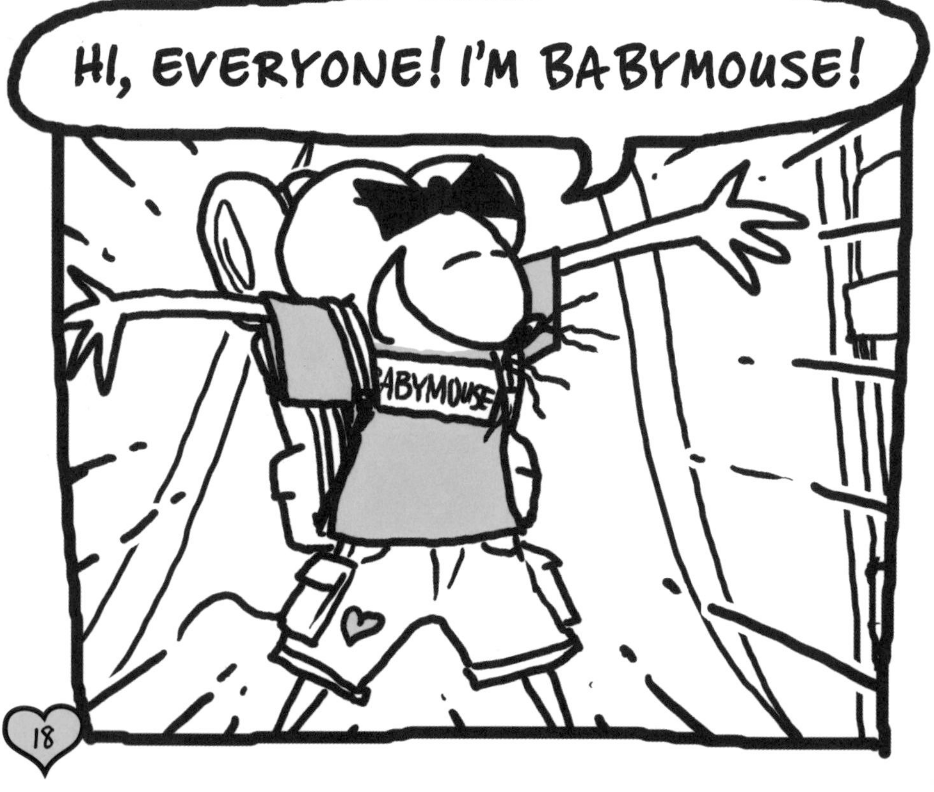
HI, EVERYONE! I'M BABYMOUSE!
ABYMOUSE

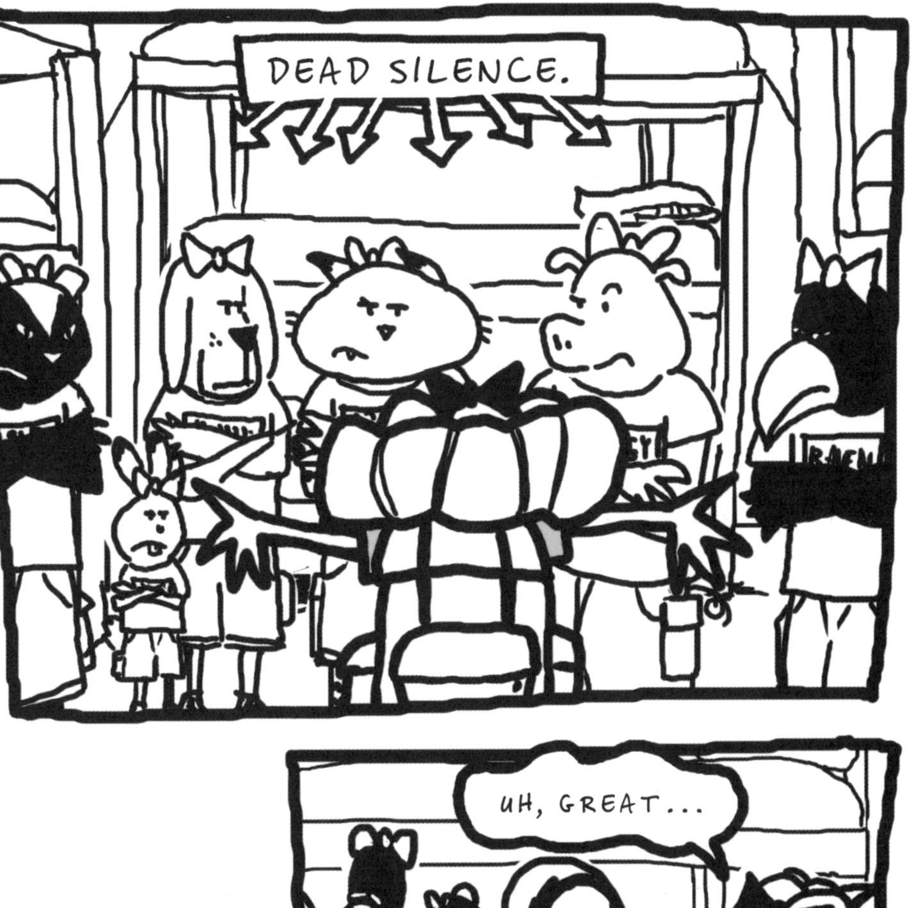
DEAD SILENCE.

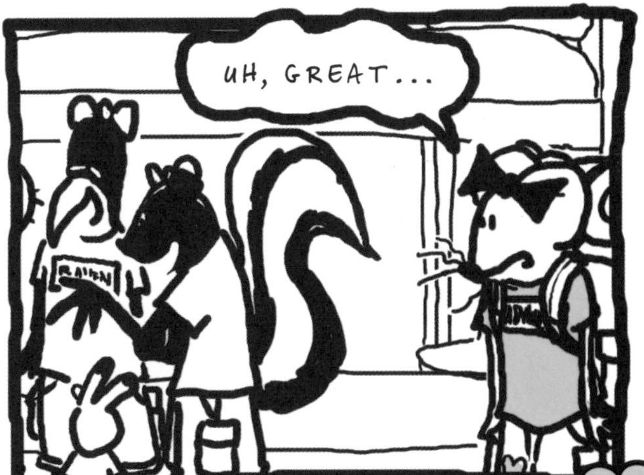
UH, GREAT...

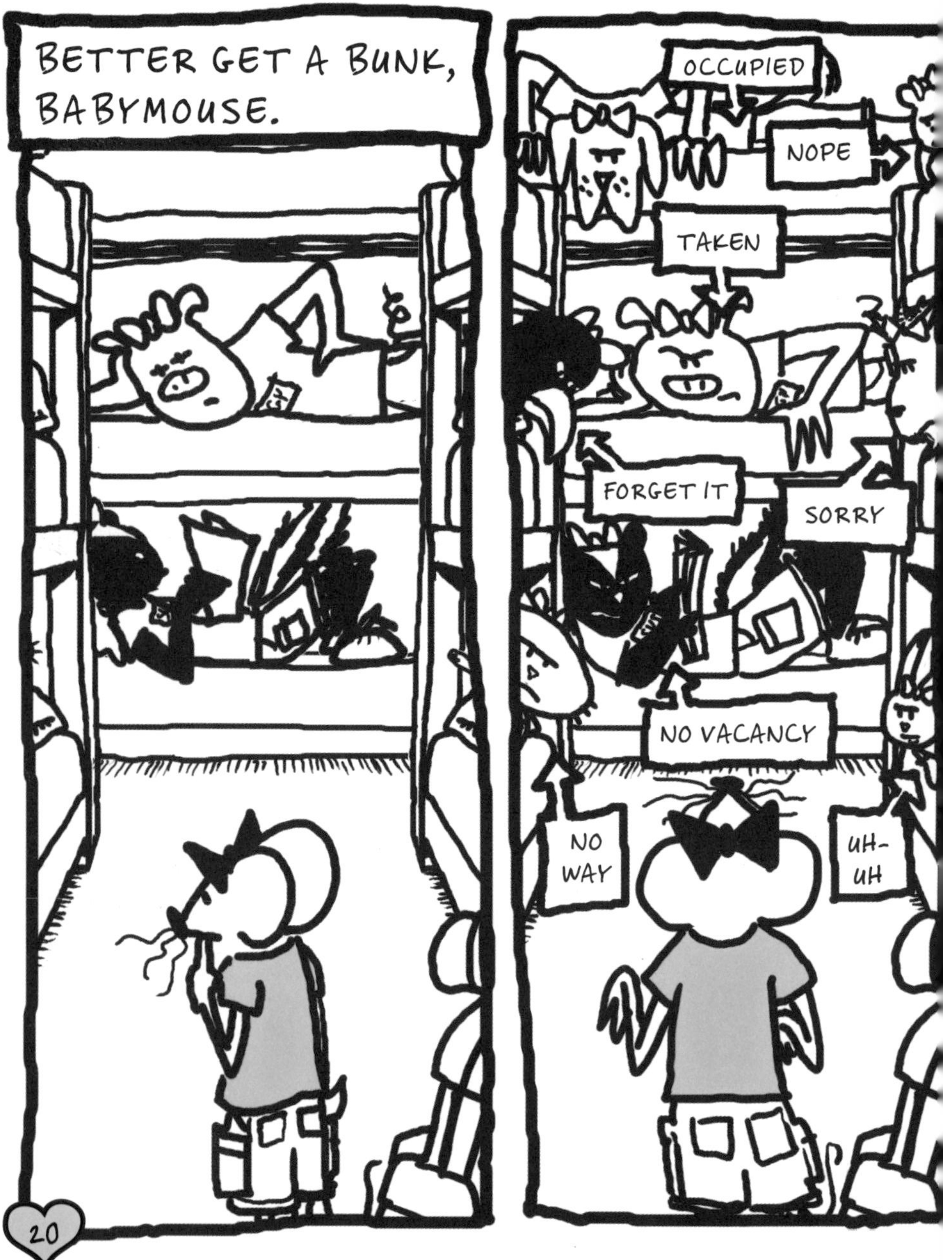
BETTER GET A BUNK, BABYMOUSE.
OCCUPIED
NOPE
TAKEN
FORGET IT
SORRY
NO VACANCY
NO WAY
UH-UH

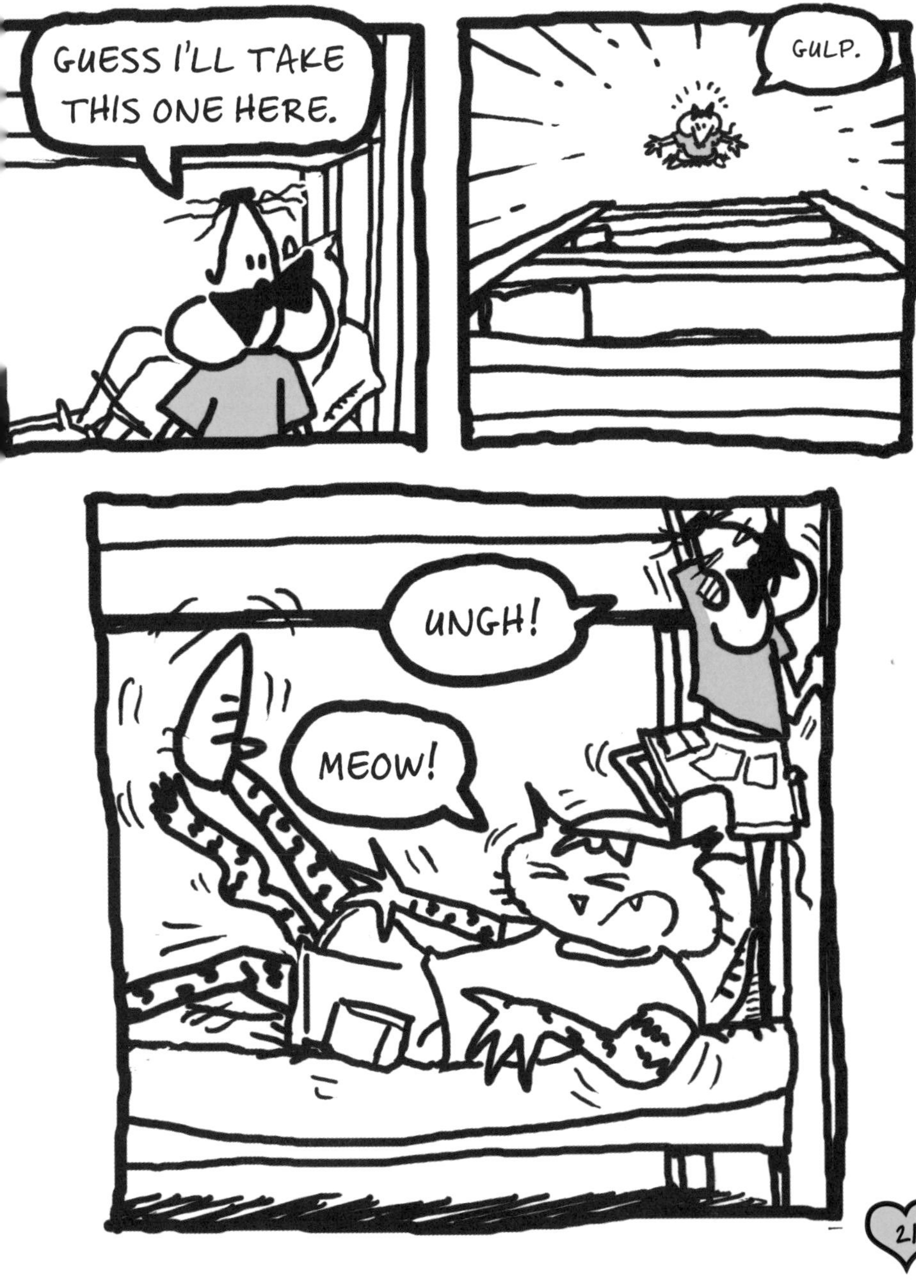
GUESS I'LL TAKE THIS ONE HERE.
GULP.
UNGH!
MEOW!

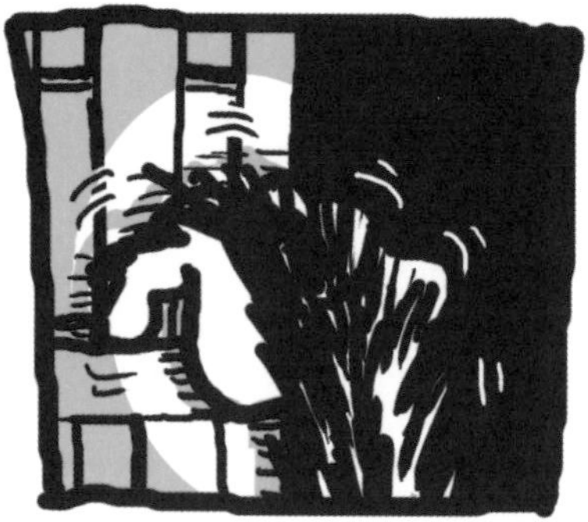

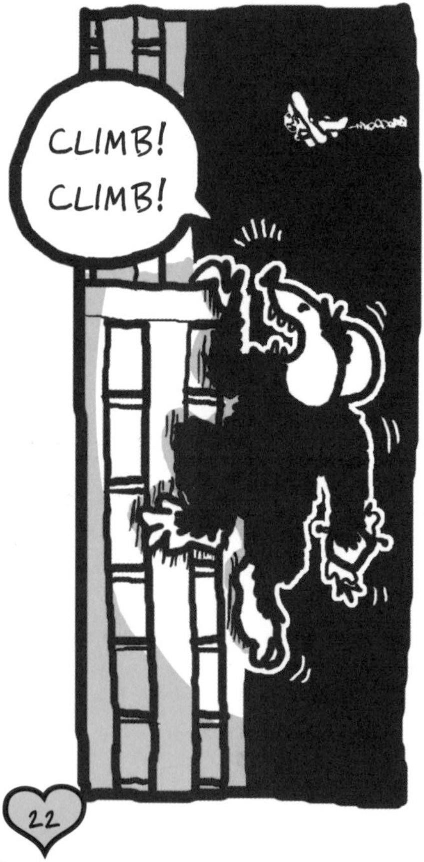
CLIMB!
CLIMB!

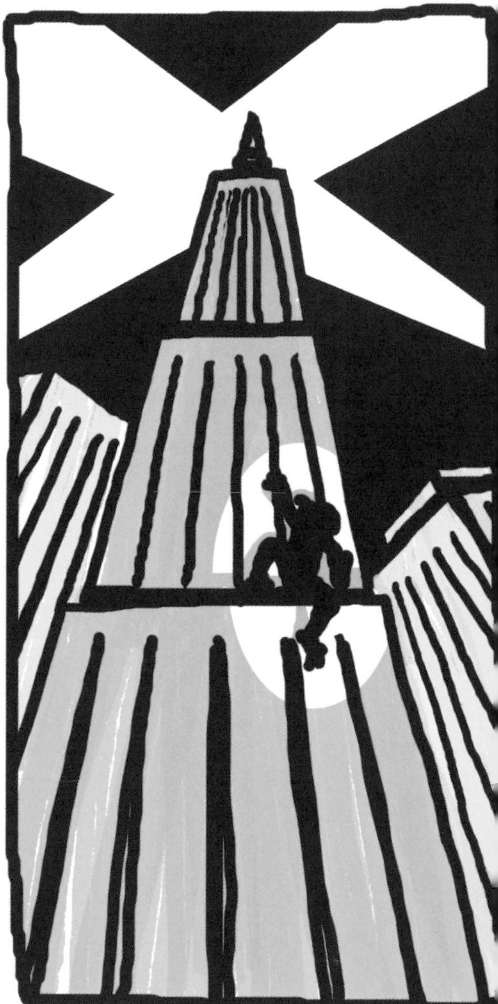

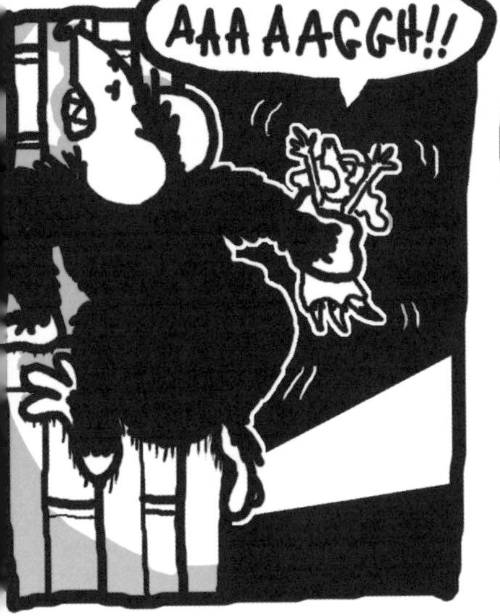
AAA AAGGH!!

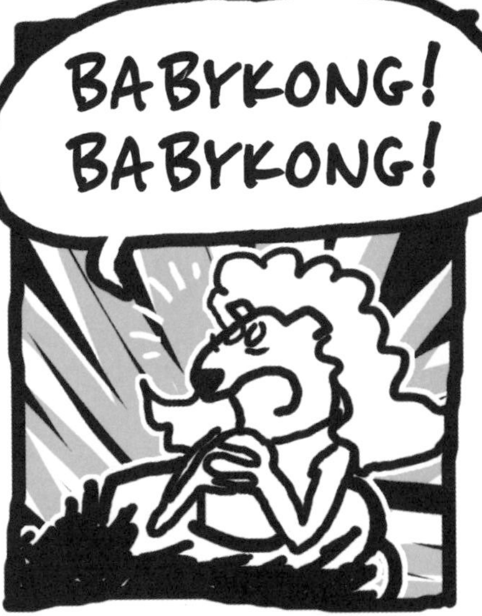
BABYKONG!
BABYKONG!

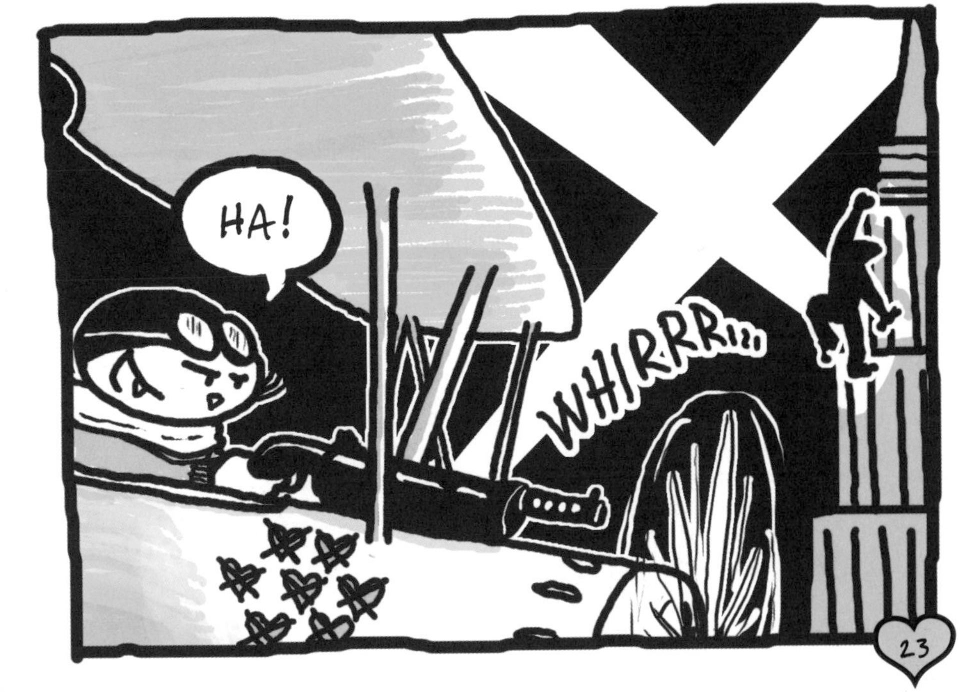
HA!
WHIRRR...

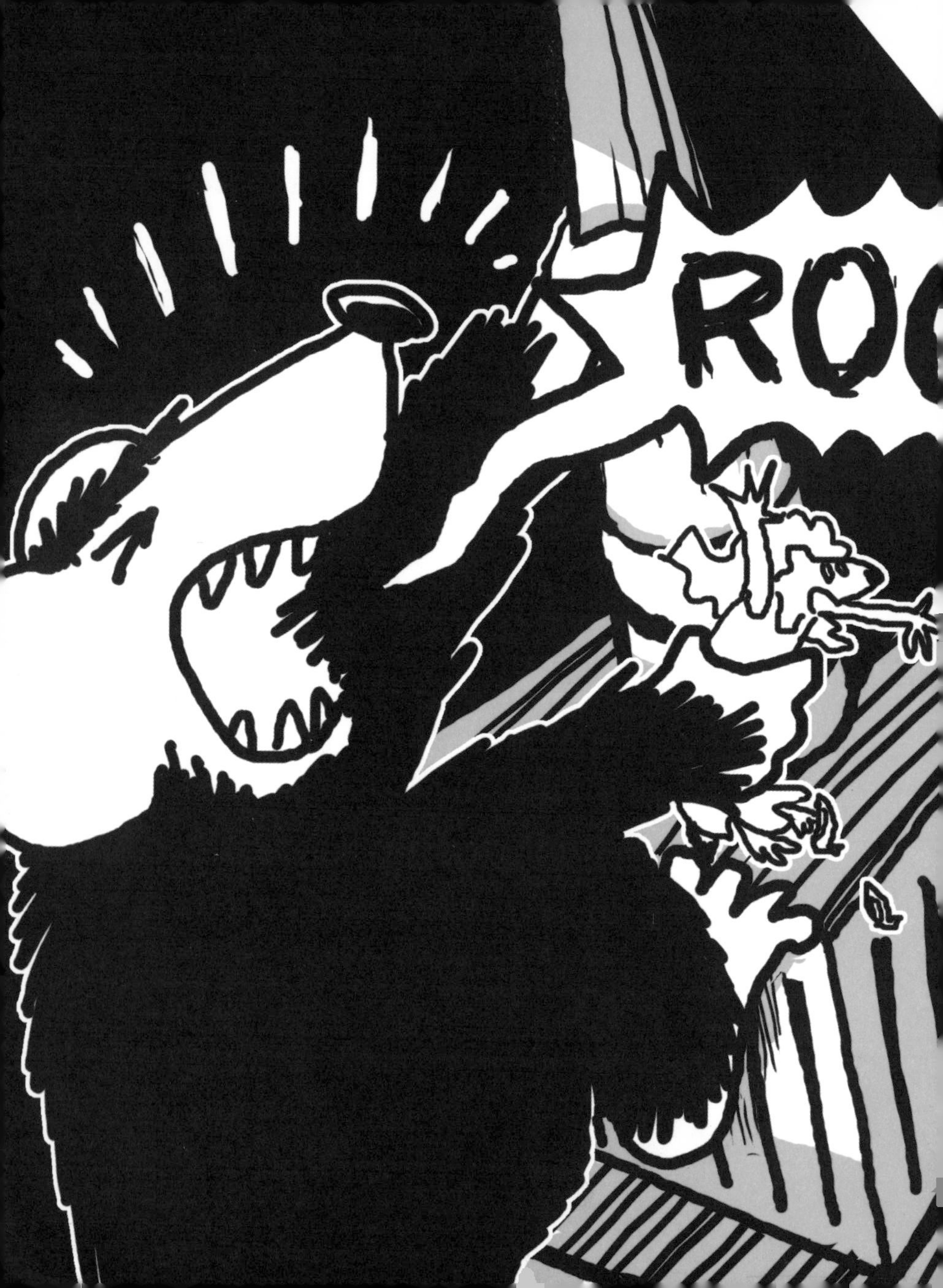
ROO

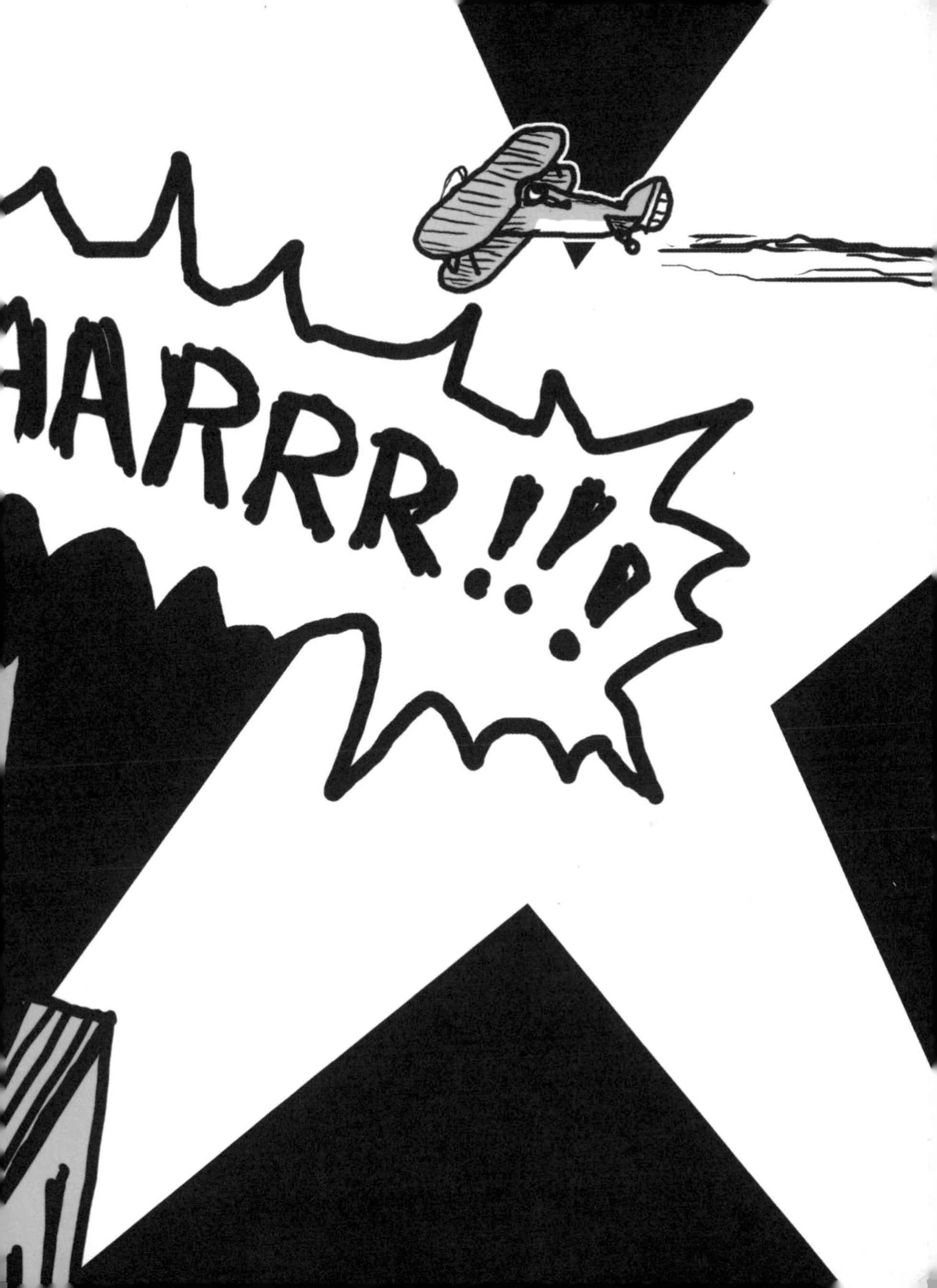
HARRR!!!

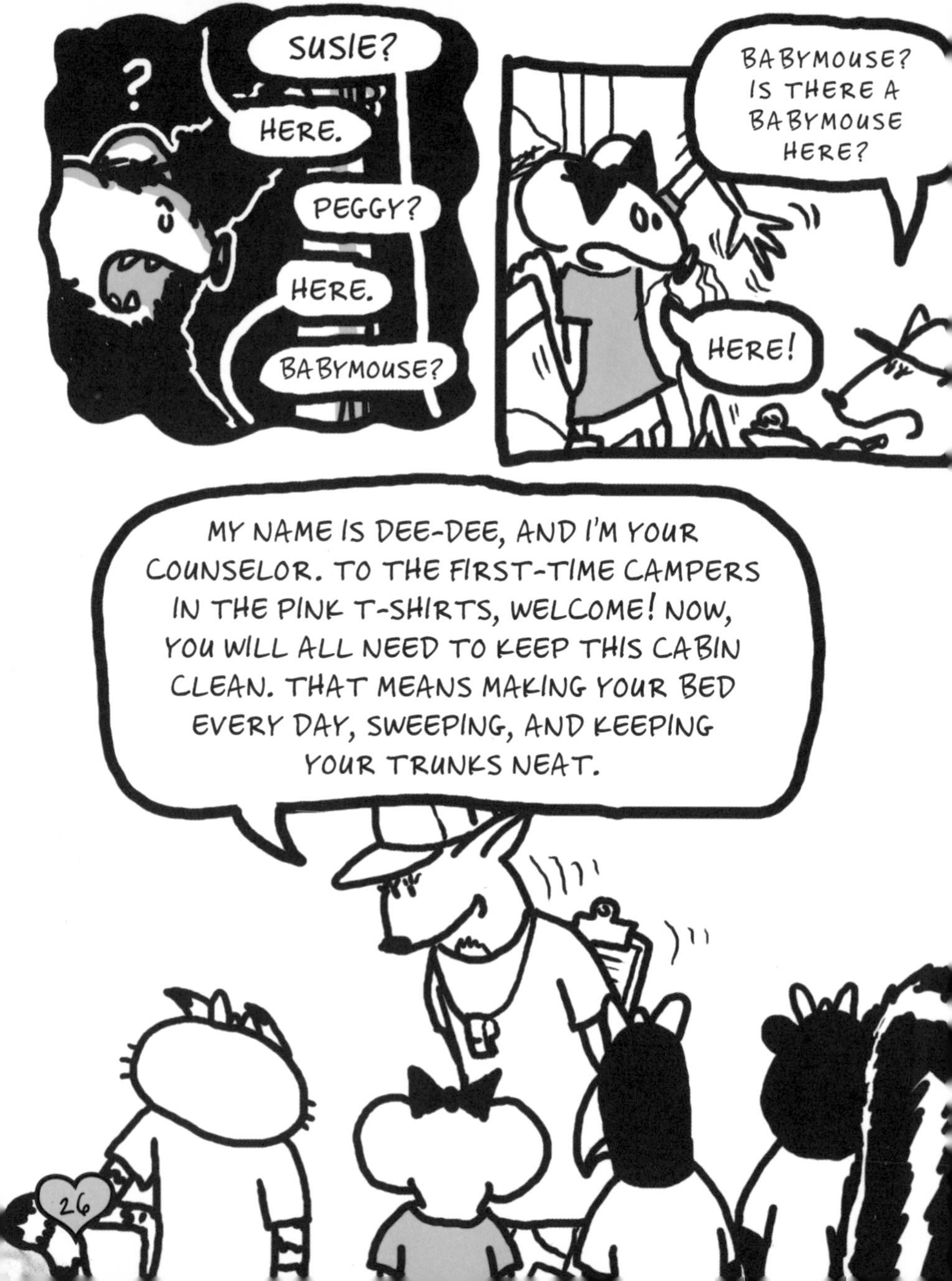
?
SUSIE?
HERE.
PEGGY?
HERE.
BABYMOUSE?
BABYMOUSE? IS THERE A BABYMOUSE HERE?
HERE!
MY NAME IS DEE-DEE, AND I'M YOUR COUNSELOR. TO THE FIRST-TIME CAMPERS IN THE PINK T-SHIRTS, WELCOME! NOW, YOU WILL ALL NEED TO KEEP THIS CABIN CLEAN. THAT MEANS MAKING YOUR BED EVERY DAY, SWEEPING, AND KEEPING YOUR TRUNKS NEAT.

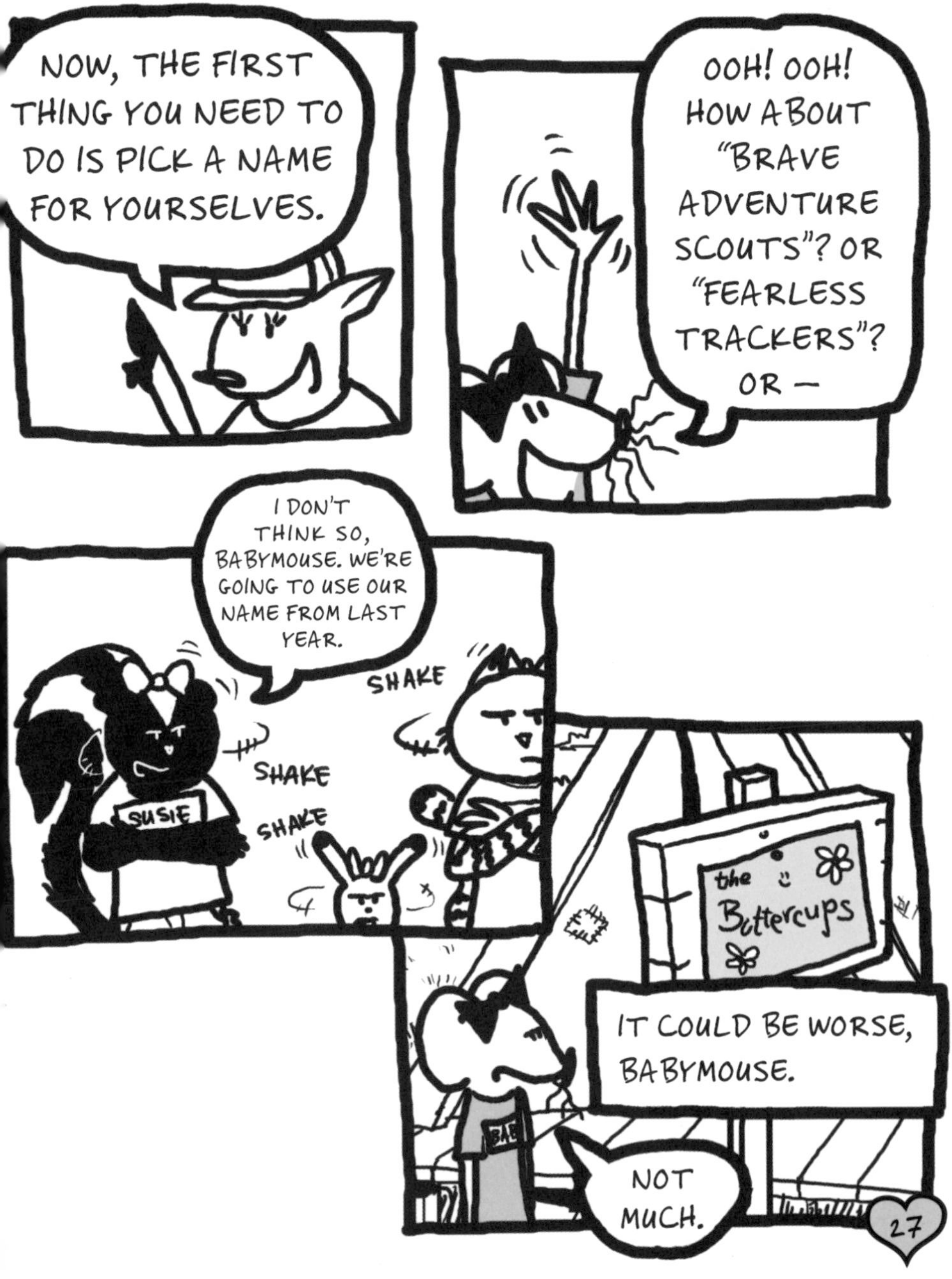

NOW, THE FIRST THING YOU NEED TO DO IS PICK A NAME FOR YOURSELVES.
OOH! OOH! HOW ABOUT "BRAVE ADVENTURE SCOUTS"? OR "FEARLESS TRACKERS"? OR —
I DON'T THINK SO, BABYMOUSE. WE'RE GOING TO USE OUR NAME FROM LAST YEAR.
SHAKE
SHAKE
SHAKE
SUSIE
the Buttercups
IT COULD BE WORSE, BABYMOUSE.
NOT MUCH.

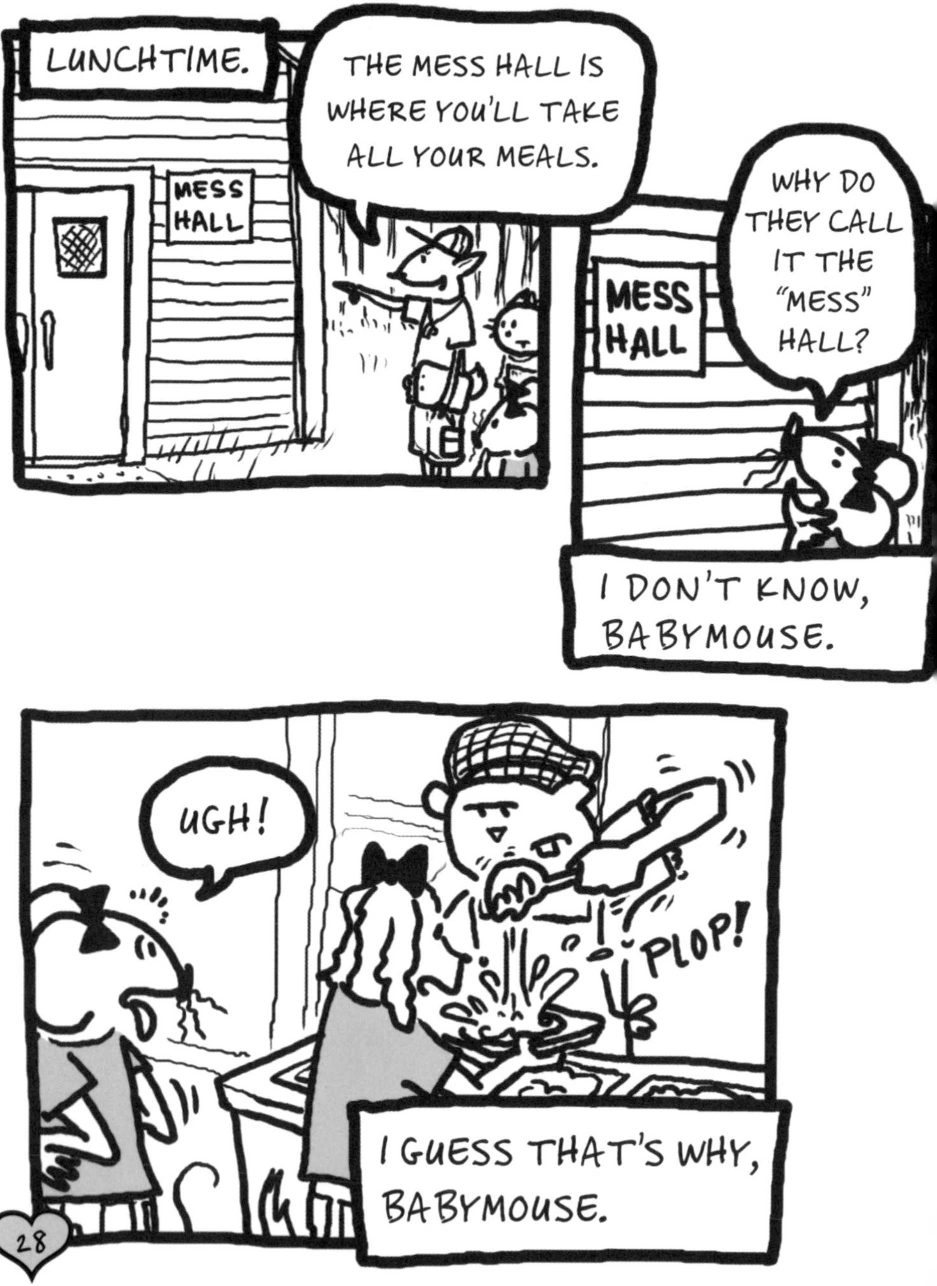

LUNCHTIME.
THE MESS HALL IS WHERE YOU'LL TAKE ALL YOUR MEALS.
MESS HALL
MESS HALL
WHY DO THEY CALL IT THE "MESS" HALL?
I DON'T KNOW, BABYMOUSE.
UGH!
PLOP!
I GUESS THAT'S WHY, BABYMOUSE.

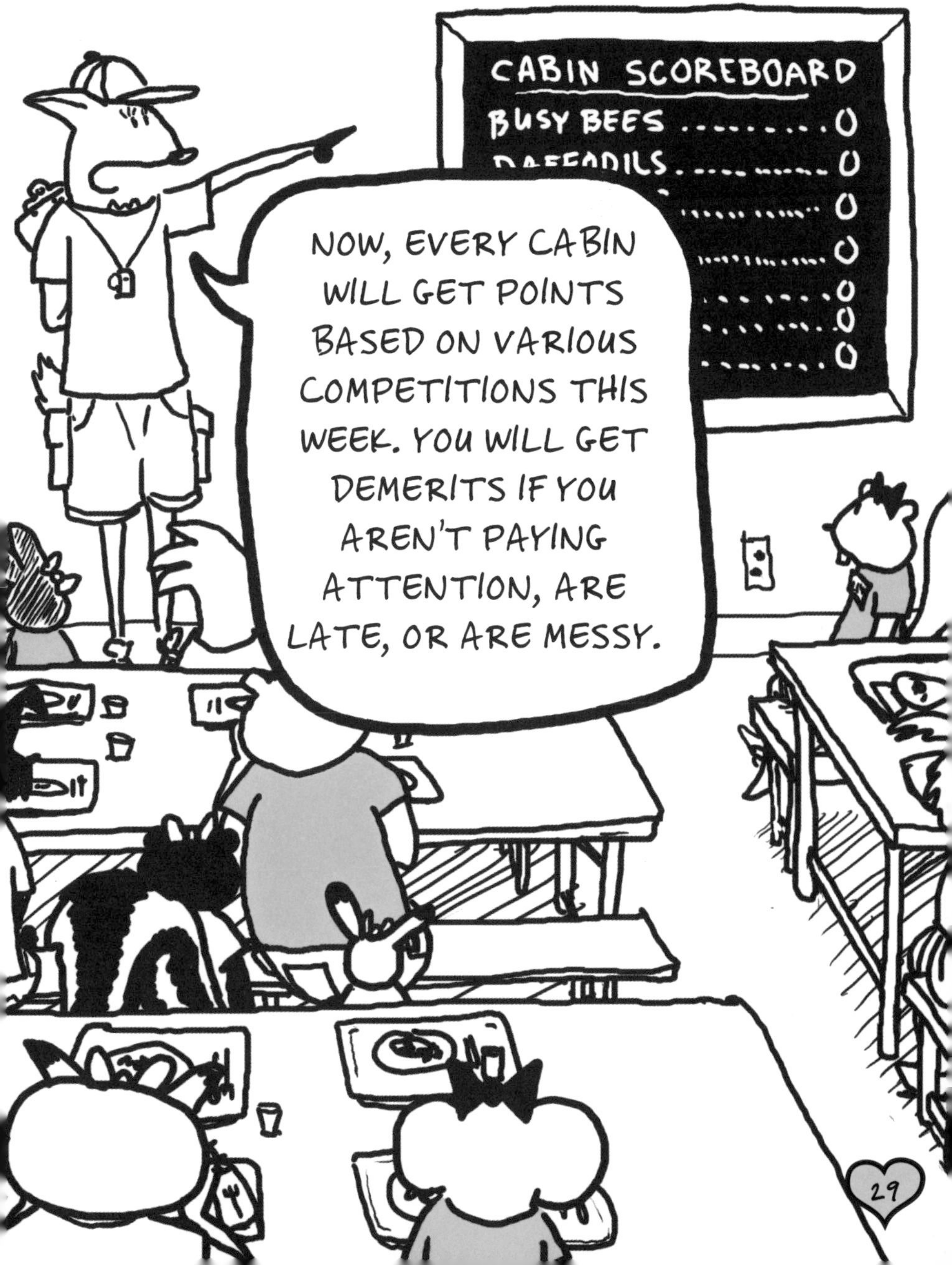
CABIN SCOREBOARD
BUSY BEES 0
NOW, EVERY CABIN WILL GET POINTS BASED ON VARIOUS COMPETITIONS THIS WEEK. YOU WILL GET DEMERITS IF YOU AREN'T PAYING ATTENTION, ARE LATE, OR ARE MESSY.

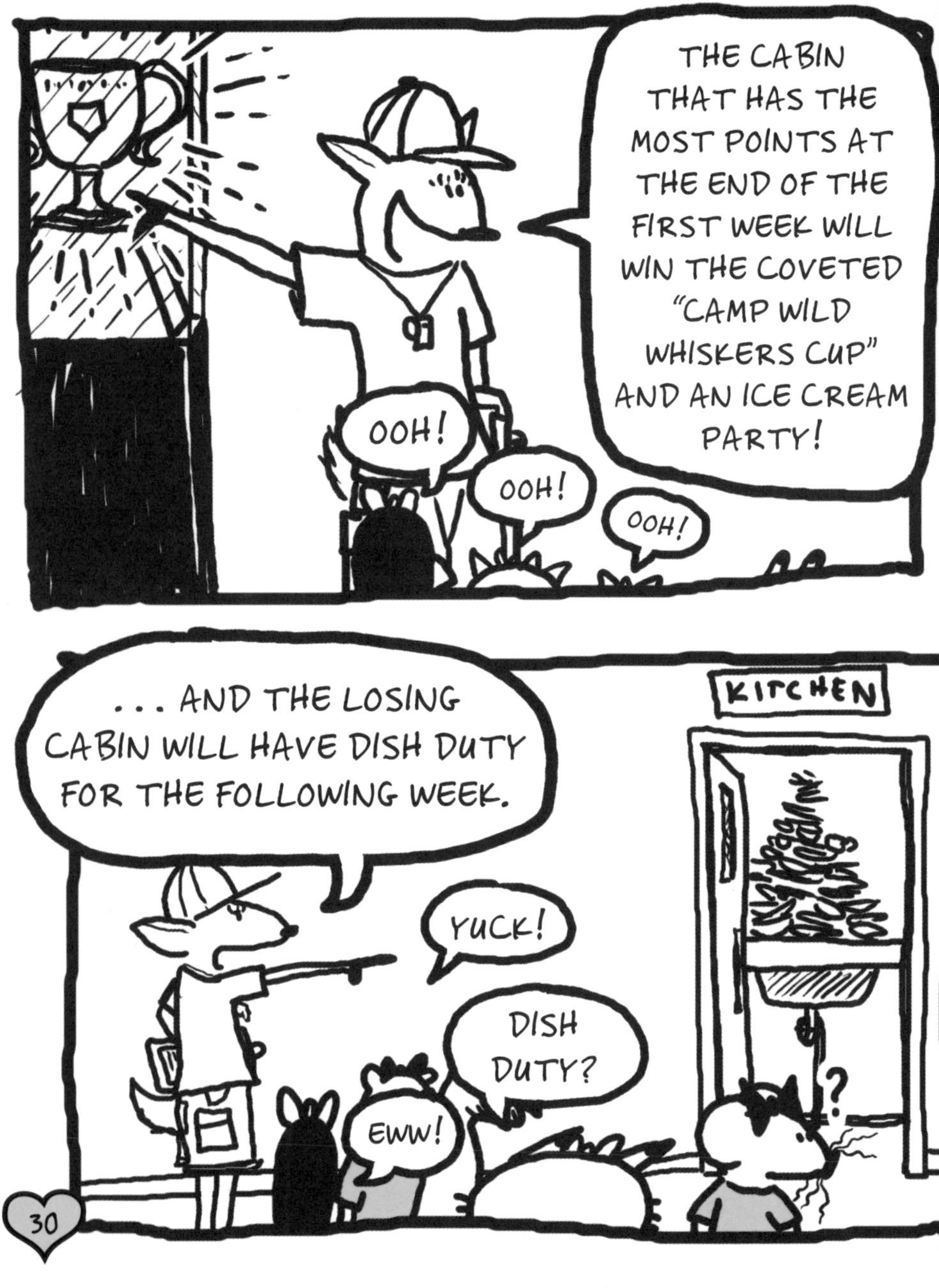
THE CABIN THAT HAS THE MOST POINTS AT THE END OF THE FIRST WEEK WILL WIN THE COVETED "CAMP WILD WHISKERS CUP" AND AN ICE CREAM PARTY!
OOH!
OOH!
OOH!
... AND THE LOSING CABIN WILL HAVE DISH DUTY FOR THE FOLLOWING WEEK.
KITCHEN
YUCK!
DISH DUTY?
EWW!
?

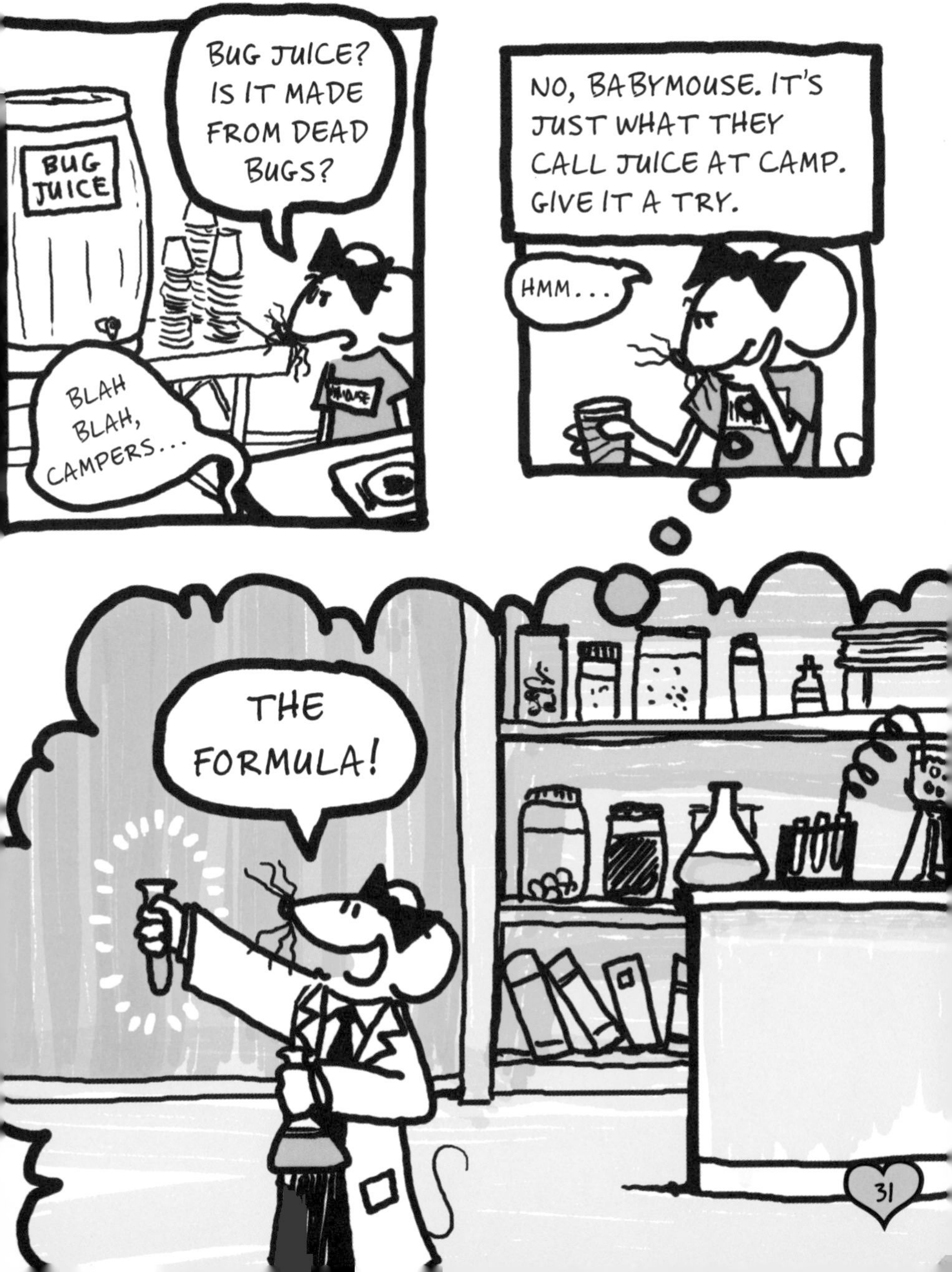
BUG JUICE
BUG JUICE? IS IT MADE FROM DEAD BUGS?
BLAH BLAH, CAMPERS...
NO, BABYMOUSE. IT'S JUST WHAT THEY CALL JUICE AT CAMP. GIVE IT A TRY.
HMM...
THE FORMULA!

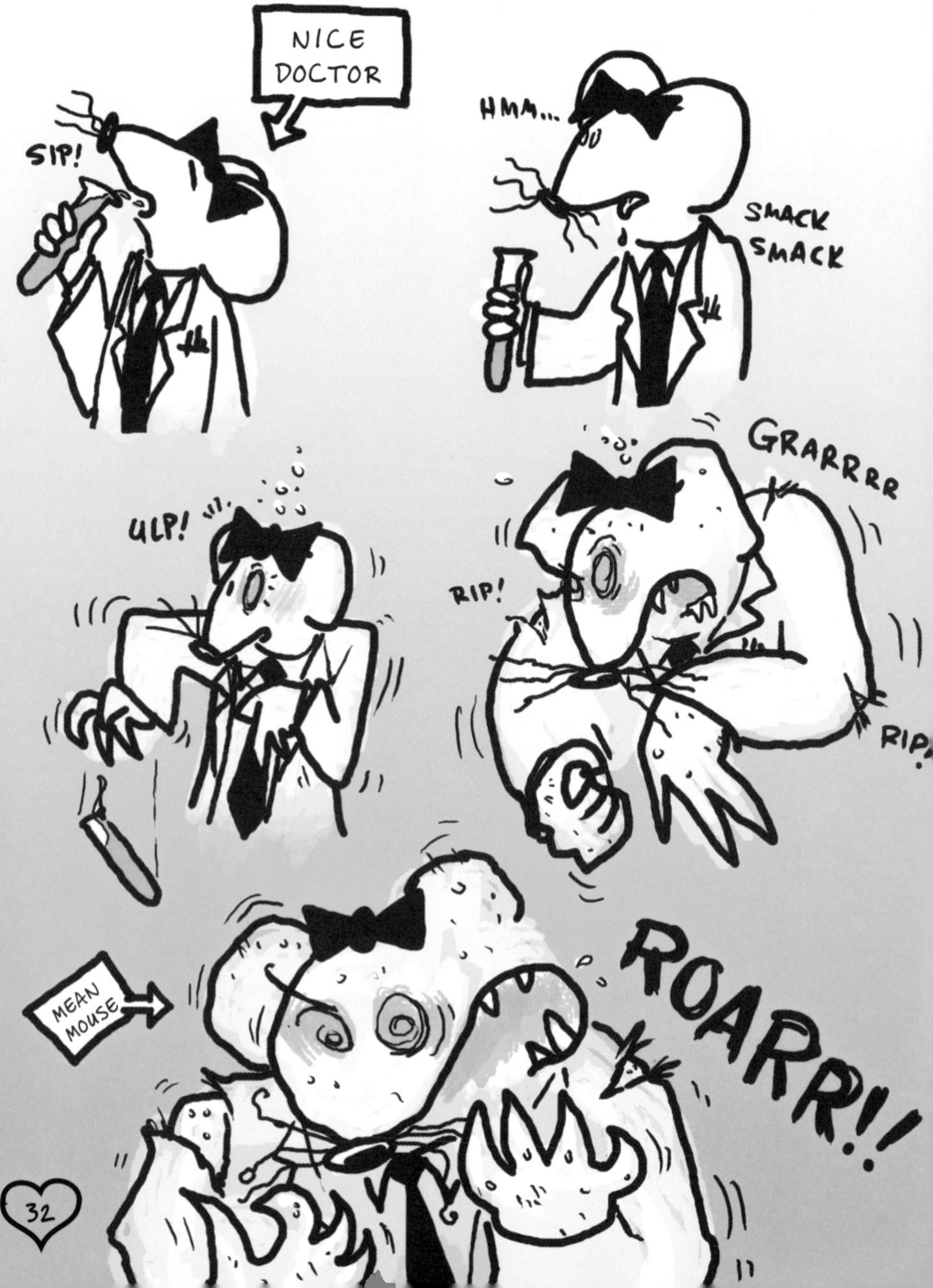
NICE DOCTOR
SIP!
HMM...
SMACK SMACK
ULP!
GRARRRRR
RIP!
RIP!
MEAN MOUSE
ROARR!!

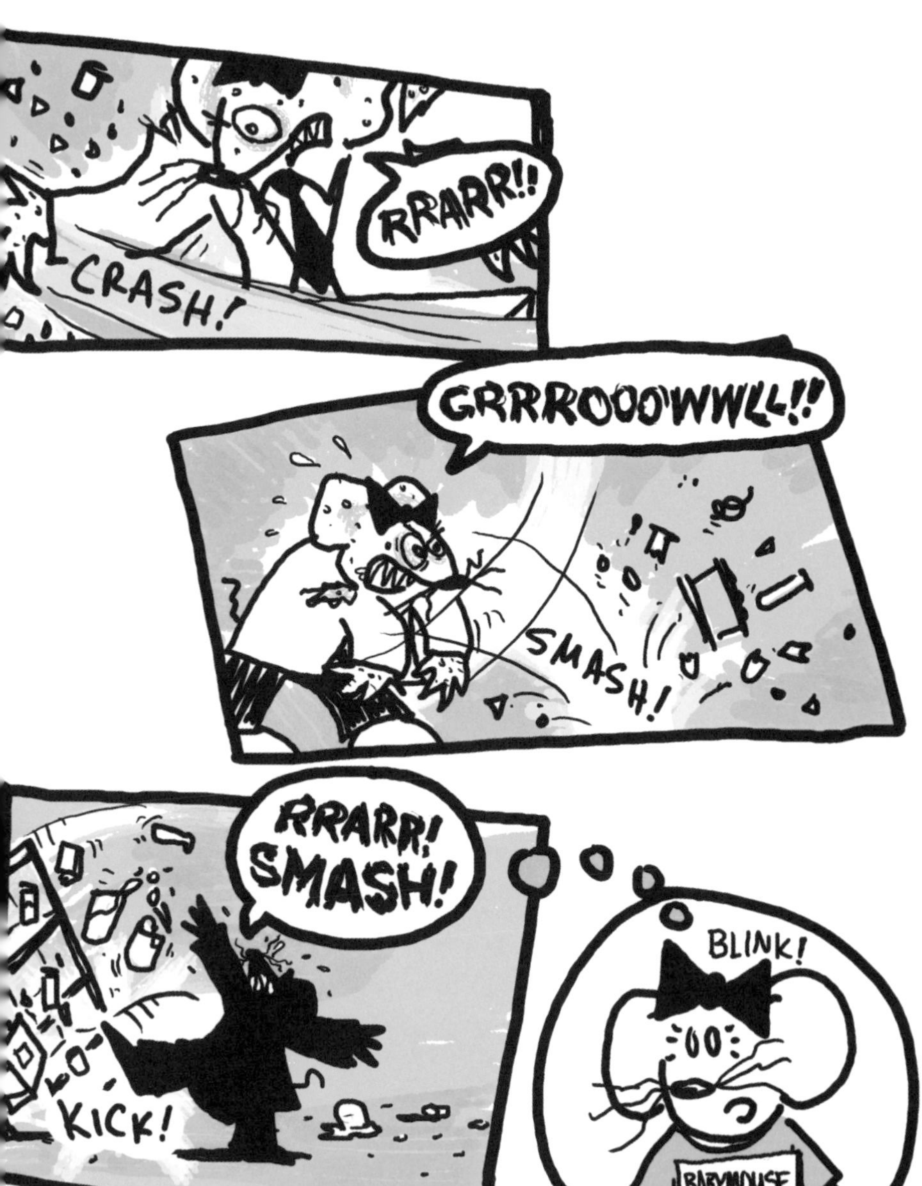
RRARR!!
CRASH!
GRRROOOWWLL!!
SMASH!
RRARR!
SMASH!
KICK!
BLINK!
BABYMOUSE

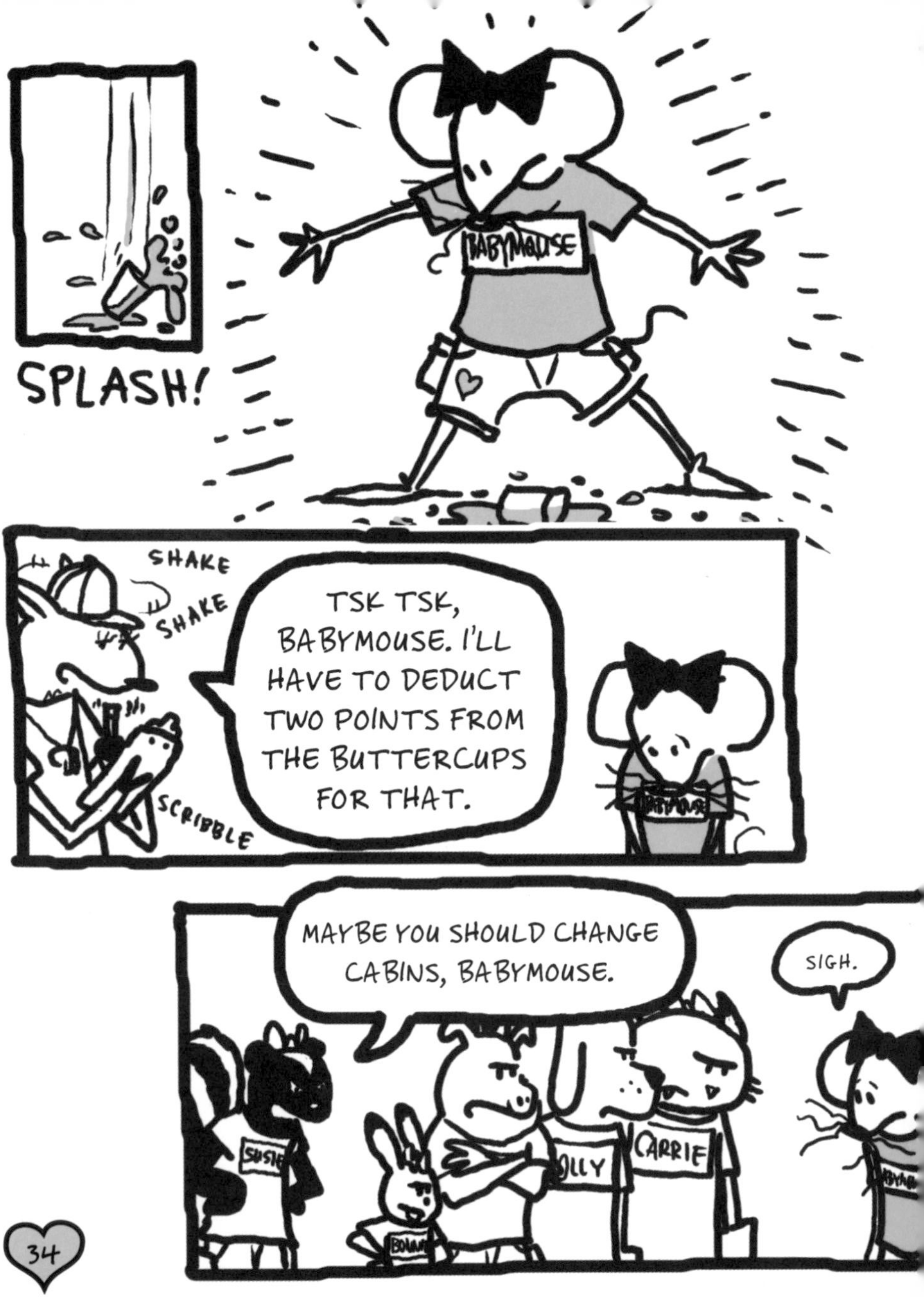
SPLASH!
BABYMOUSE
SHAKE
SHAKE
TSK TSK, BABYMOUSE. I'LL HAVE TO DEDUCT TWO POINTS FROM THE BUTTERCUPS FOR THAT.
SCRIBBLE
MAYBE YOU SHOULD CHANGE CABINS, BABYMOUSE.
SIGH.
SUSIE
CARRIE

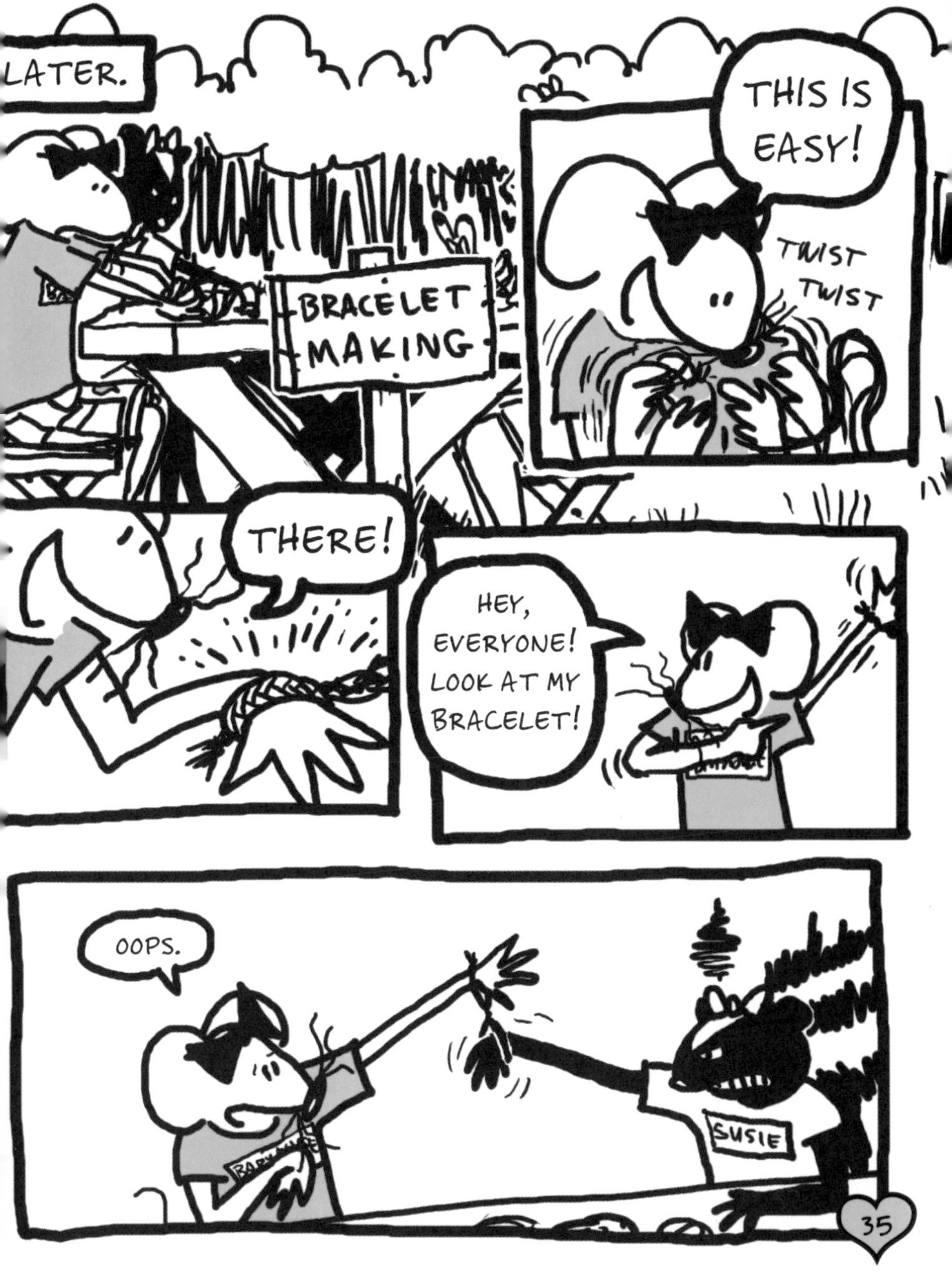
LATER.
BRACELET MAKING
THIS IS EASY!
TWIST
TWIST
THERE!
HEY, EVERYONE! LOOK AT MY BRACELET!
OOPS.
SUSIE

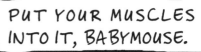

THAT AFTERNOON.

OOF!

PUT YOUR MUSCLES INTO IT, BABYMOUSE.

UNGH!

TWANG!

EMPTY.

WHERE'D IT GO?

YOU DON'T WANT TO KNOW, BABYMOUSE.

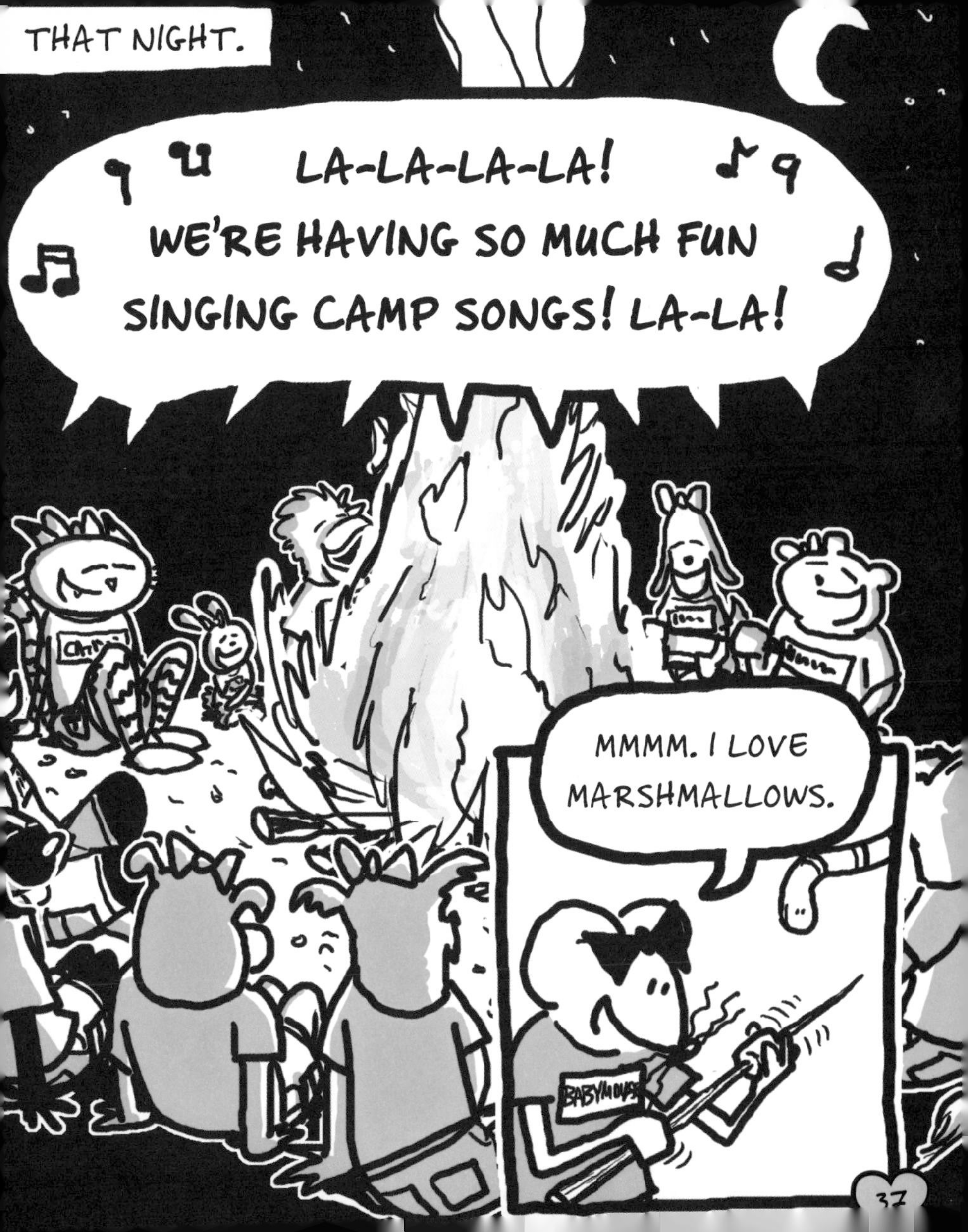
THAT NIGHT.
LA-LA-LA-LA! WE'RE HAVING SO MUCH FUN SINGING CAMP SONGS! LA-LA!
MMMM. I LOVE MARSHMALLOWS.
BABYMOUSE

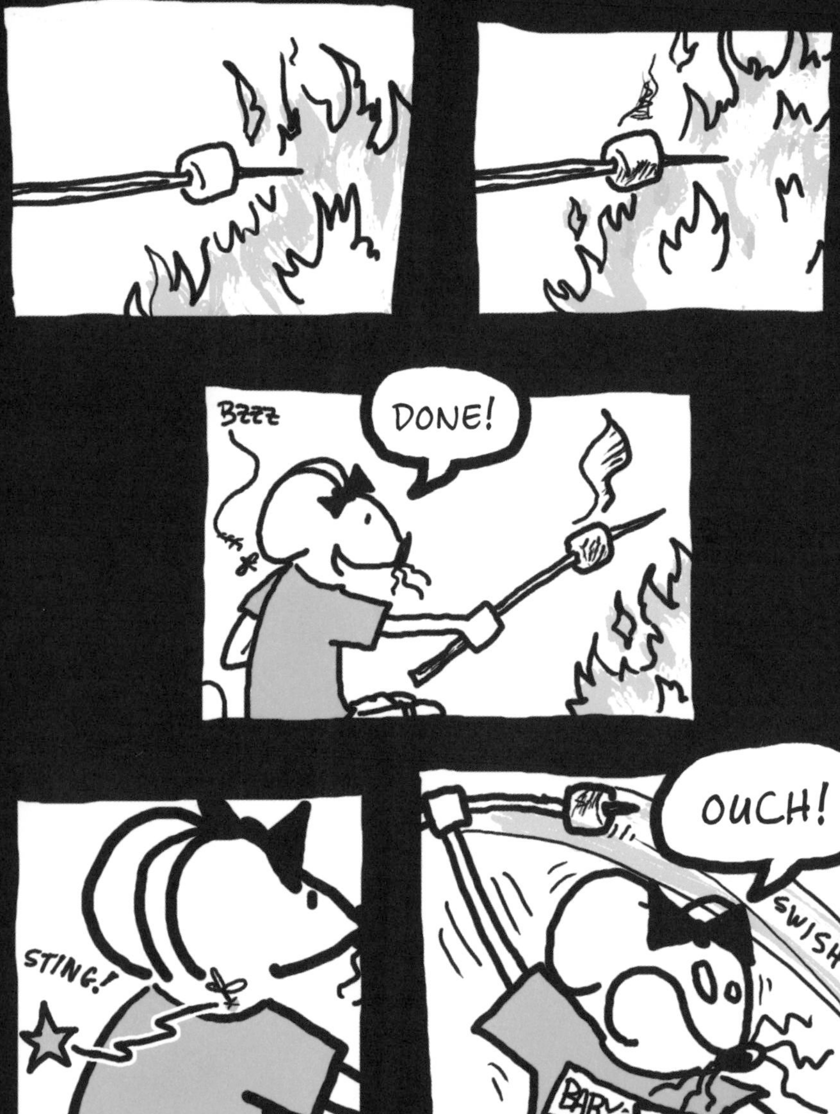
BZZZ
DONE!
STING!
OUCH!
SWISH
BABY

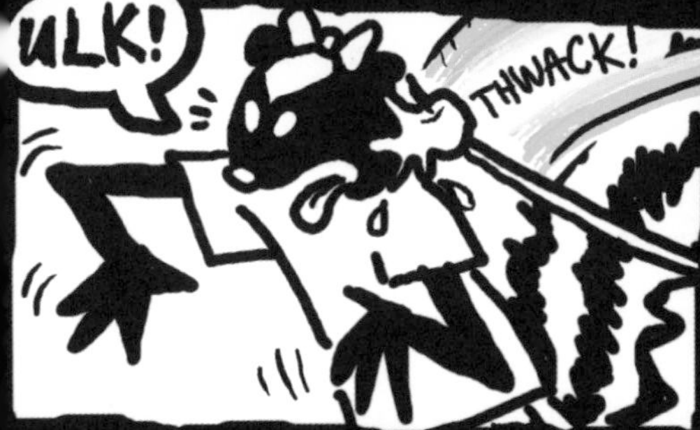
ULK!
THWACK!

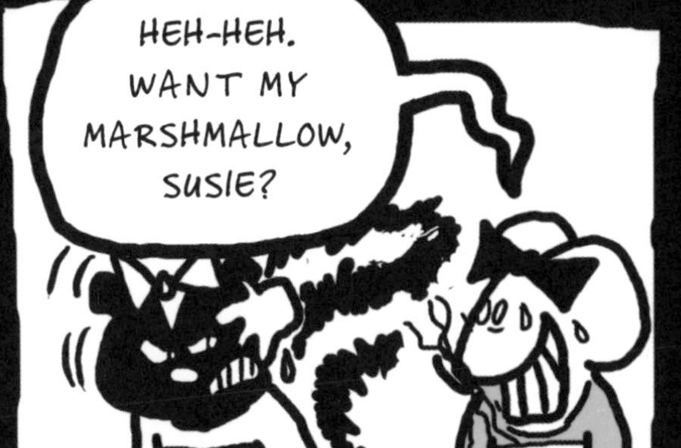
HEH-HEH.
WANT MY
MARSHMALLOW,
SUSIE?
SUSIE
BABYMOUSE
I'M TRYING
REALLY HARD
NOT TO SPRAY
YOU NOW.

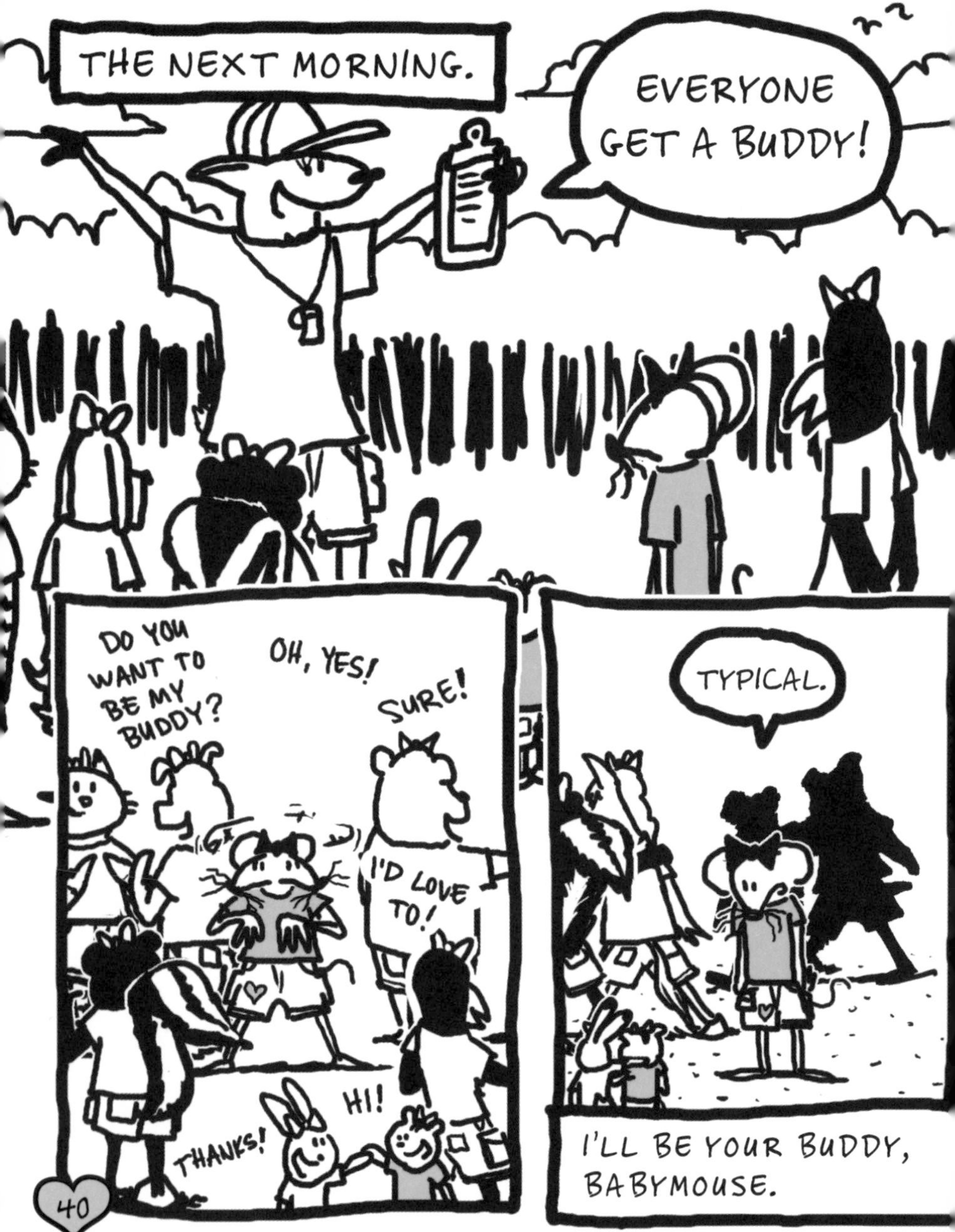
THE NEXT MORNING.
EVERYONE GET A BUDDY!
DO YOU WANT TO BE MY BUDDY?
OH, YES!
SURE!
I'D LOVE TO!
HI!
THANKS!
TYPICAL.
I'LL BE YOUR BUDDY, BABYMOUSE.

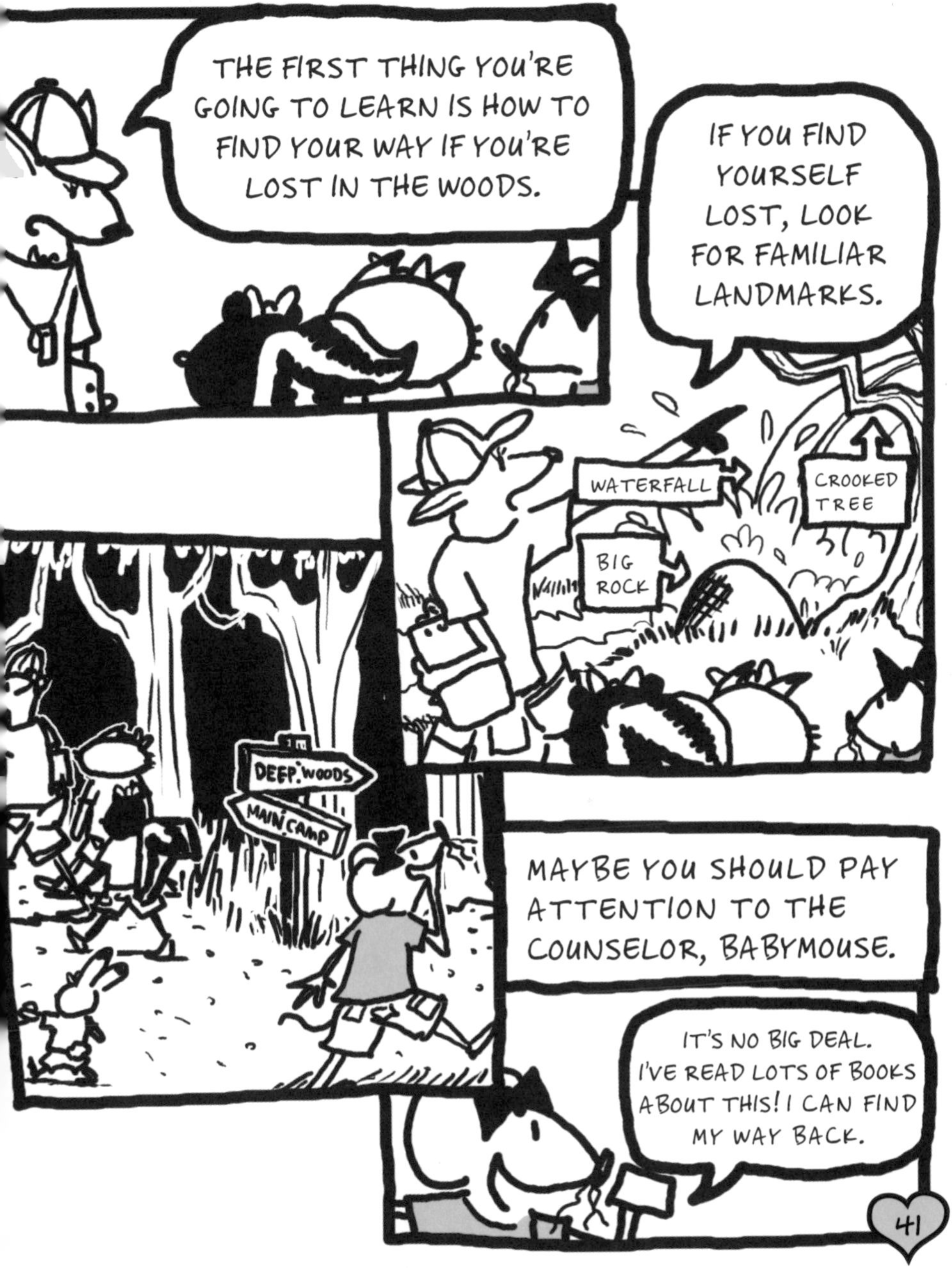
THE FIRST THING YOU'RE GOING TO LEARN IS HOW TO FIND YOUR WAY IF YOU'RE LOST IN THE WOODS.
IF YOU FIND YOURSELF LOST, LOOK FOR FAMILIAR LANDMARKS.
WATERFALL
CROOKED TREE
BIG ROCK
DEEP WOODS
MAIN CAMP
MAYBE YOU SHOULD PAY ATTENTION TO THE COUNSELOR, BABYMOUSE.
IT'S NO BIG DEAL. I'VE READ LOTS OF BOOKS ABOUT THIS! I CAN FIND MY WAY BACK.

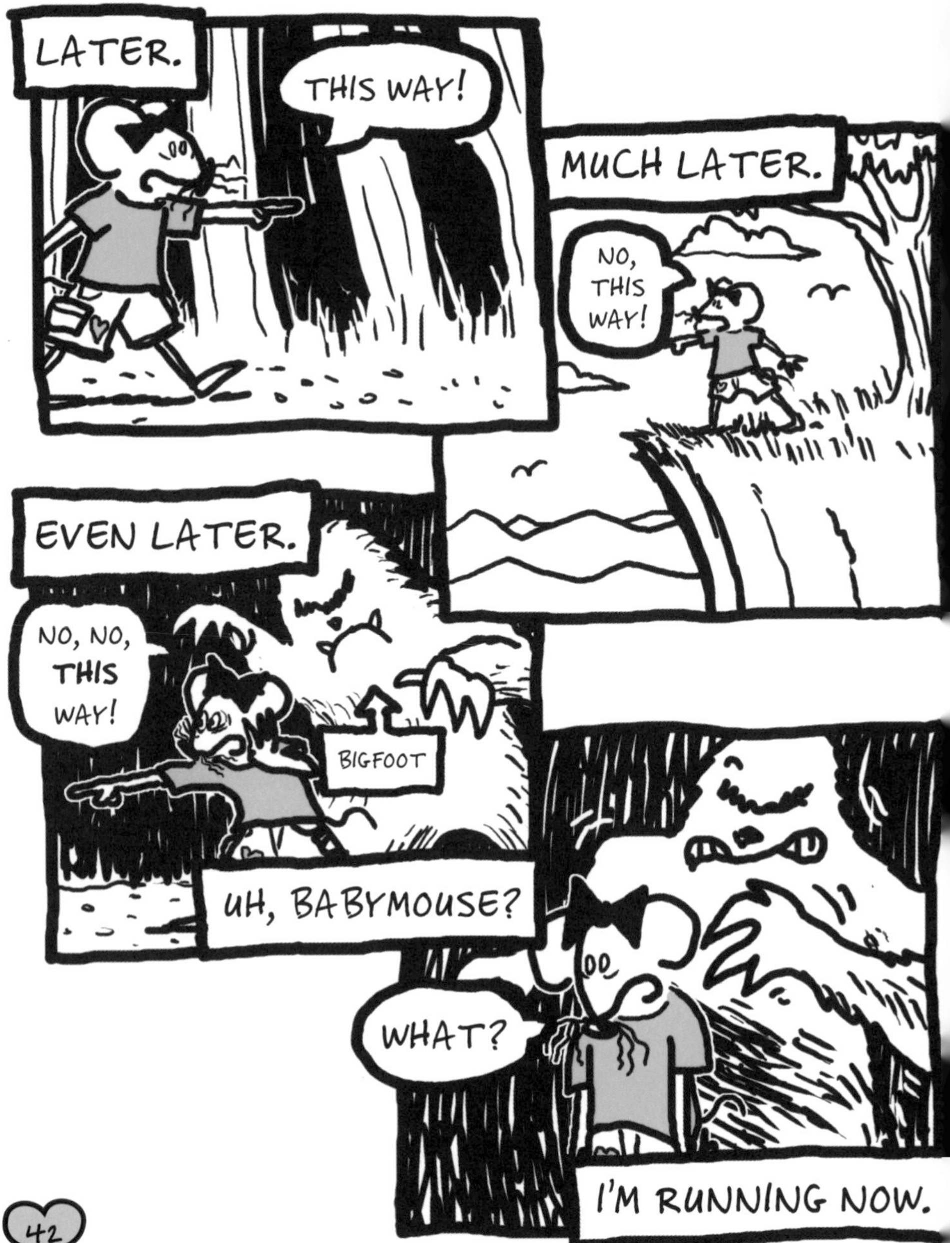
LATER.
THIS WAY!
MUCH LATER.
NO, THIS WAY!
EVEN LATER.
NO, NO, THIS WAY!
BIGFOOT
UH, BABYMOUSE?
WHAT?
I'M RUNNING NOW.

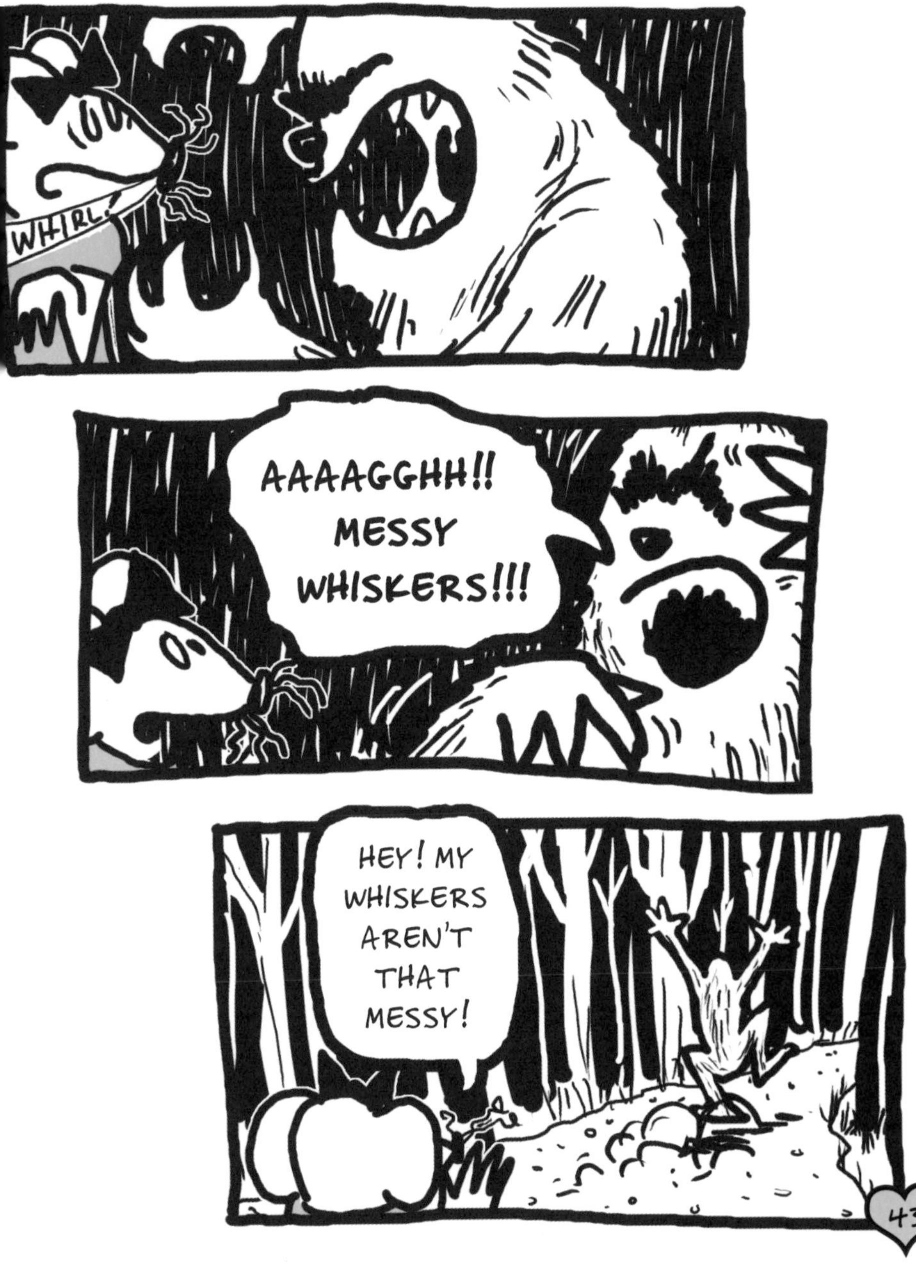
WHIRL!
AAAAGGHH!! MESSY WHISKERS!!!
HEY! MY WHISKERS AREN'T THAT MESSY!

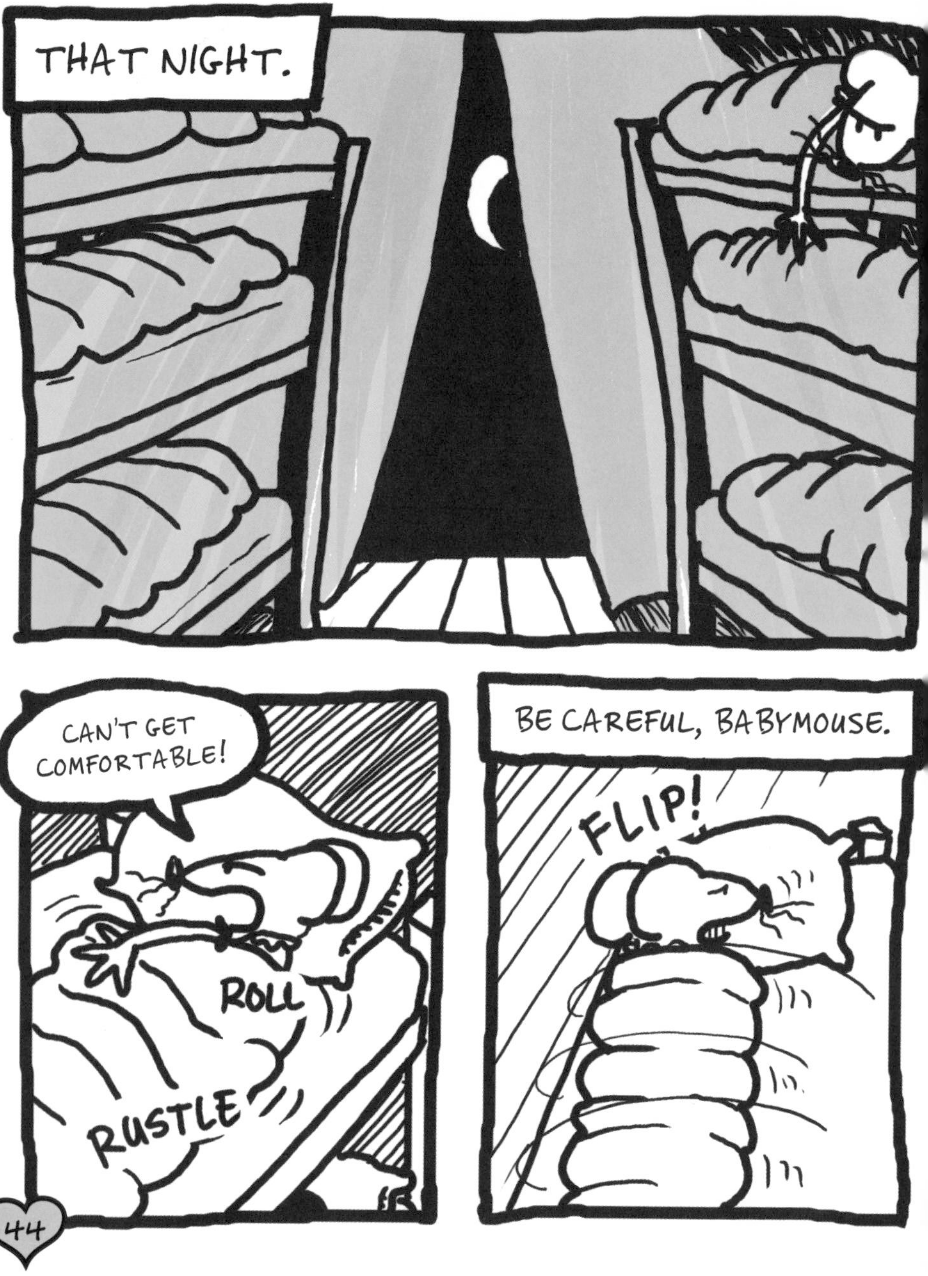
THAT NIGHT.
CAN'T GET COMFORTABLE!
ROLL
RUSTLE
BE CAREFUL, BABYMOUSE.
FLIP!

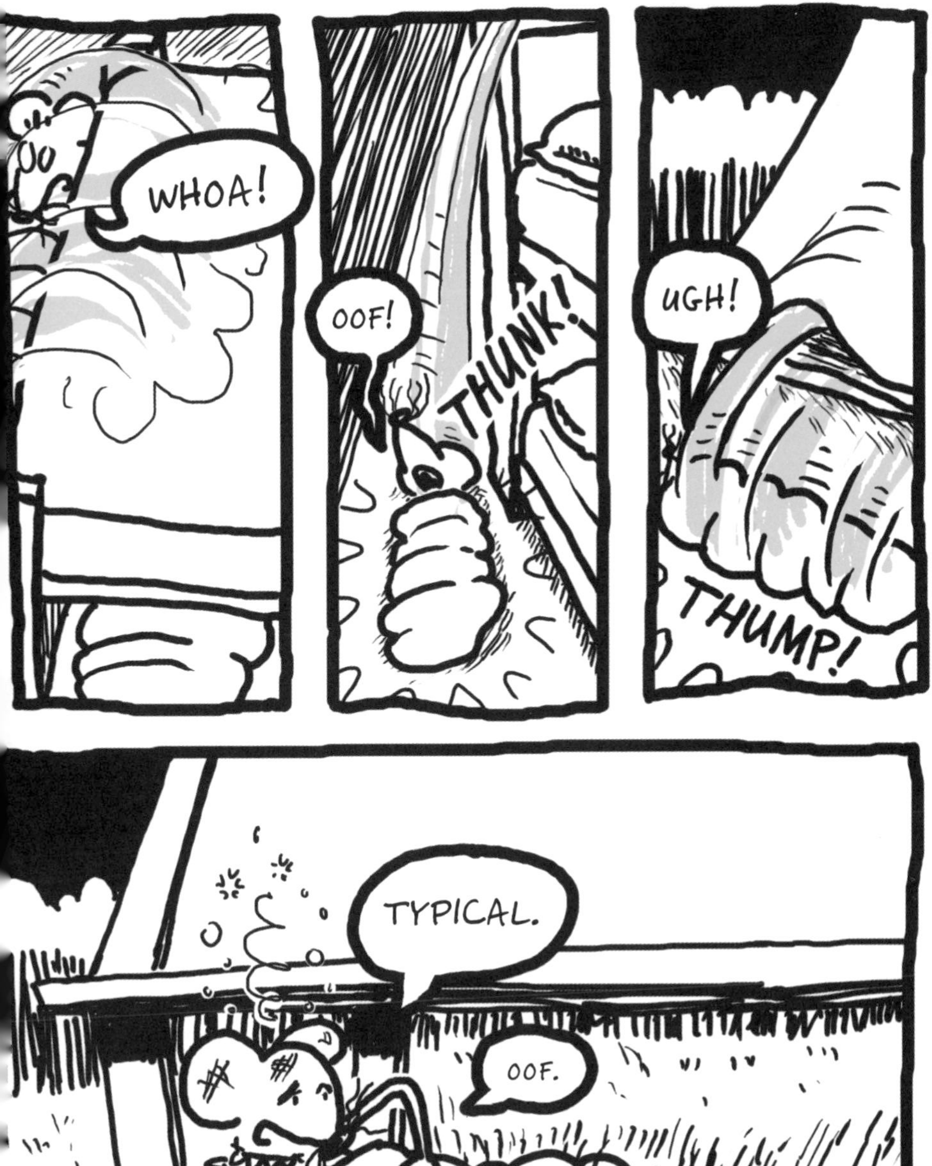
WHOA!
OOF!
THUNK!
UGH!
THUMP!
TYPICAL.
OOF.

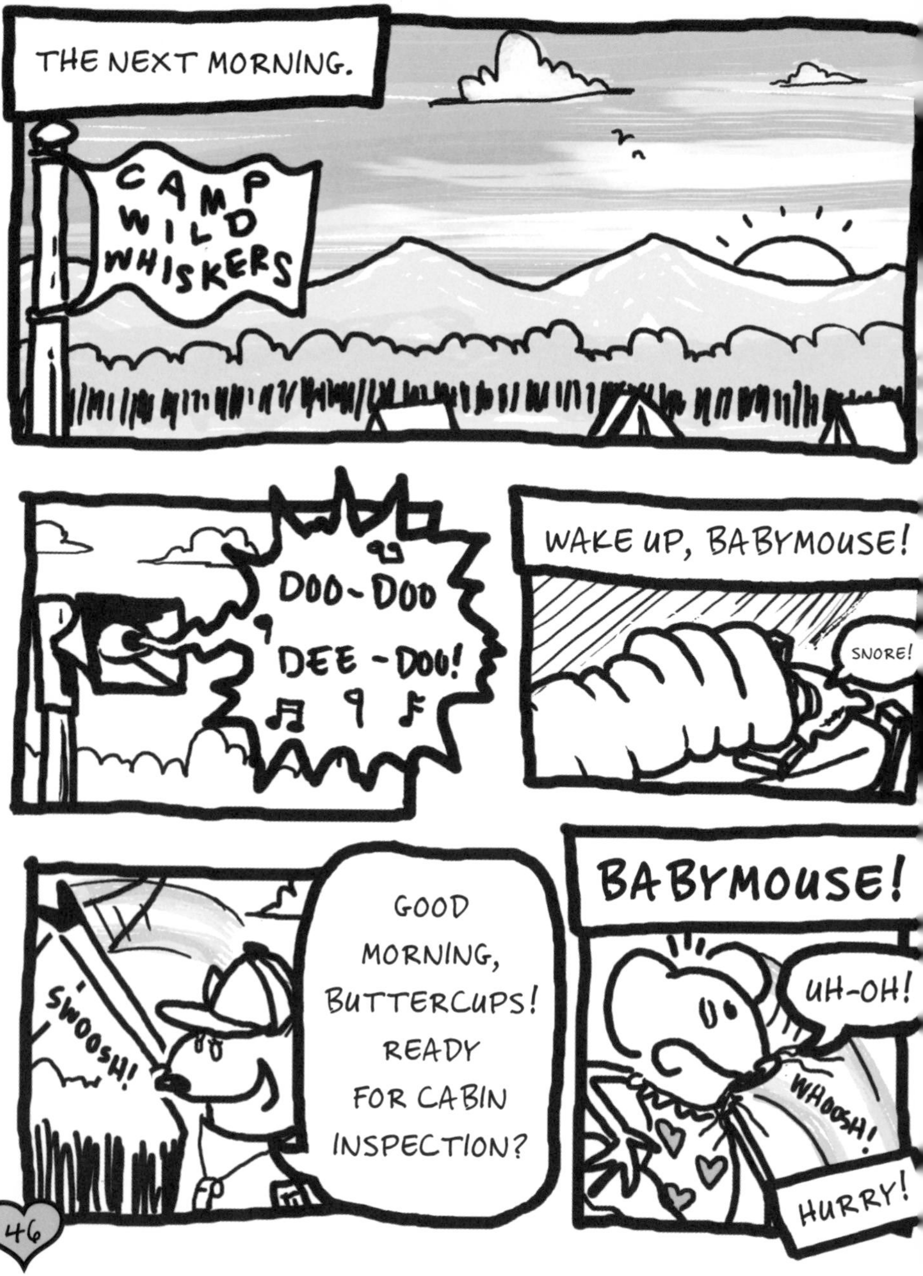
THE NEXT MORNING.
CAMP WILD WHISKERS
DOO-DOO DEE-DOO!
WAKE UP, BABYMOUSE!
SNORE!
SWOOSH!
GOOD MORNING, BUTTERCUPS! READY FOR CABIN INSPECTION?
BABYMOUSE!
UH-OH!
WHOOSH!
HURRY!

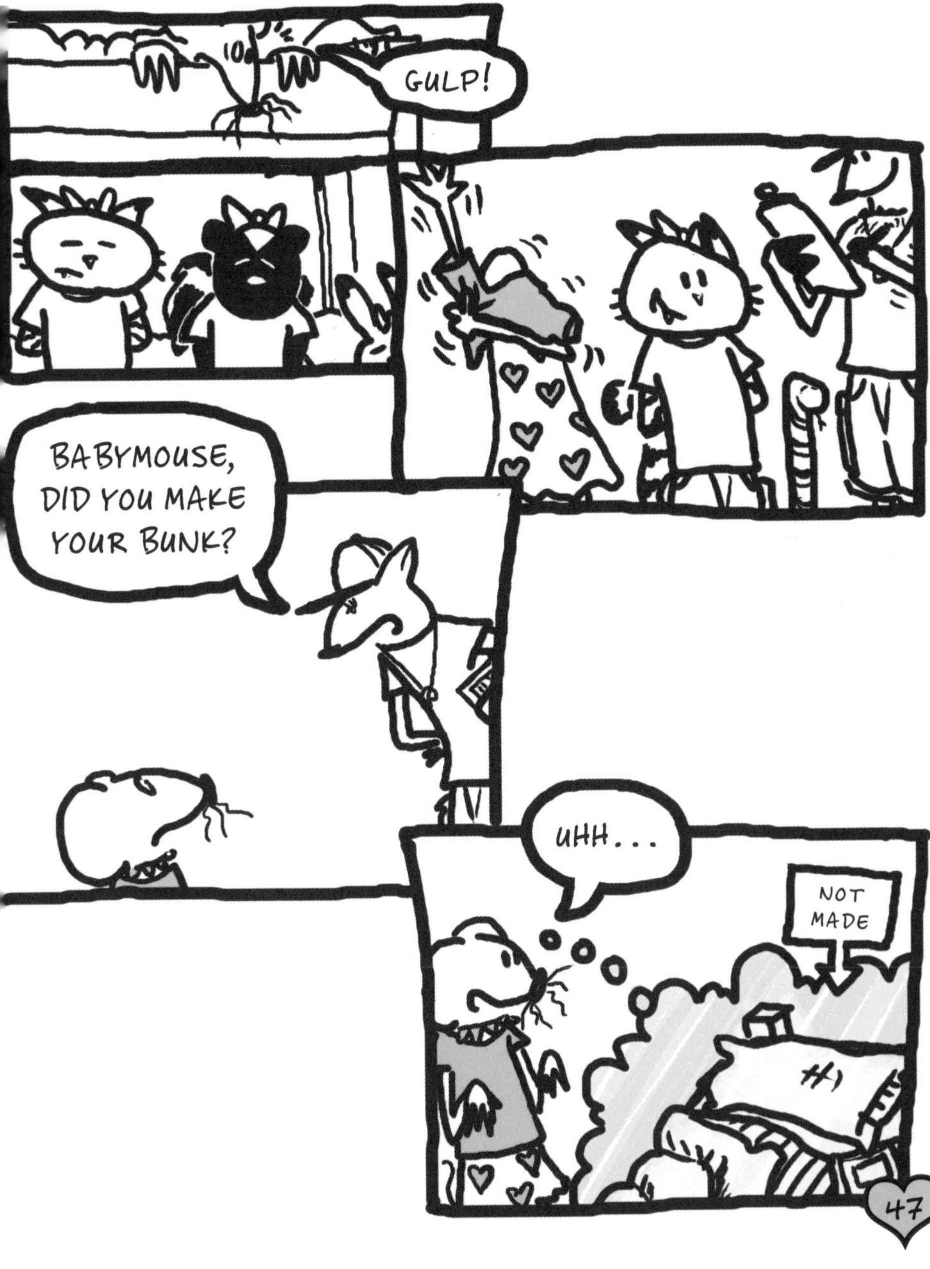
GULP!
BABYMOUSE, DID YOU MAKE YOUR BUNK?
UHH...
NOT MADE

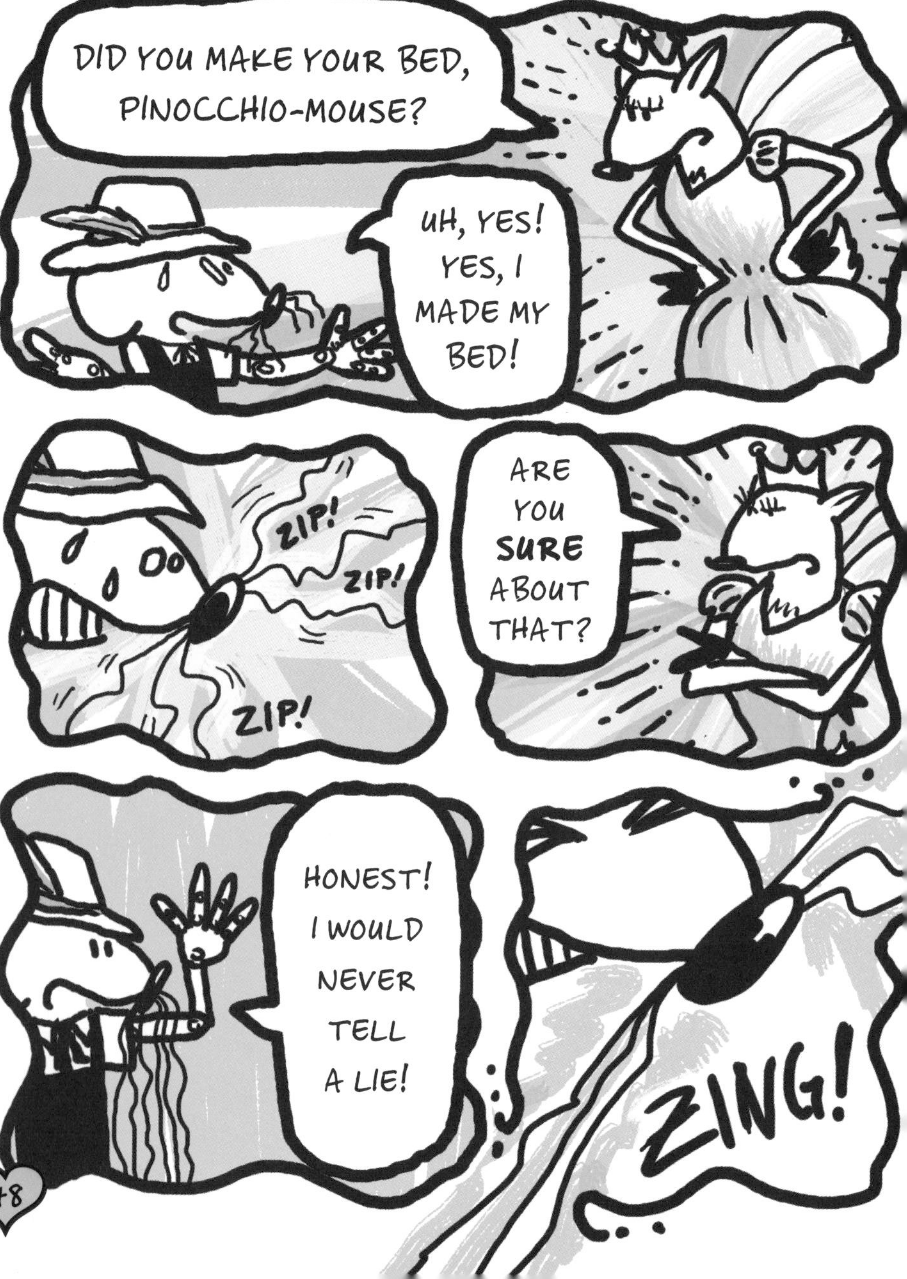
DID YOU MAKE YOUR BED, PINOCCHIO-MOUSE?
UH, YES! YES, I MADE MY BED!
ZIP!
ZIP!
ZIP!
ARE YOU **SURE** ABOUT THAT?
HONEST! I WOULD NEVER TELL A LIE!
ZING!

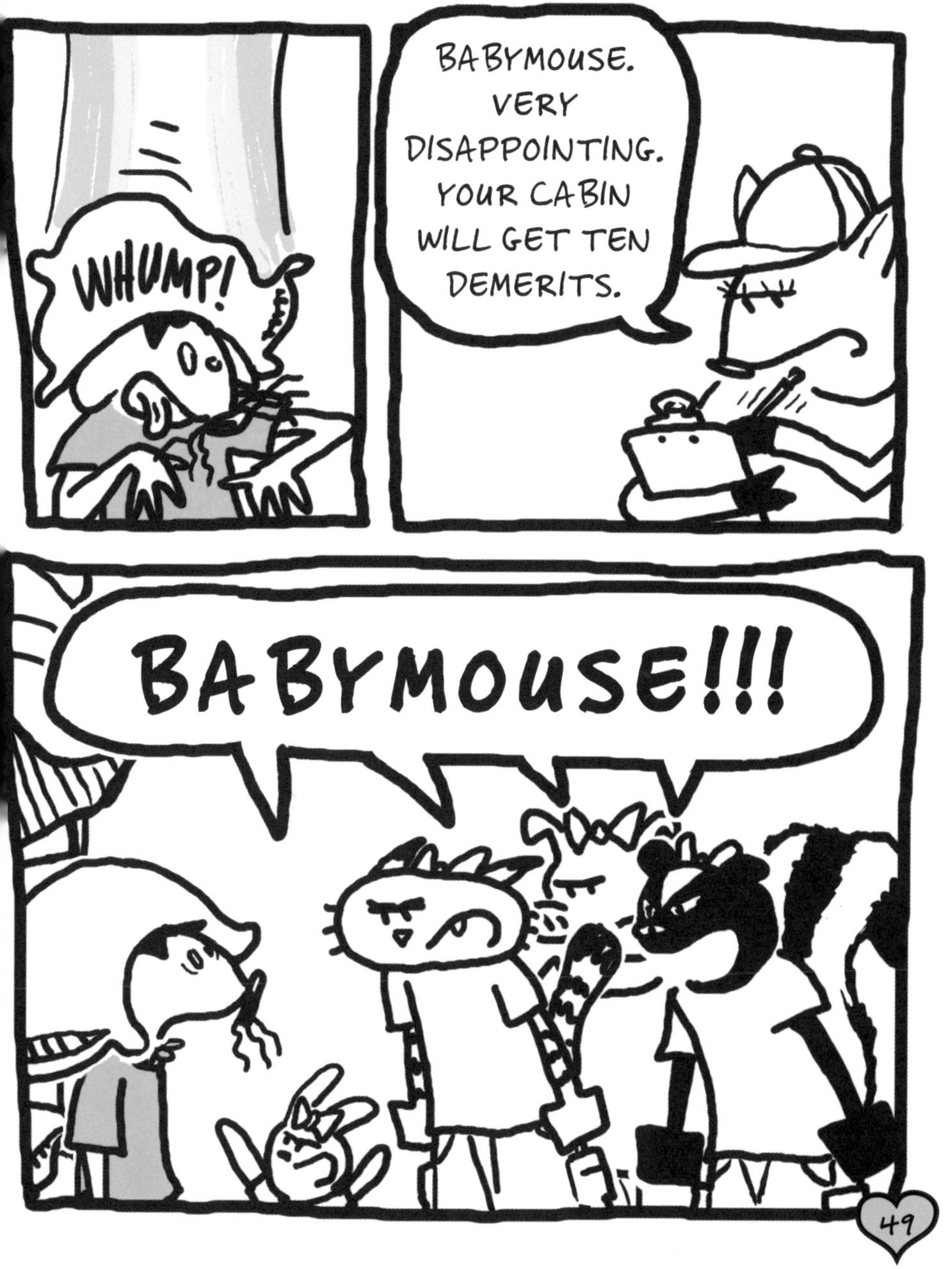
WHUMP!
BABYMOUSE. VERY DISAPPOINTING. YOUR CABIN WILL GET TEN DEMERITS.
BABYMOUSE!!!

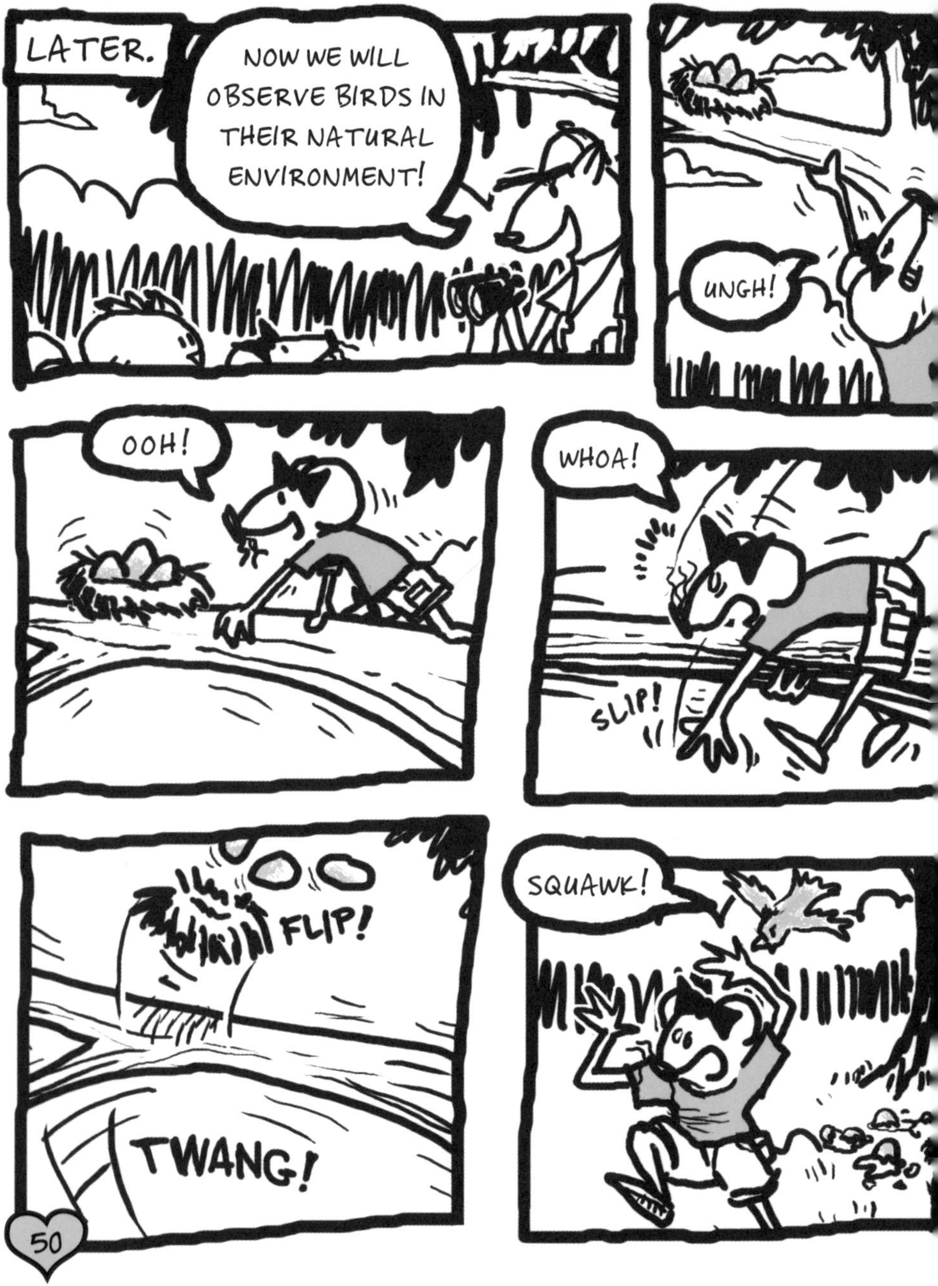
LATER.
NOW WE WILL OBSERVE BIRDS IN THEIR NATURAL ENVIRONMENT!
UNGH!
OOH!
WHOA!
SLIP!
FLIP!
TWANG!
SQUAWK!

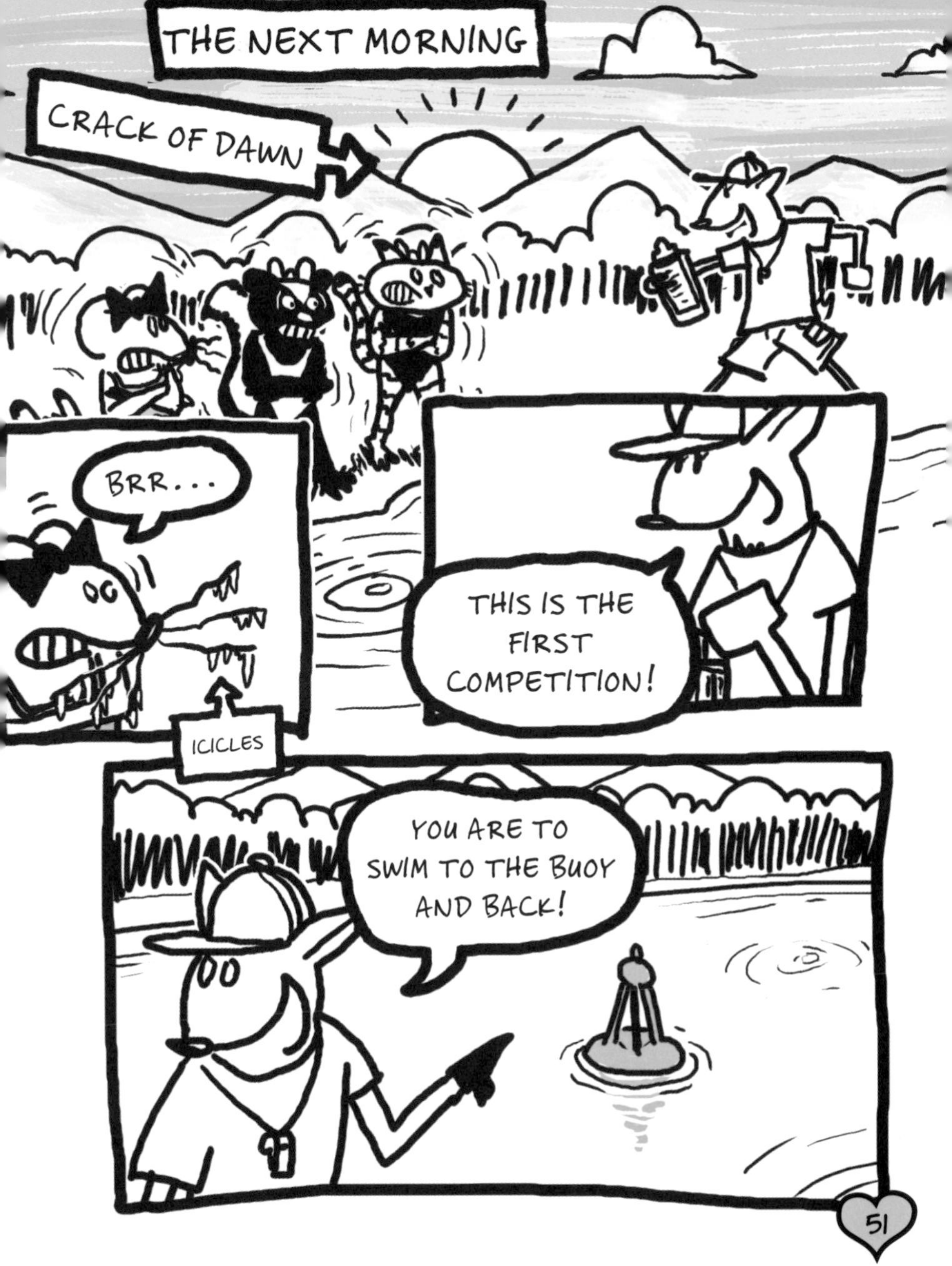
THE NEXT MORNING
CRACK OF DAWN
BRR...
ICICLES
THIS IS THE FIRST COMPETITION!
YOU ARE TO SWIM TO THE BUOY AND BACK!

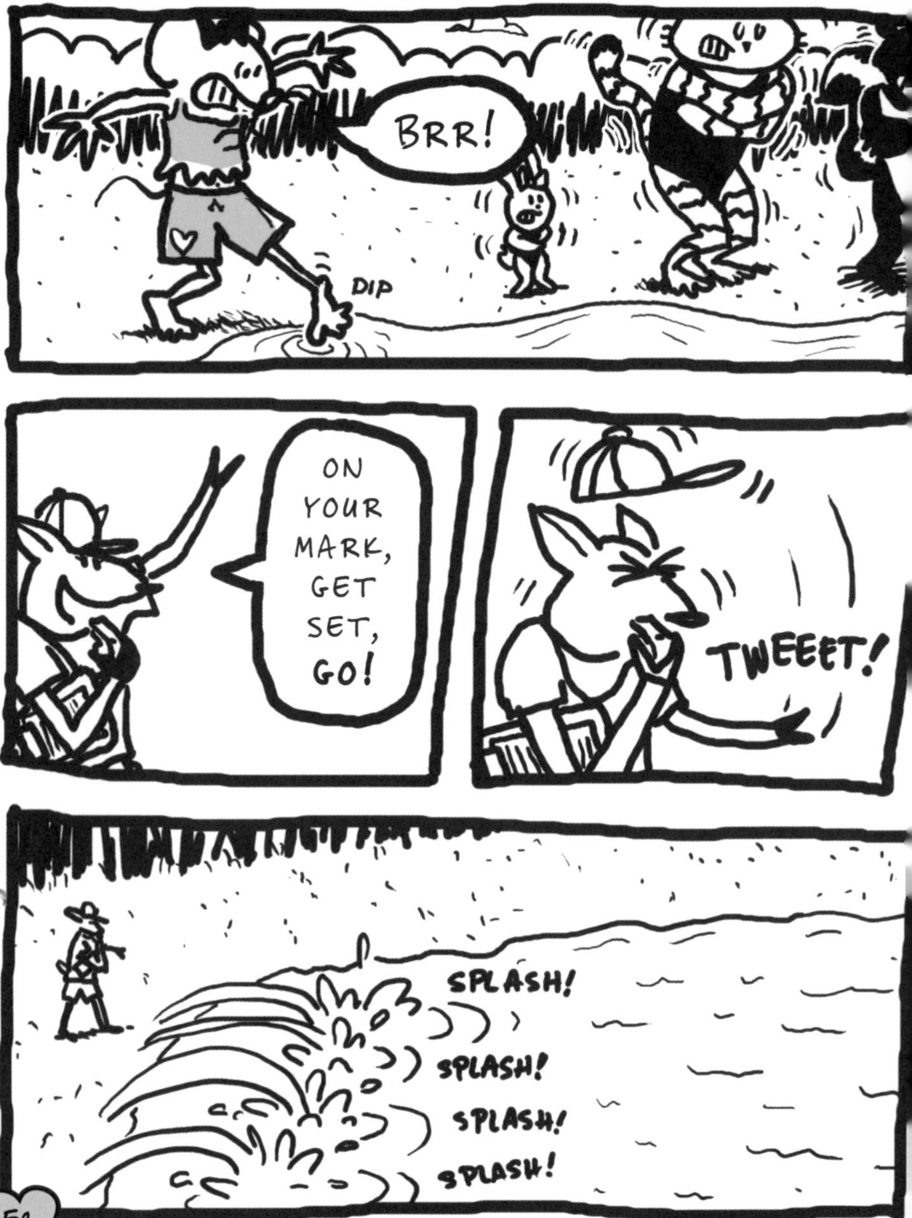
BRR!
DIP
ON YOUR MARK, GET SET, GO!
TWEEET!
SPLASH!
SPLASH!
SPLASH!
SPLASH!

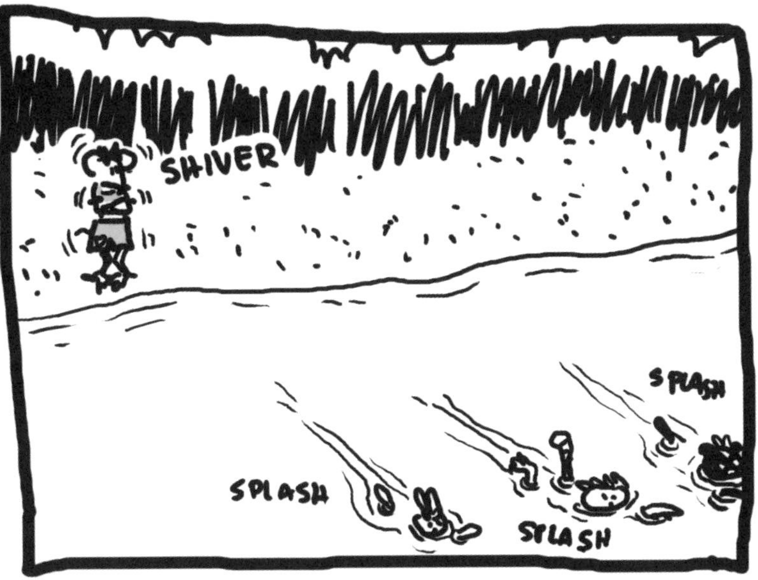
SHIVER
SPLASH
SPLASH
SPLASH

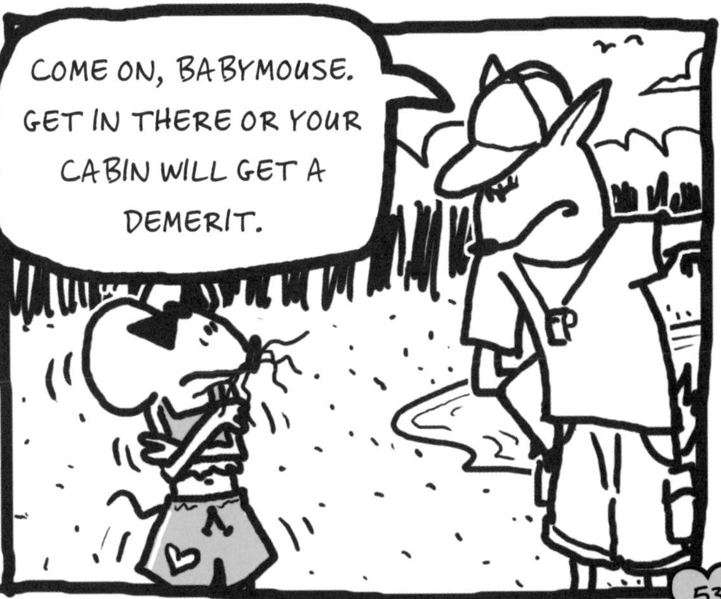
COME ON, BABYMOUSE. GET IN THERE OR YOUR CABIN WILL GET A DEMERIT.

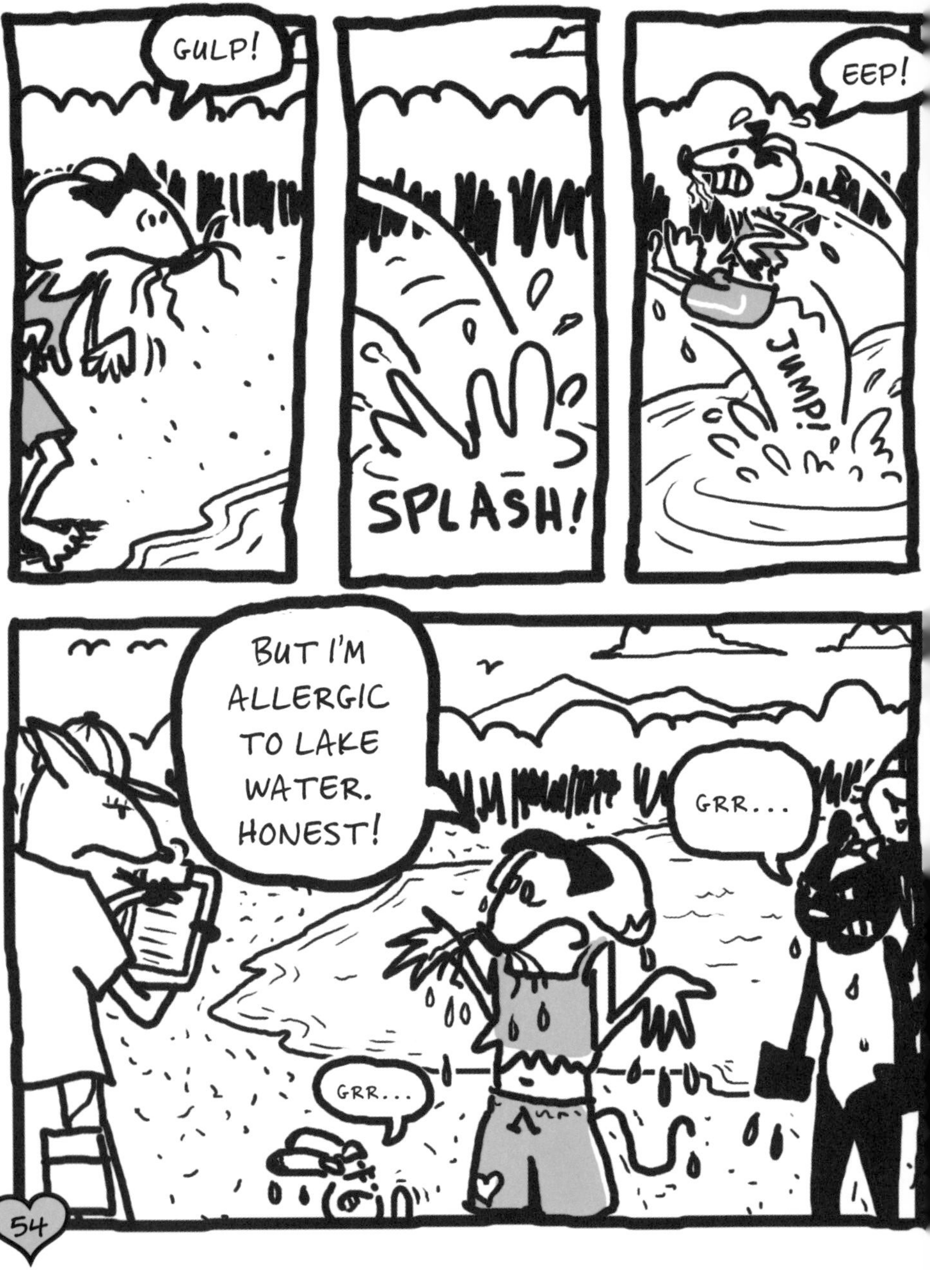
GULP!
SPLASH!
EEP!
JUMP!
BUT I'M ALLERGIC TO LAKE WATER. HONEST!
GRR...
GRR...

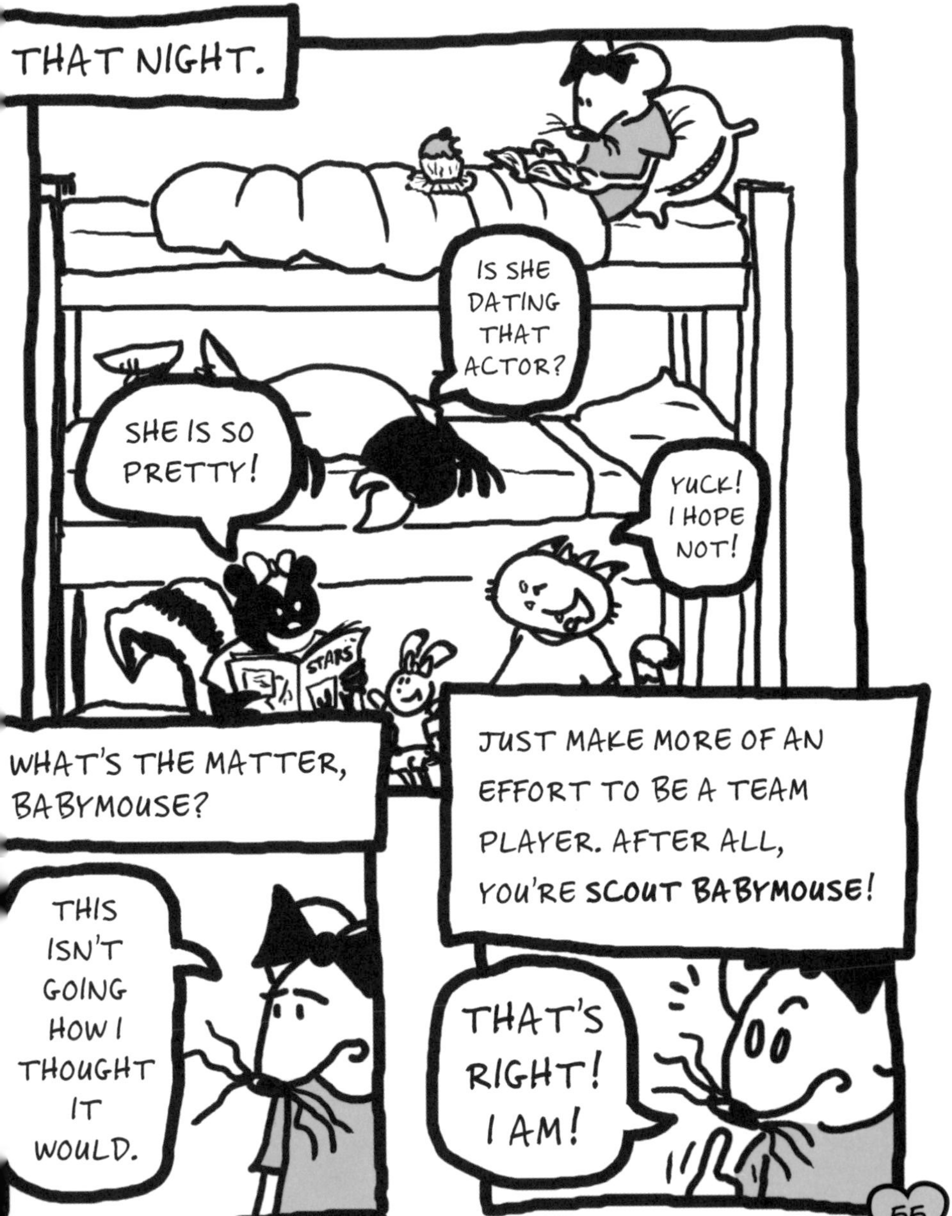
THAT NIGHT.
IS SHE DATING THAT ACTOR?
SHE IS SO PRETTY!
YUCK! I HOPE NOT!
STARS
WHAT'S THE MATTER, BABYMOUSE?
JUST MAKE MORE OF AN EFFORT TO BE A TEAM PLAYER. AFTER ALL, YOU'RE **SCOUT BABYMOUSE**!
THIS ISN'T GOING HOW I THOUGHT IT WOULD.
THAT'S RIGHT! I AM!

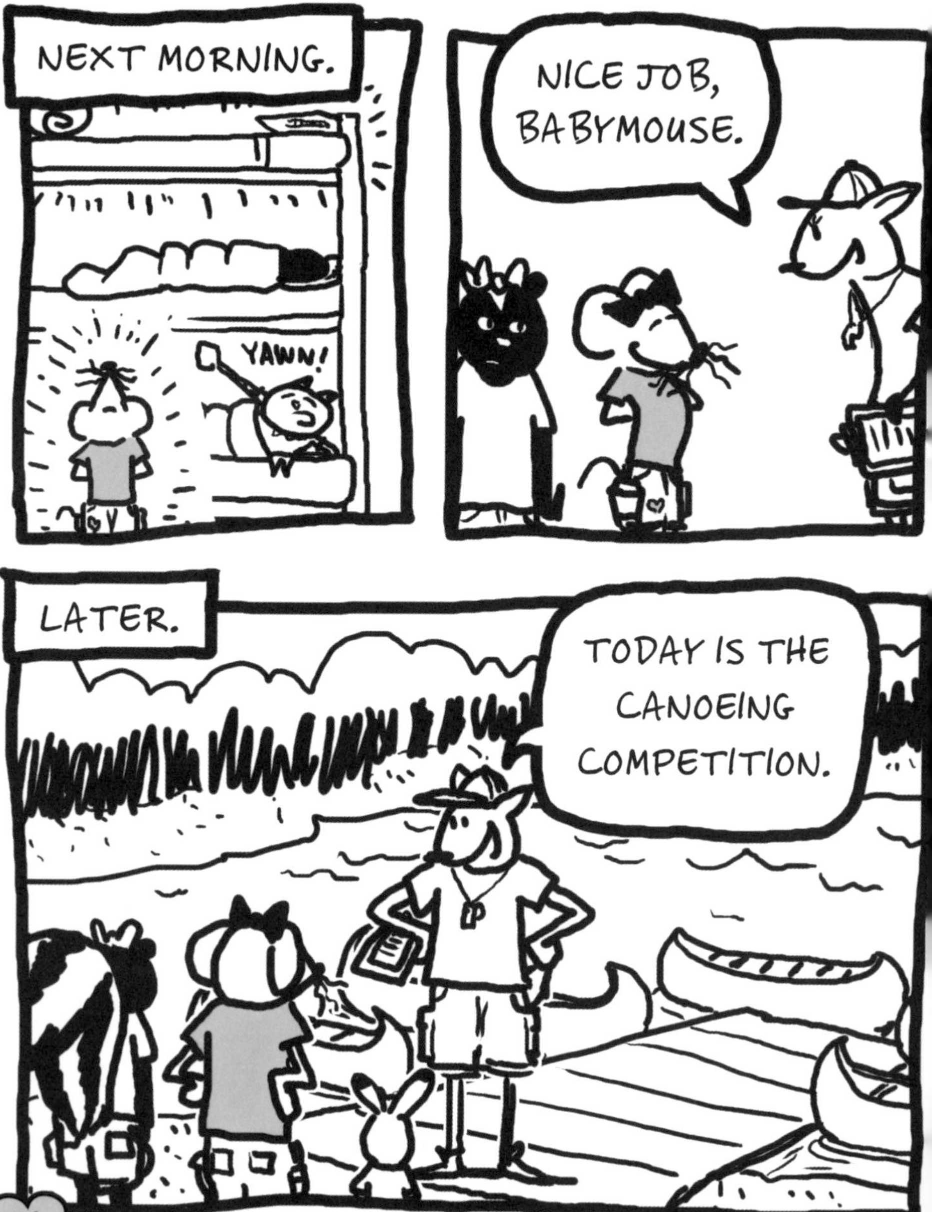
NEXT MORNING.
YAWN!
NICE JOB, BABYMOUSE.
LATER.
TODAY IS THE CANOEING COMPETITION.

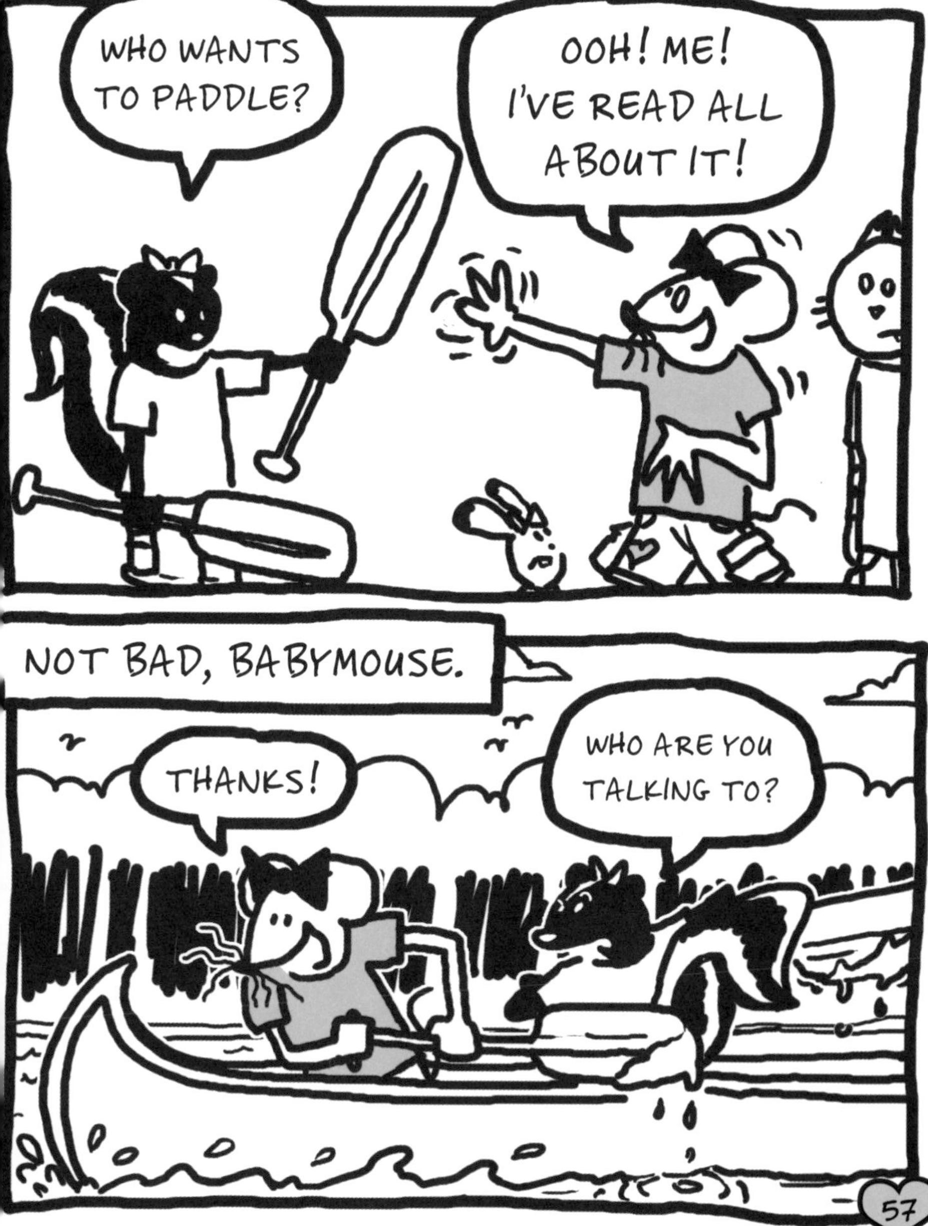
WHO WANTS TO PADDLE?
OOH! ME! I'VE READ ALL ABOUT IT!
NOT BAD, BABYMOUSE.
THANKS!
WHO ARE YOU TALKING TO?

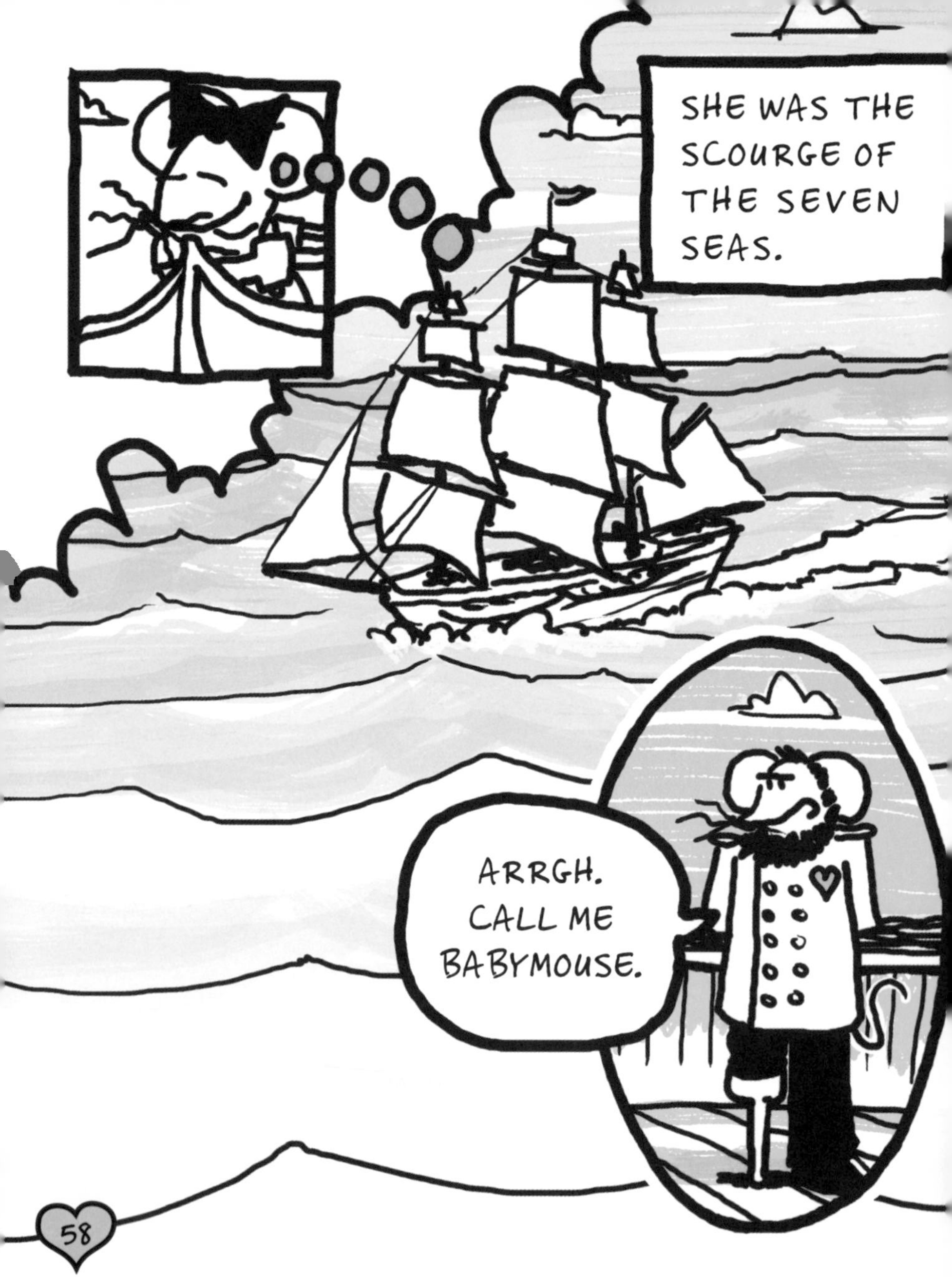
SHE WAS THE SCOURGE OF THE SEVEN SEAS.
ARRGH. CALL ME BABYMOUSE.

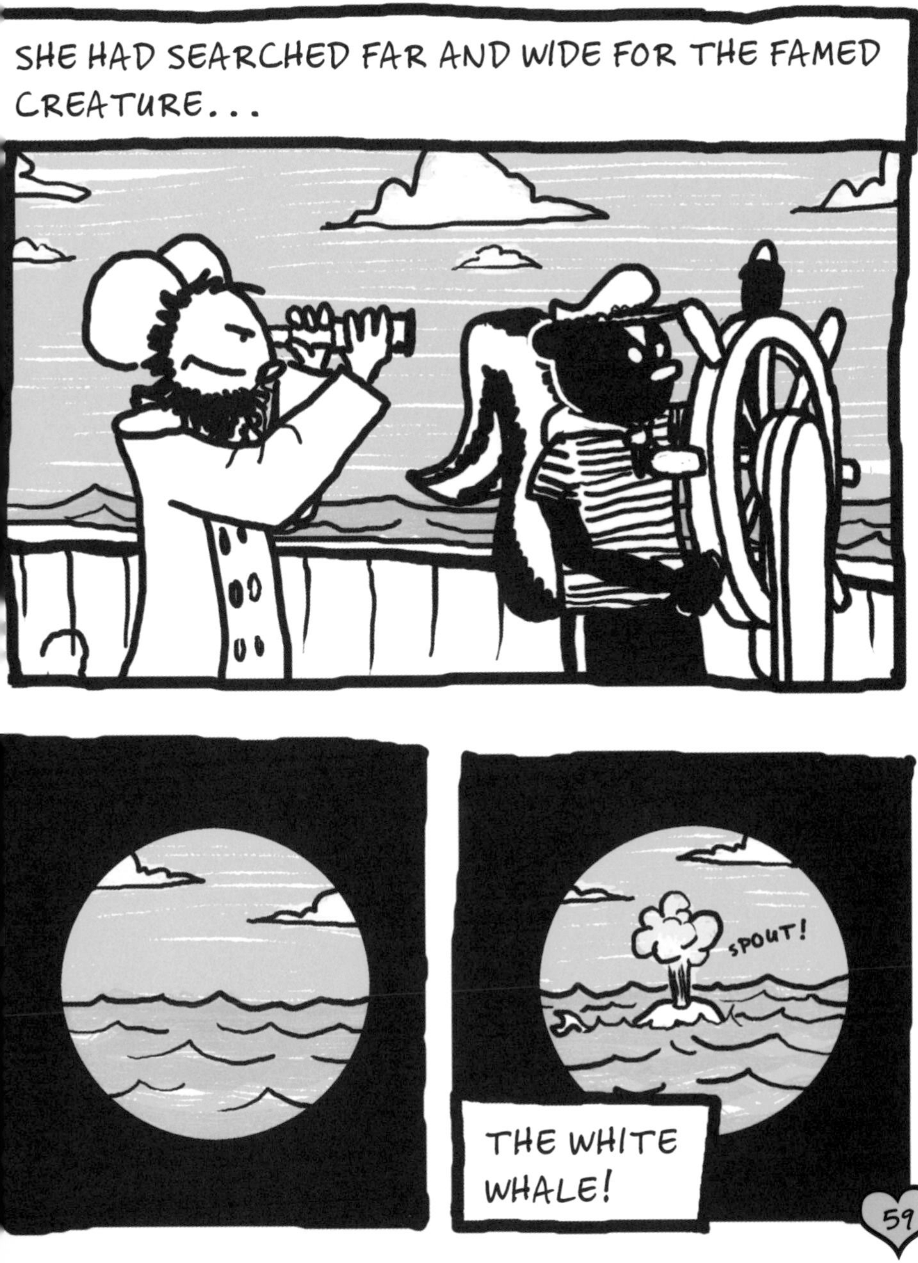
SHE HAD SEARCHED FAR AND WIDE FOR THE FAMED CREATURE...
SPOUT!
THE WHITE WHALE!

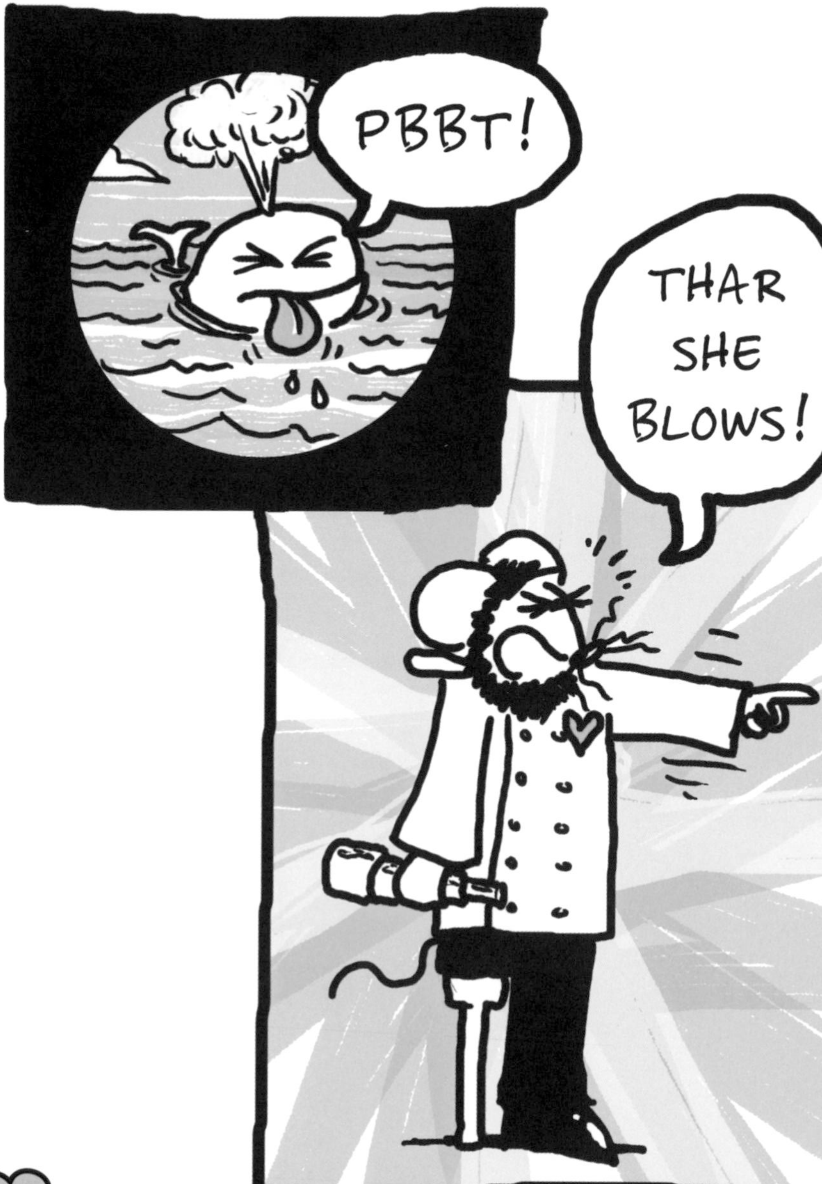
PBBT!
THAR SHE BLOWS!

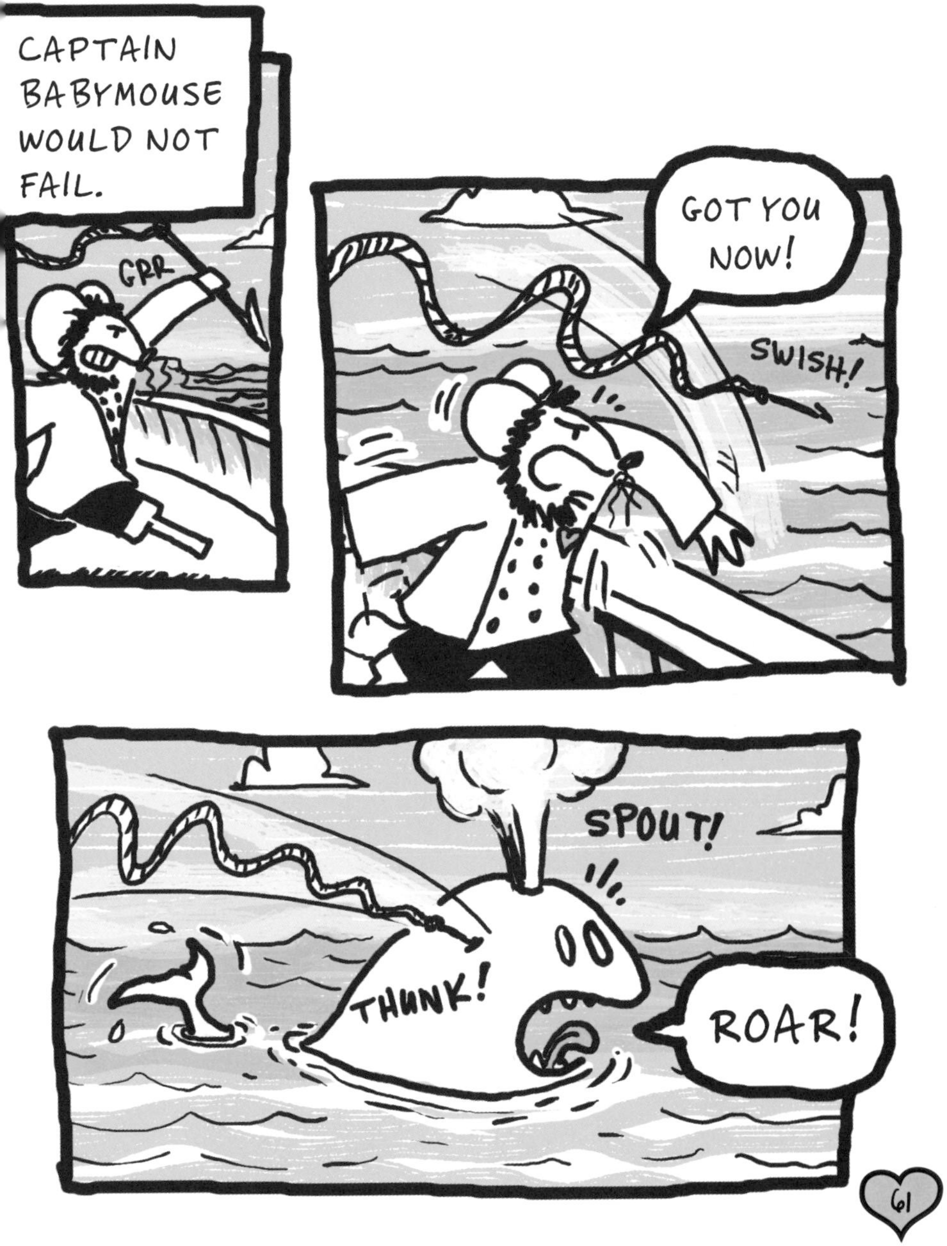
CAPTAIN BABYMOUSE WOULD NOT FAIL.
GRR
GOT YOU NOW!
SWISH!
SPOUT!
THUNK!
ROAR!

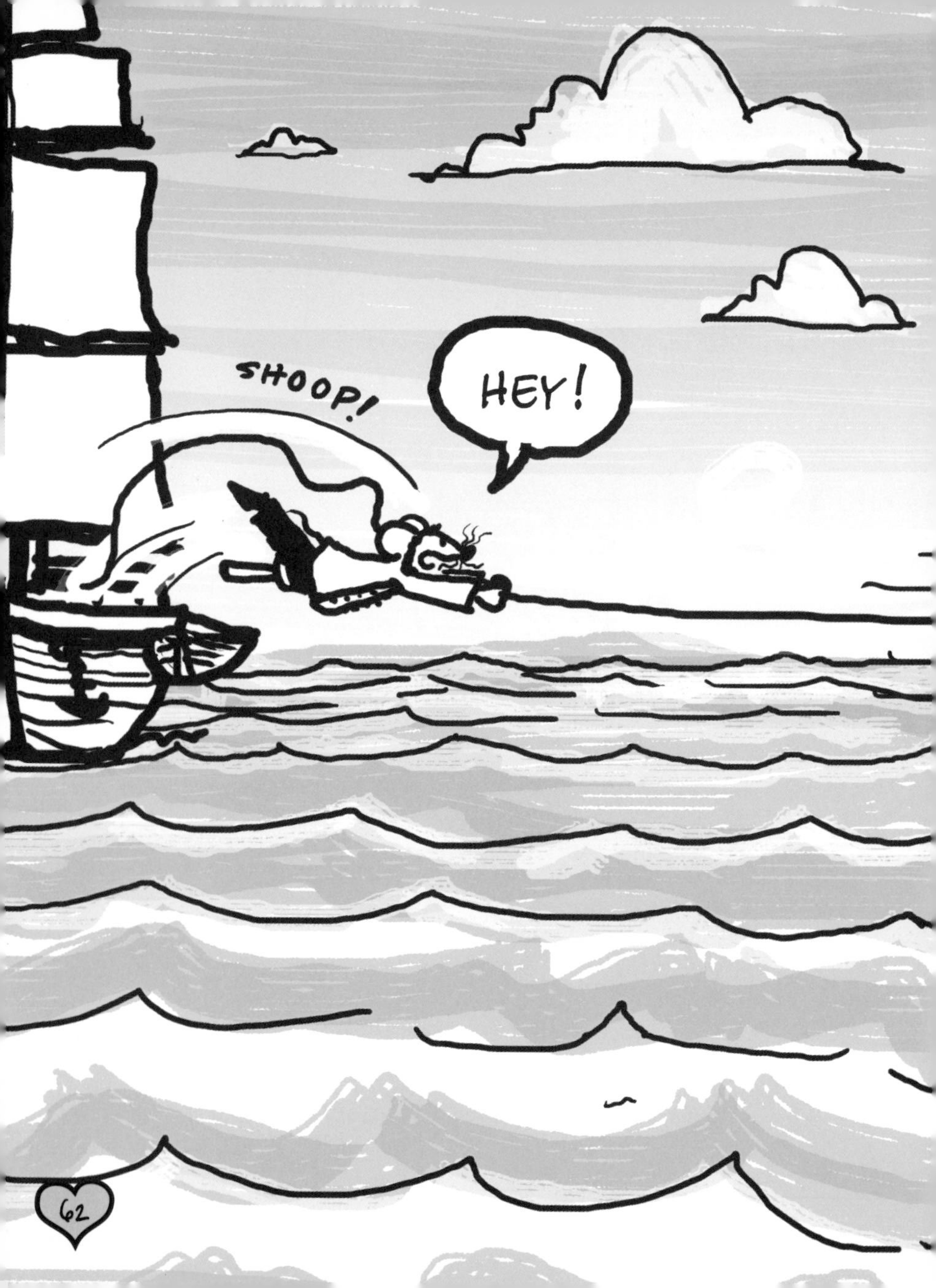
SHOOP!
HEY!

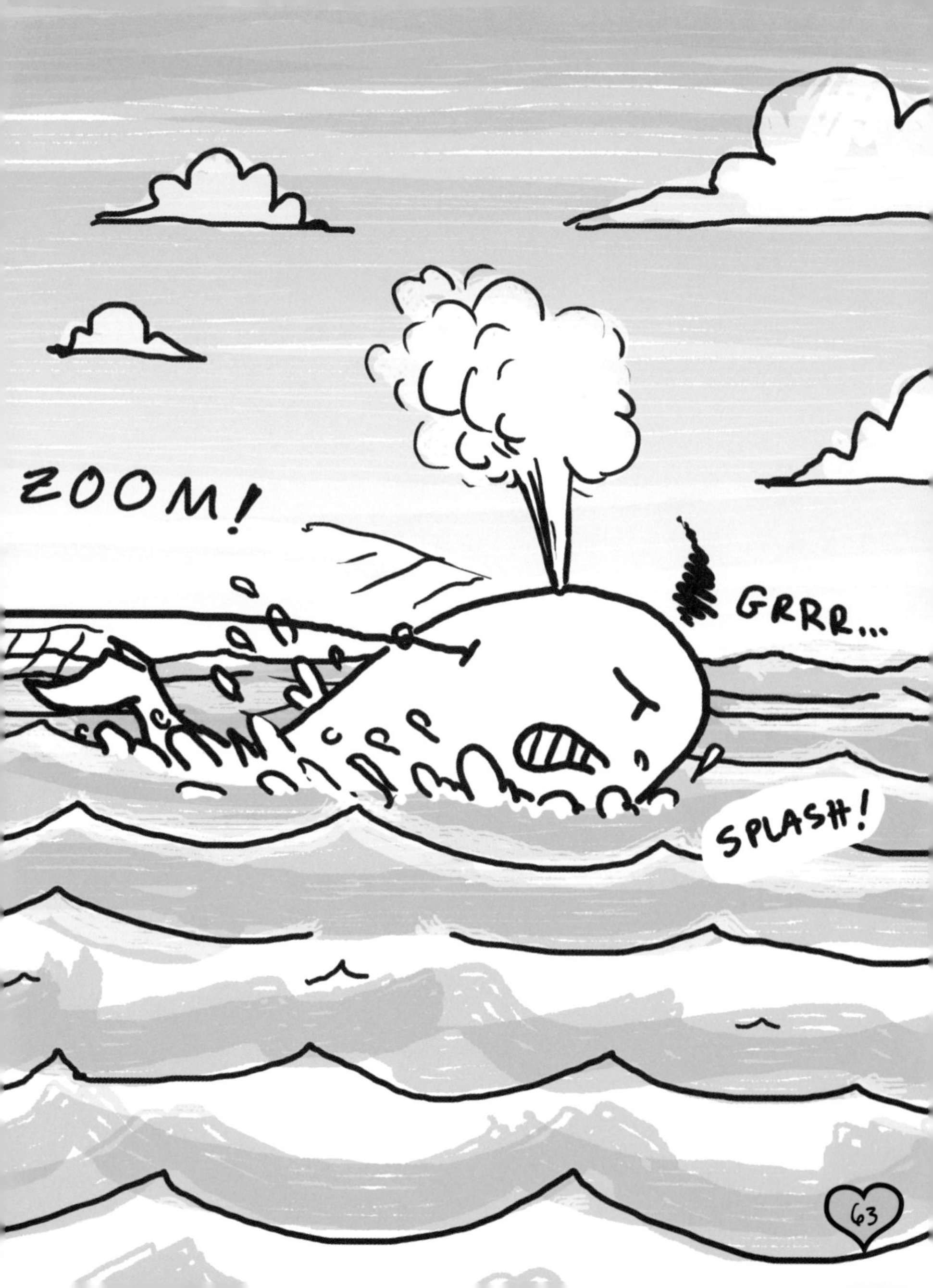
ZOOM!
GRRR...
SPLASH!

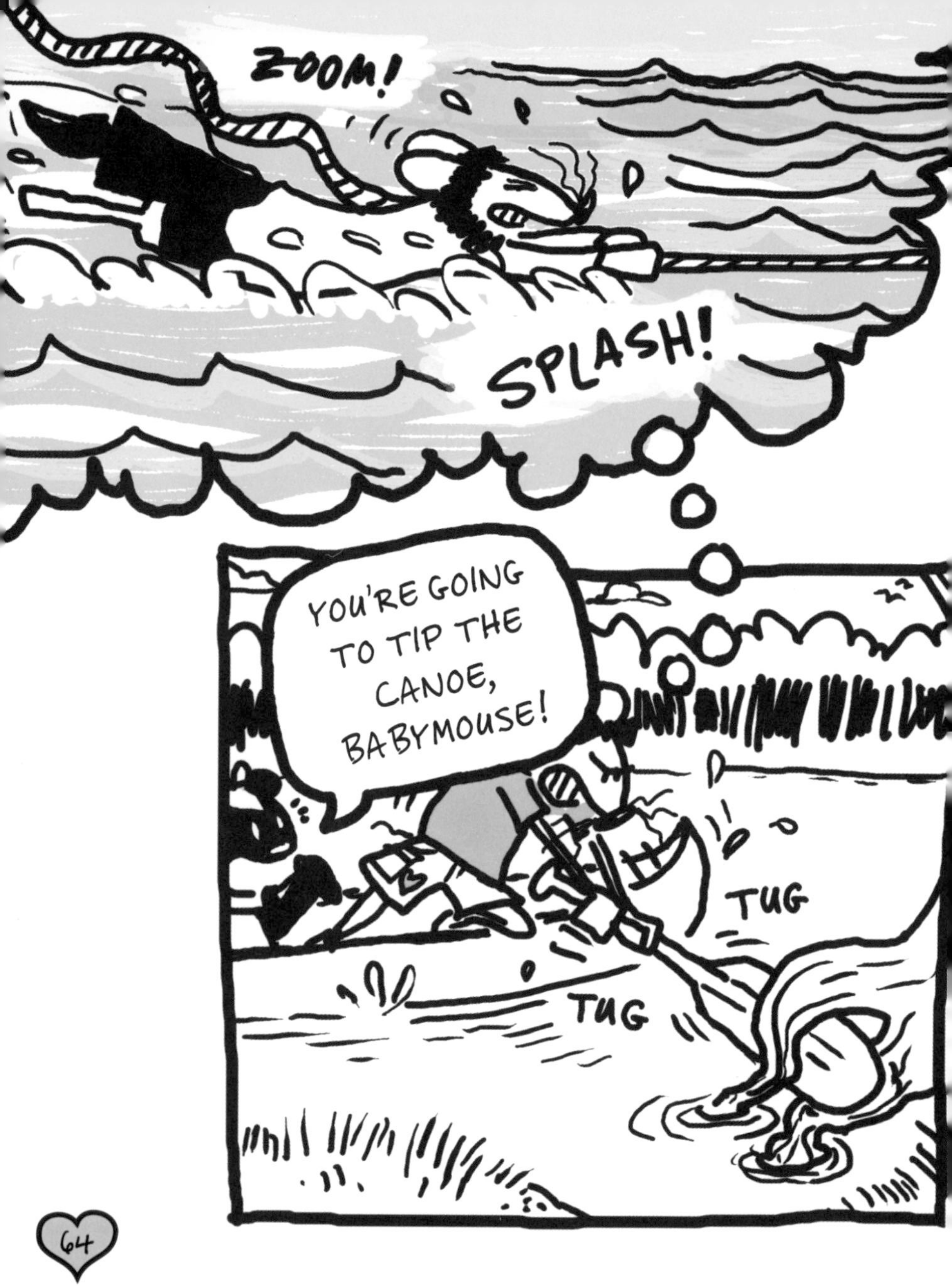
ZOOM!
SPLASH!
YOU'RE GOING TO TIP THE CANOE, BABYMOUSE!
TUG
TUG

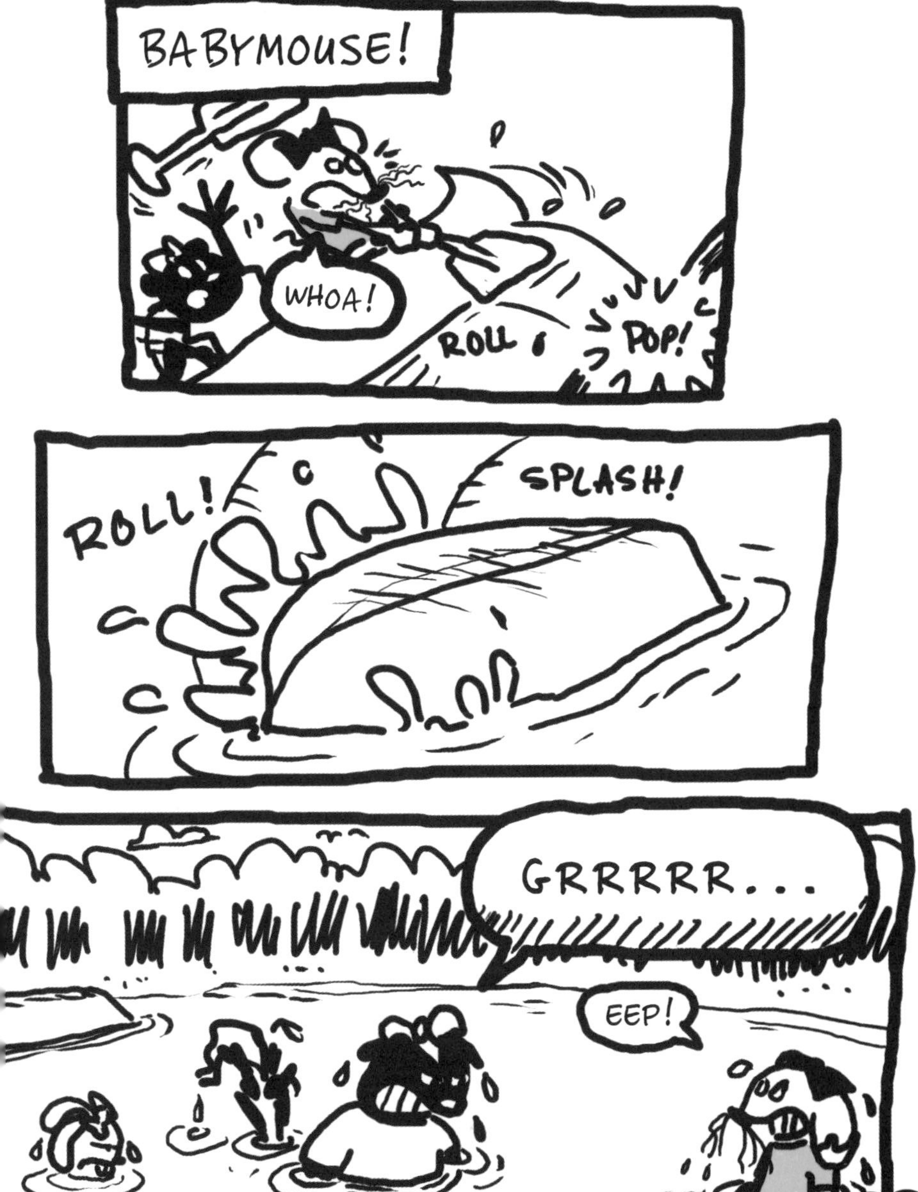
BABYMOUSE!
WHOA!
ROLL
POP!
ROLL!
SPLASH!
GRRRRR...
EEP!

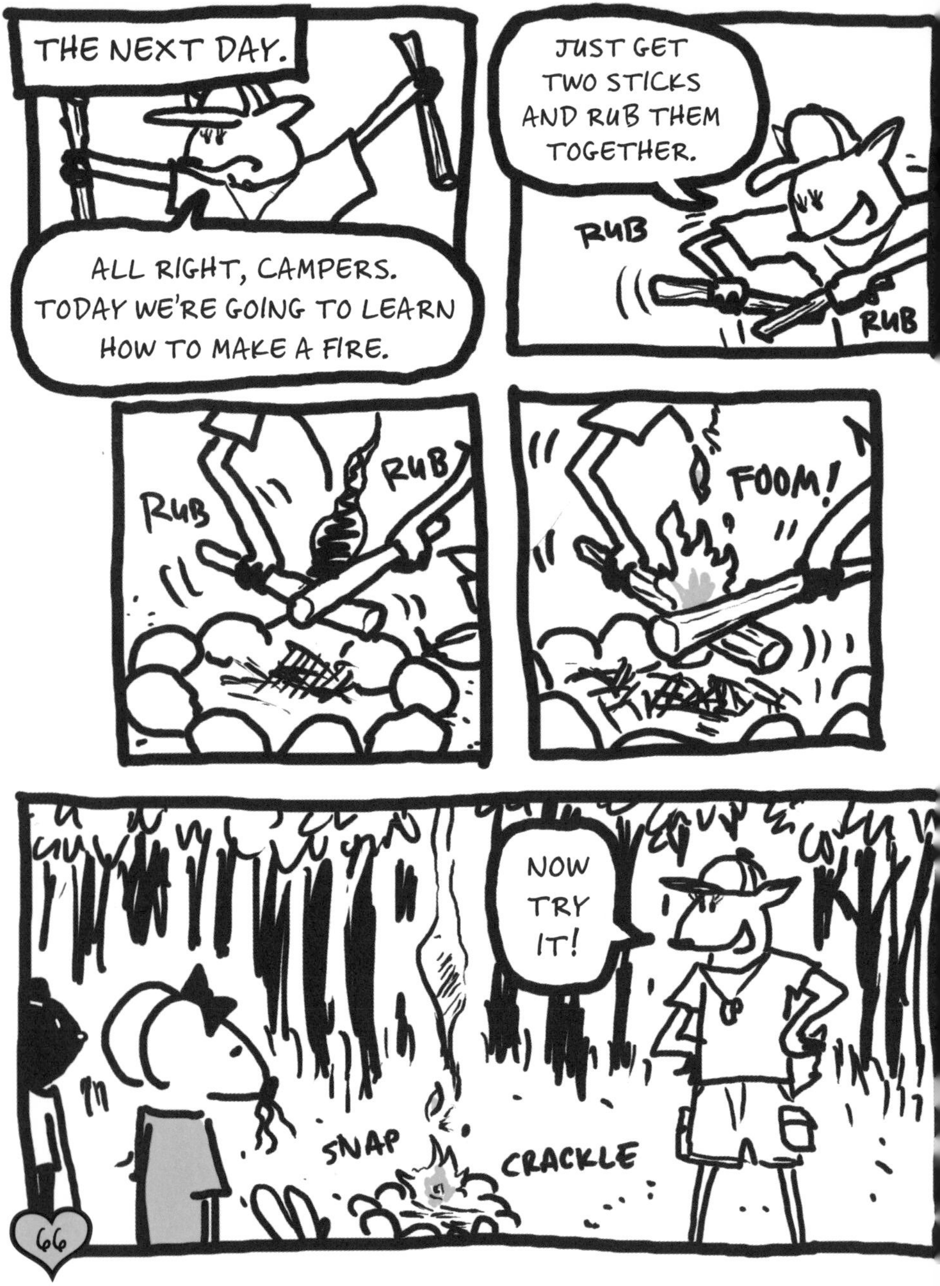
THE NEXT DAY.
ALL RIGHT, CAMPERS. TODAY WE'RE GOING TO LEARN HOW TO MAKE A FIRE.
JUST GET TWO STICKS AND RUB THEM TOGETHER.
RUB
RUB
RUB
RUB
FOOM!
NOW TRY IT!
SNAP
CRACKLE

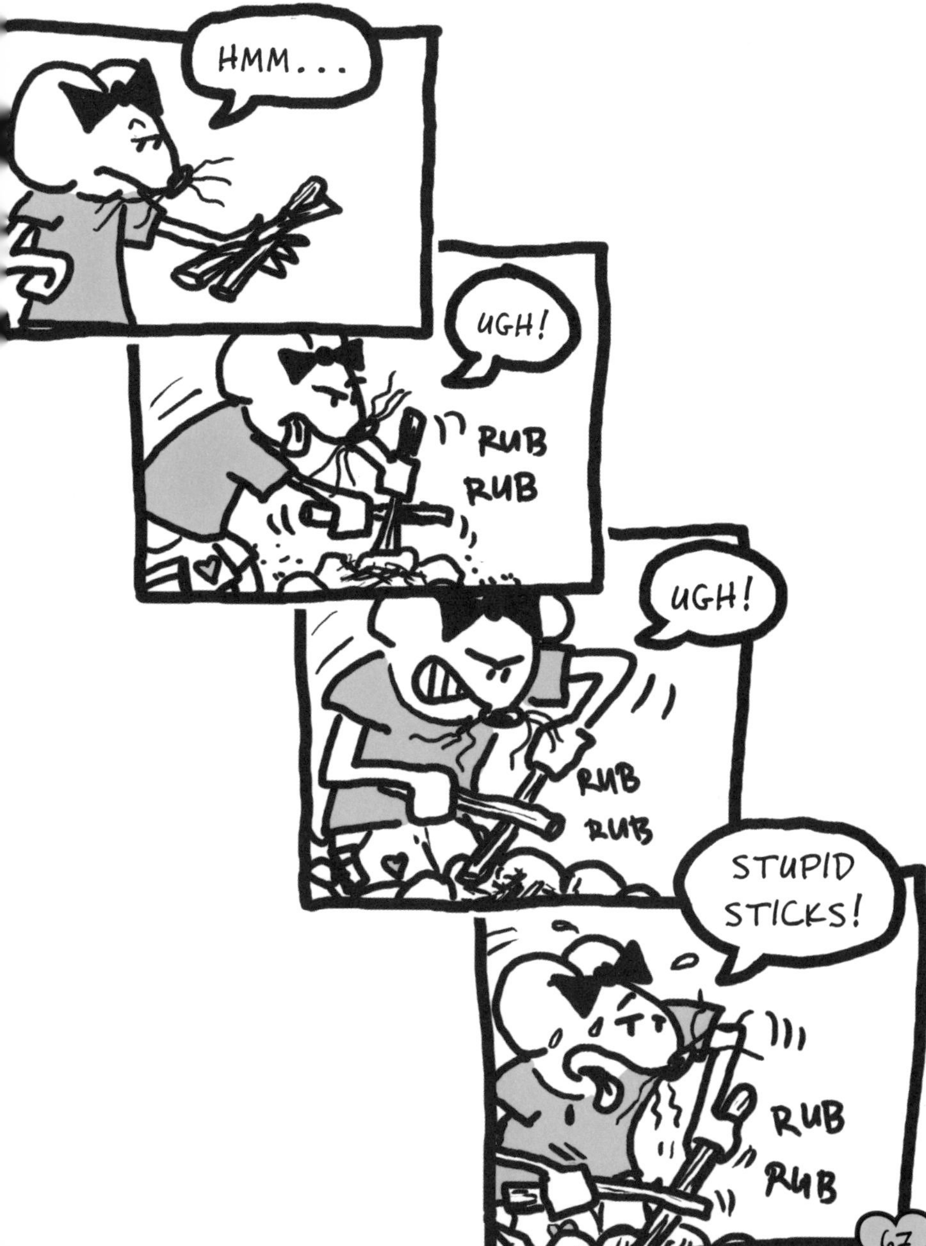
HMM...
UGH!
RUB
RUB
UGH!
RUB
RUB
STUPID STICKS!
RUB
RUB

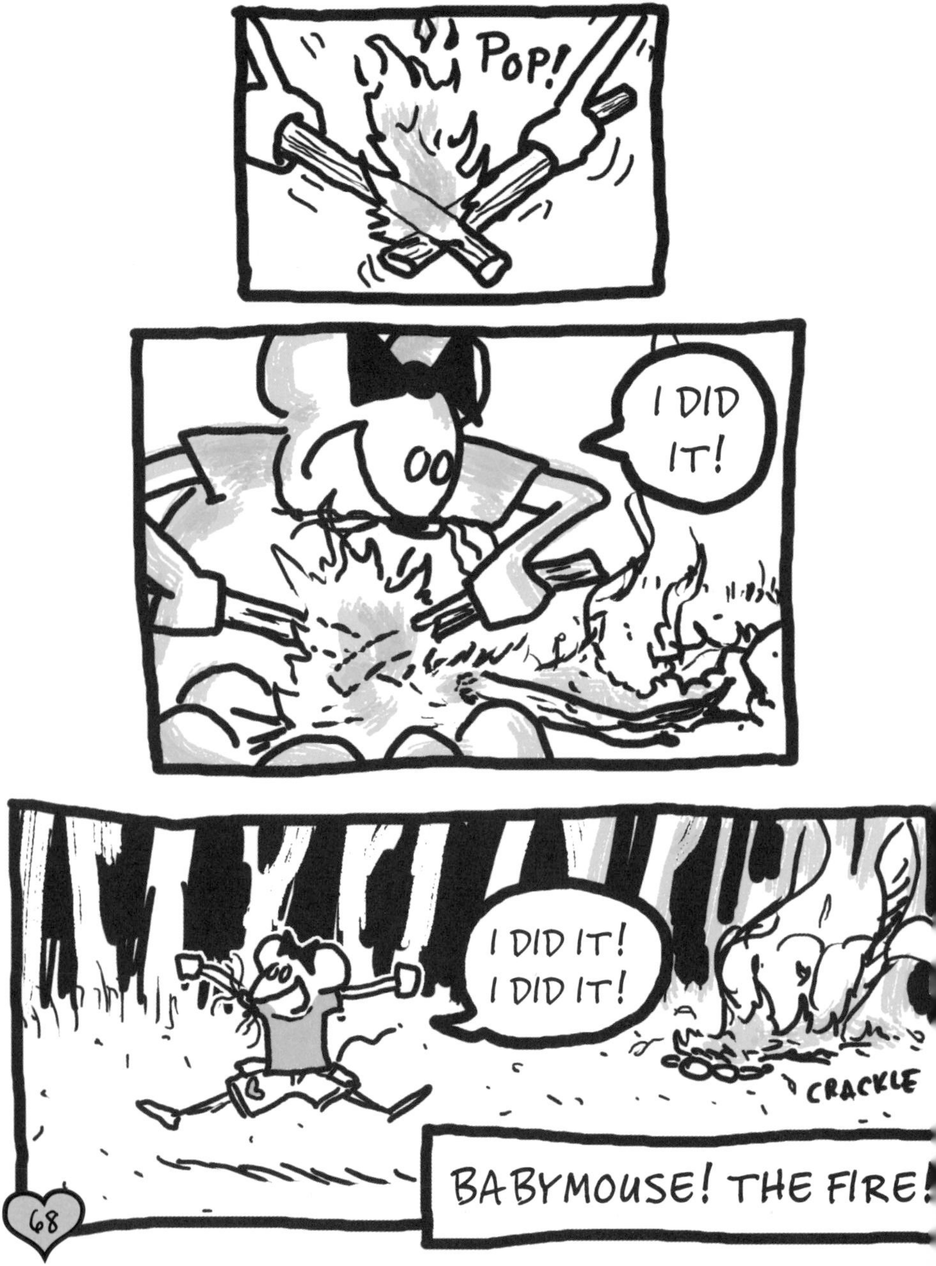

POP!
I DID IT!
I DID IT! I DID IT!
CRACKLE
BABYMOUSE! THE FIRE!

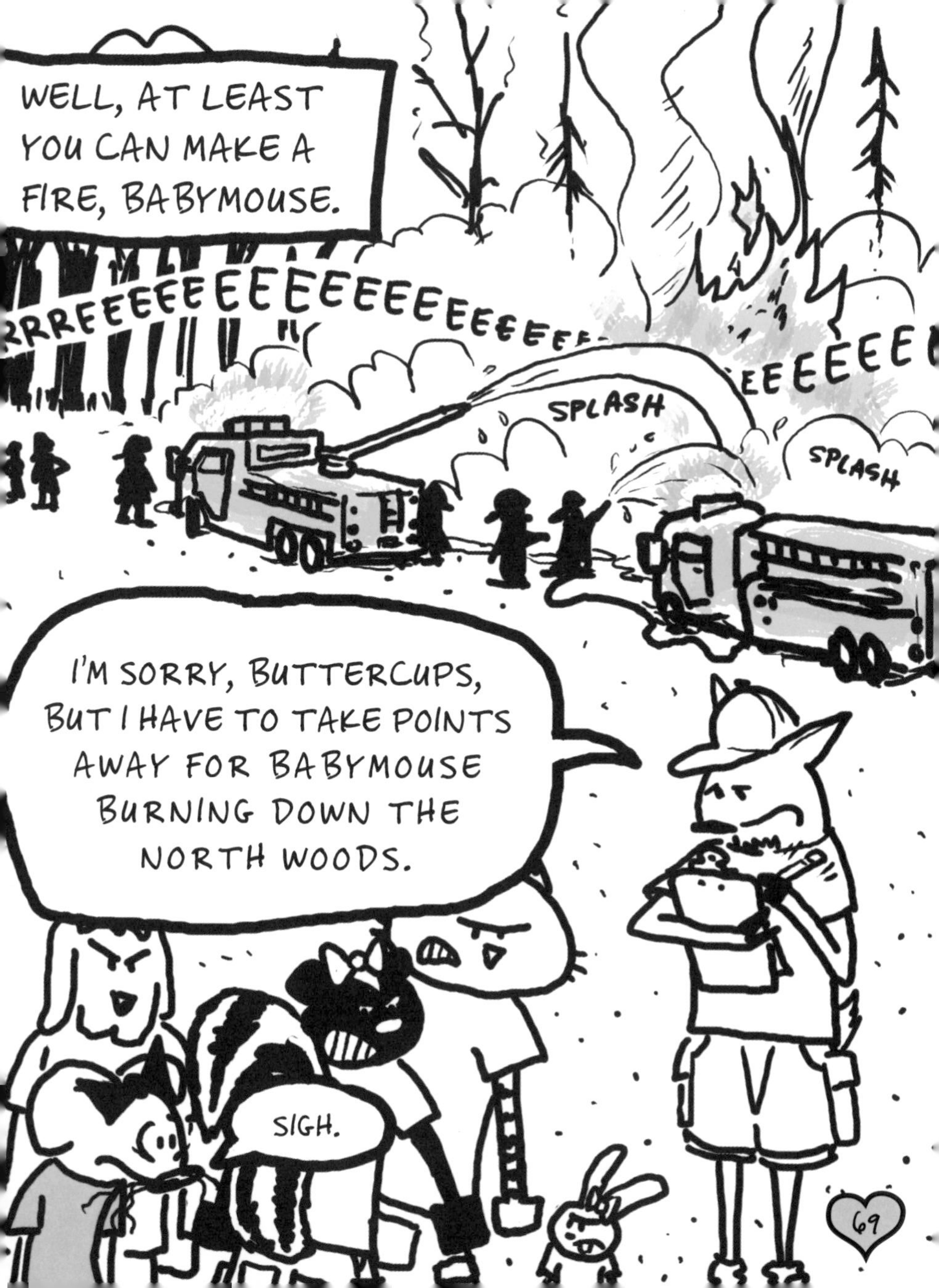
WELL, AT LEAST YOU CAN MAKE A FIRE, BABYMOUSE.
RRREEEEEEEEEEEEEEEEEEEEEEEEE
EEEEEEE
SPLASH
SPLASH
I'M SORRY, BUTTERCUPS, BUT I HAVE TO TAKE POINTS AWAY FOR BABYMOUSE BURNING DOWN THE NORTH WOODS.
SIGH.

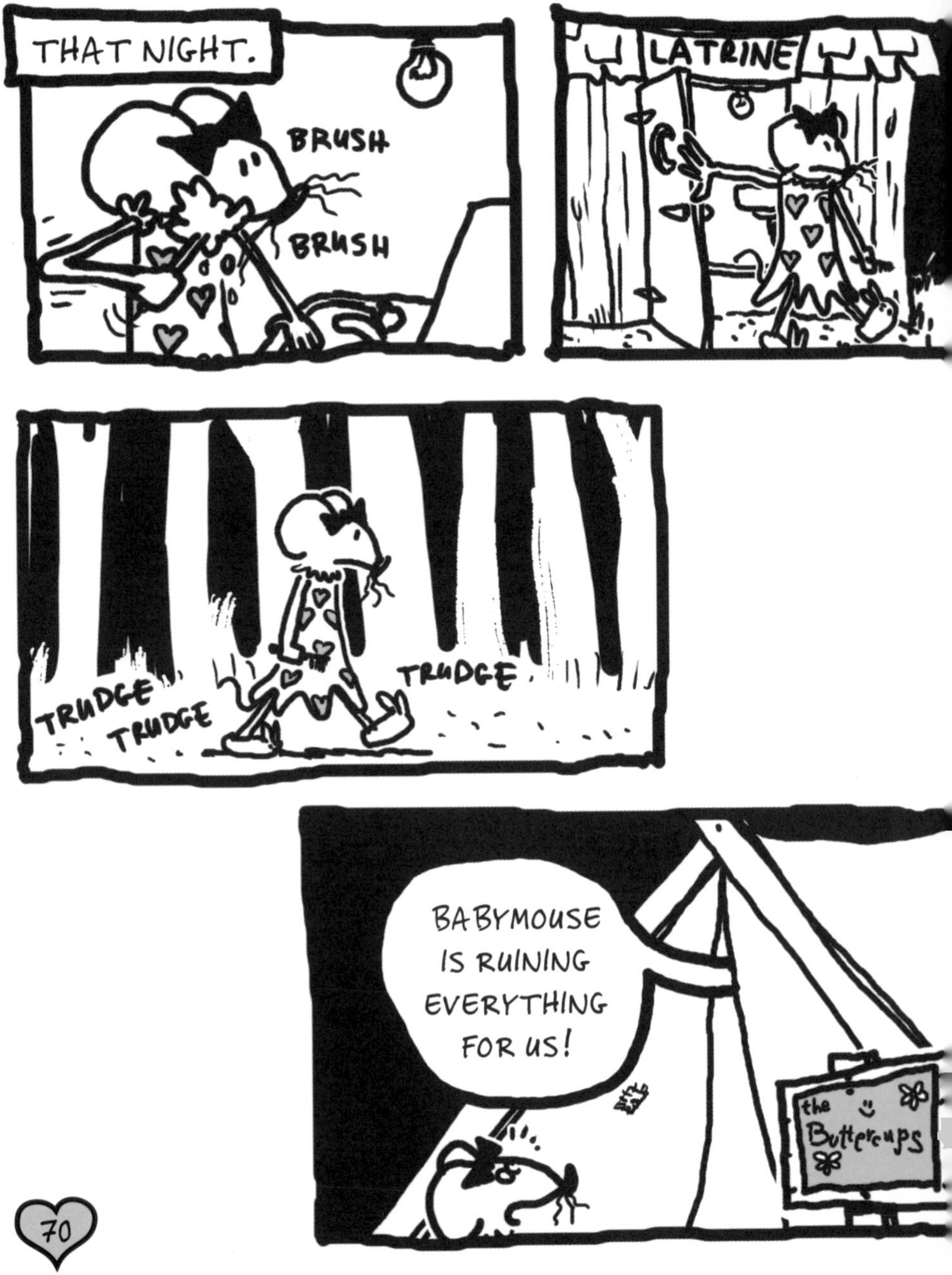
THAT NIGHT.
BRUSH
BRUSH
LATRINE
TRUDGE
TRUDGE
TRUDGE
BABYMOUSE IS RUINING EVERYTHING FOR US!
the Buttercups

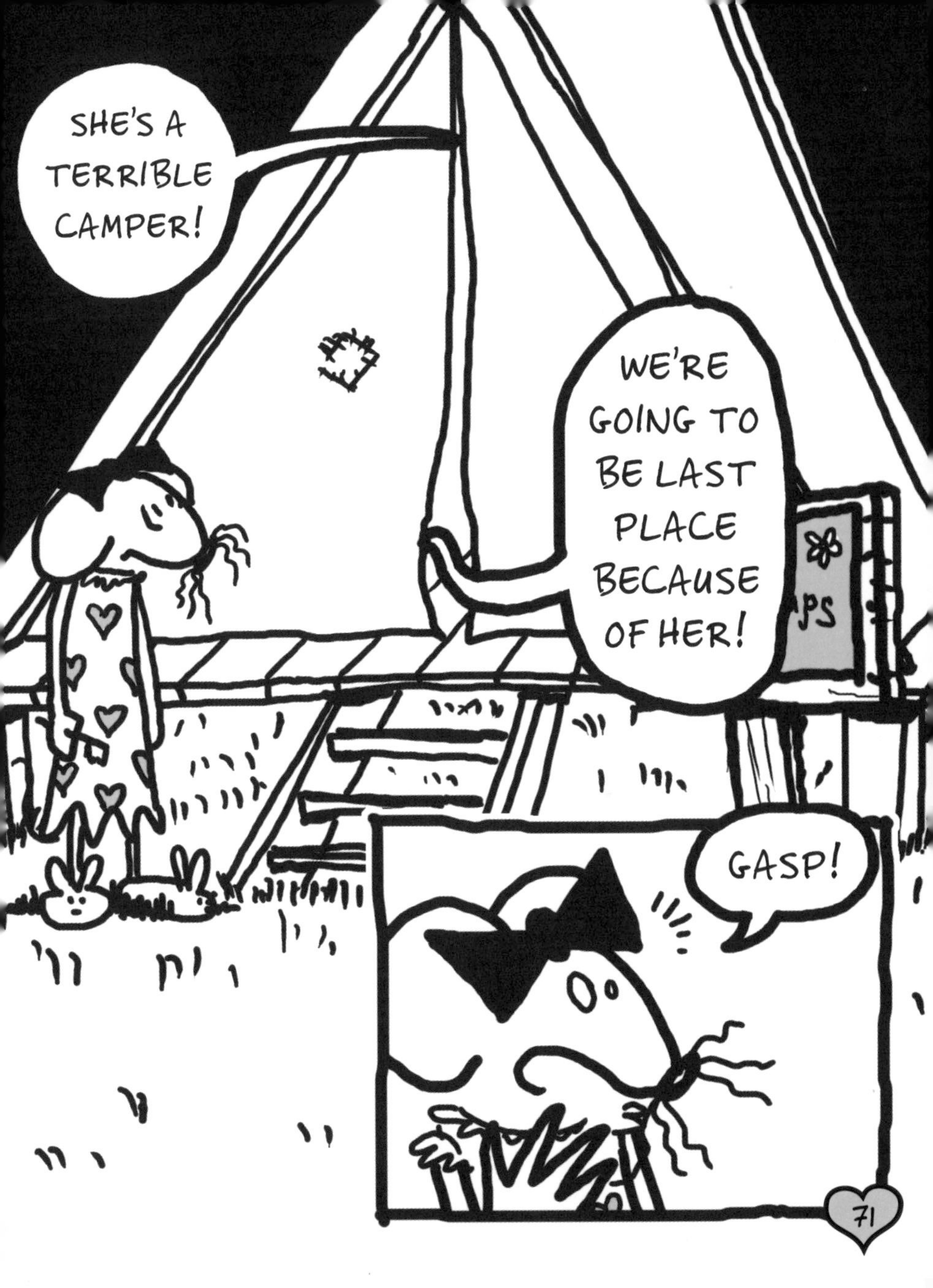
SHE'S A TERRIBLE CAMPER!
WE'RE GOING TO BE LAST PLACE BECAUSE OF HER!
GASP!

We're not home right now. Leave a message at the beep. *BEEP!*
PHONE
PHONE

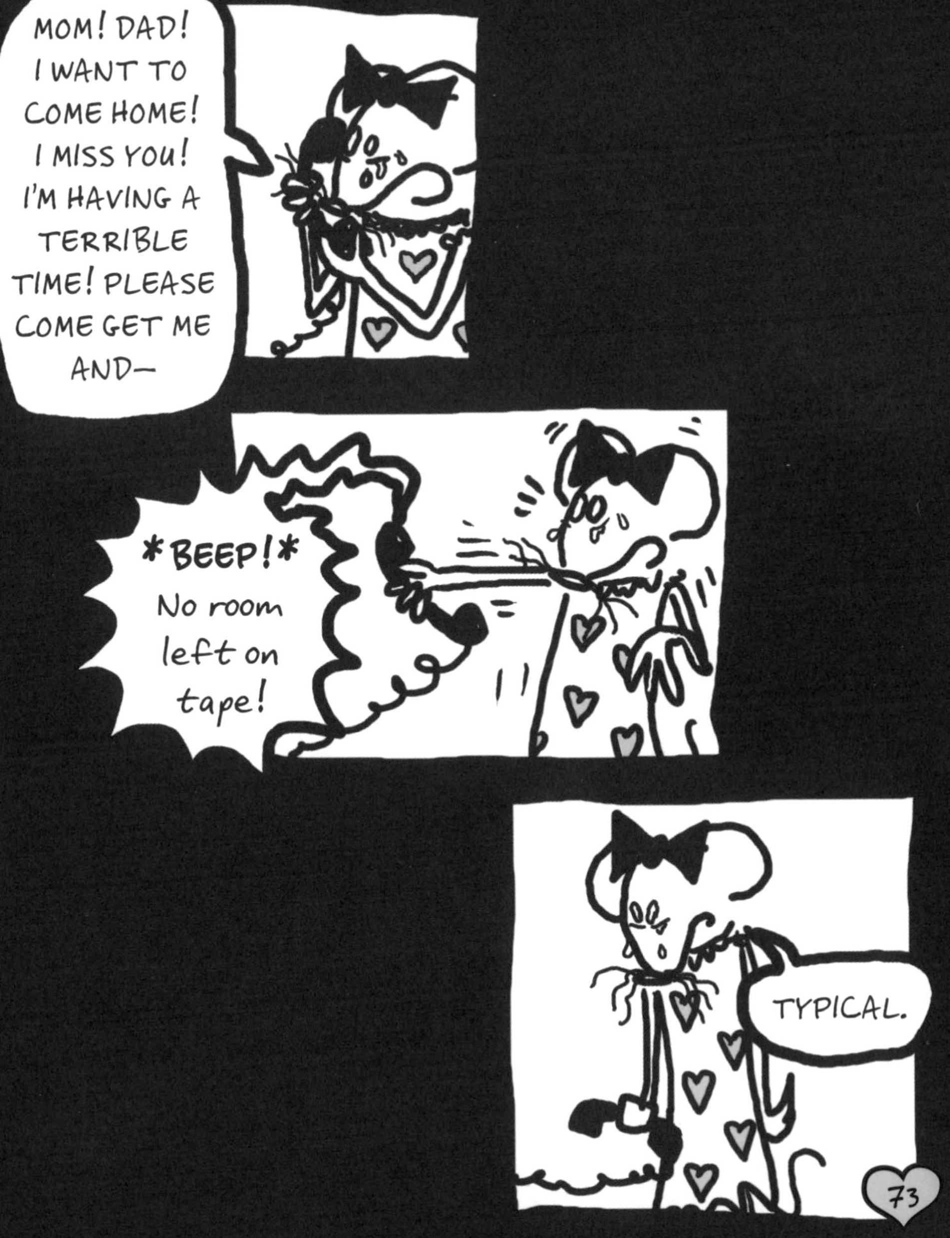
MOM! DAD! I WANT TO COME HOME! I MISS YOU! I'M HAVING A TERRIBLE TIME! PLEASE COME GET ME AND—
BEEP! No room left on tape!
TYPICAL.

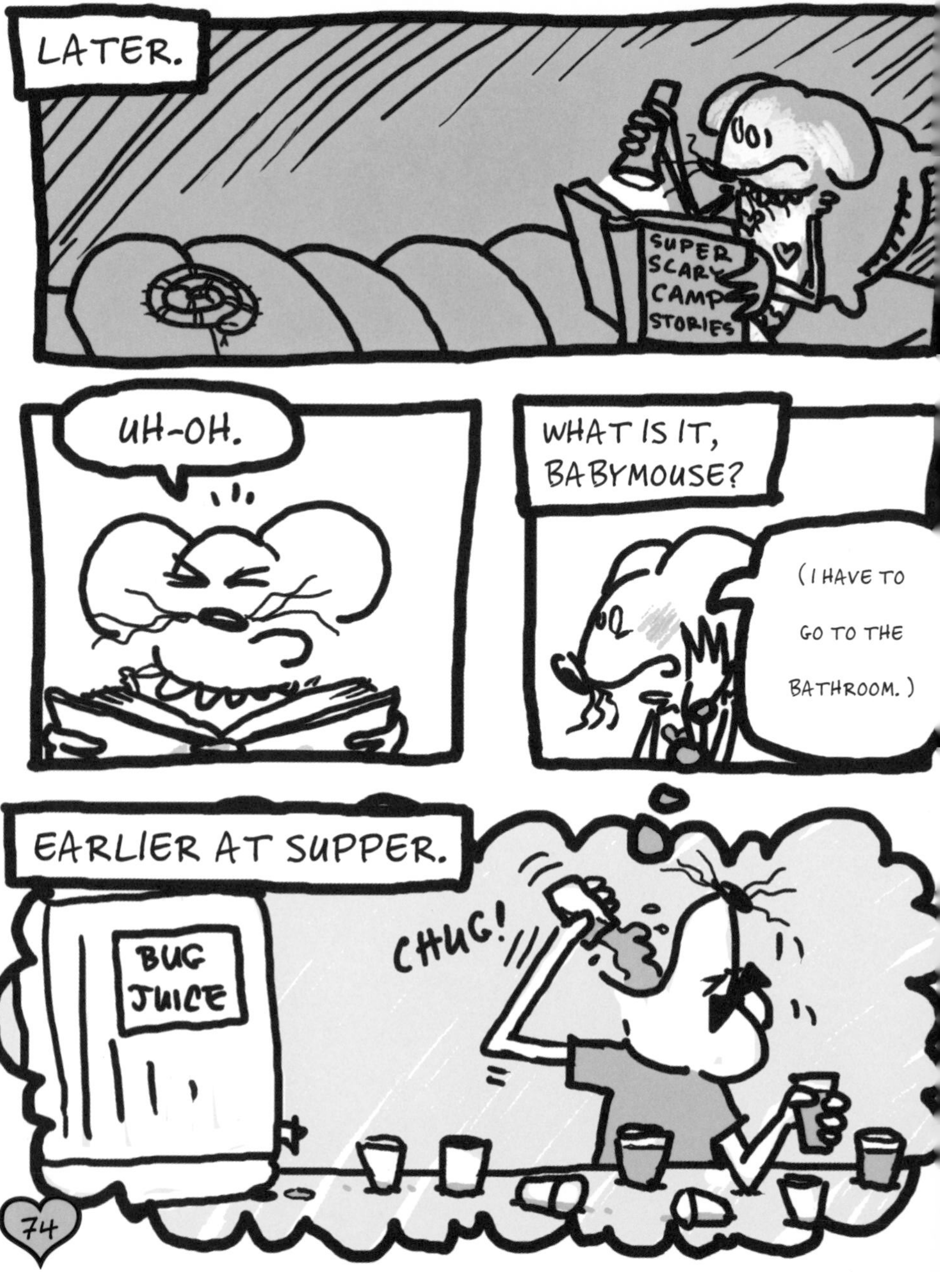
LATER.
SUPER SCARY CAMP STORIES
UH-OH.
WHAT IS IT, BABYMOUSE?
(I HAVE TO GO TO THE BATHROOM.)
EARLIER AT SUPPER.
BUG JUICE
CHUG!

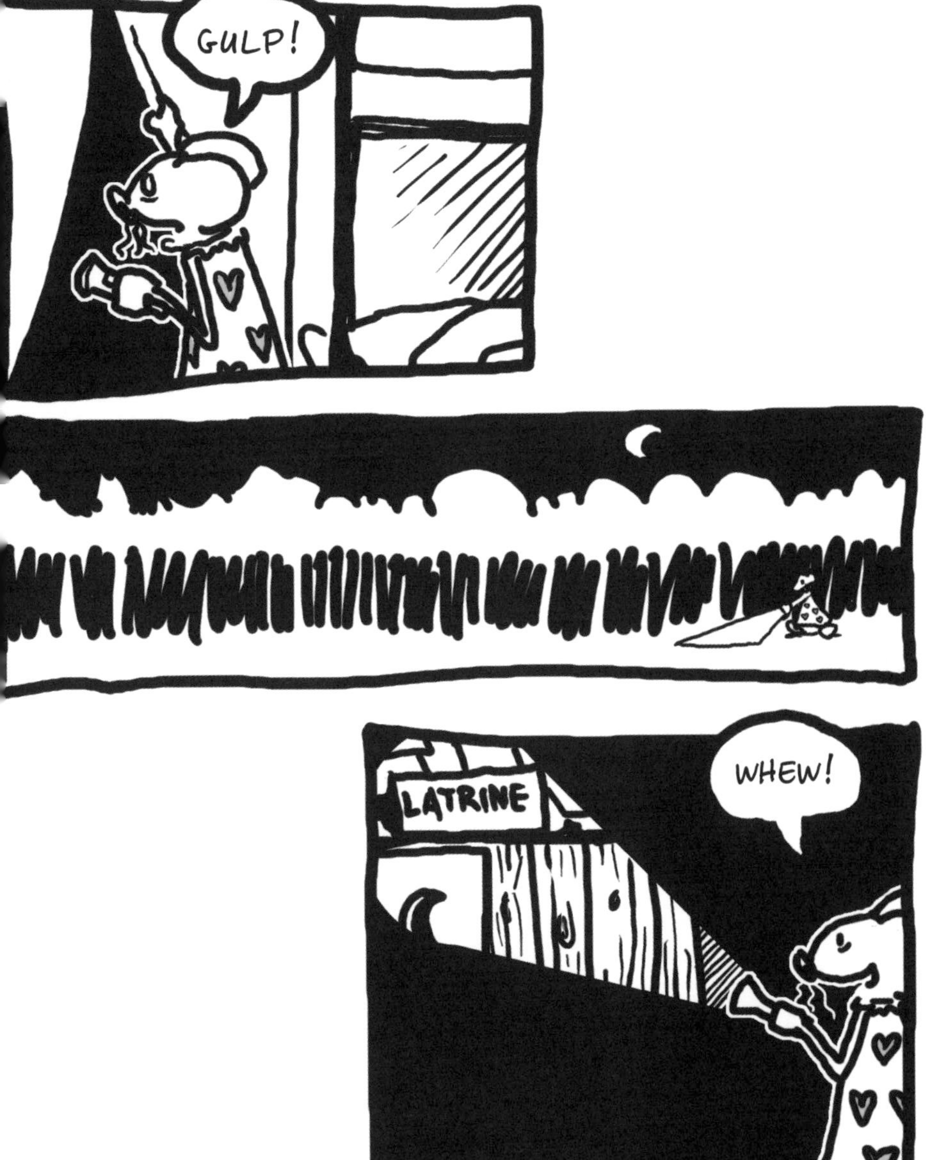
GULP!
LATRINE
WHEW!

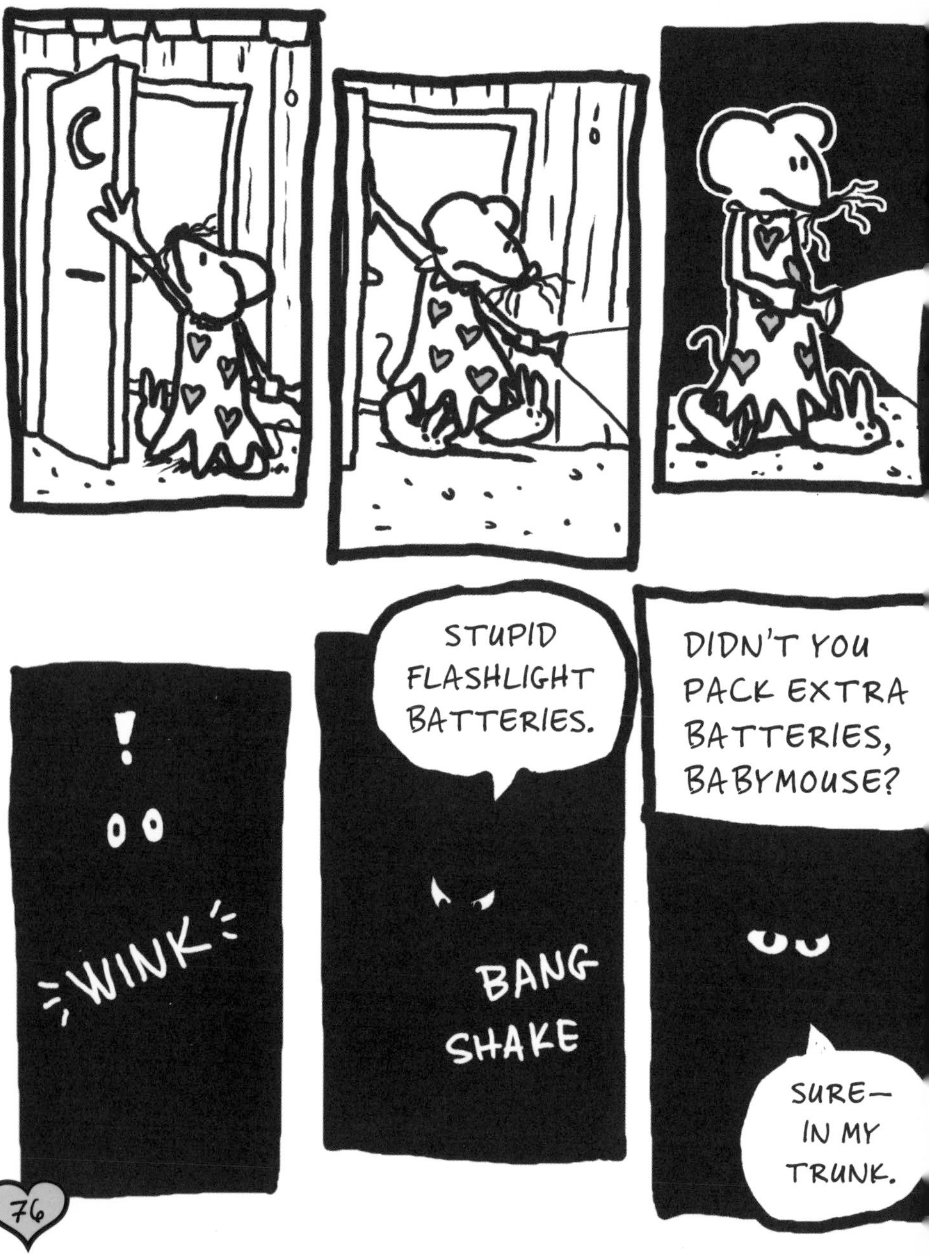
!
WINK
STUPID FLASHLIGHT BATTERIES.
BANG
SHAKE
DIDN'T YOU PACK EXTRA BATTERIES, BABYMOUSE?
SURE— IN MY TRUNK.

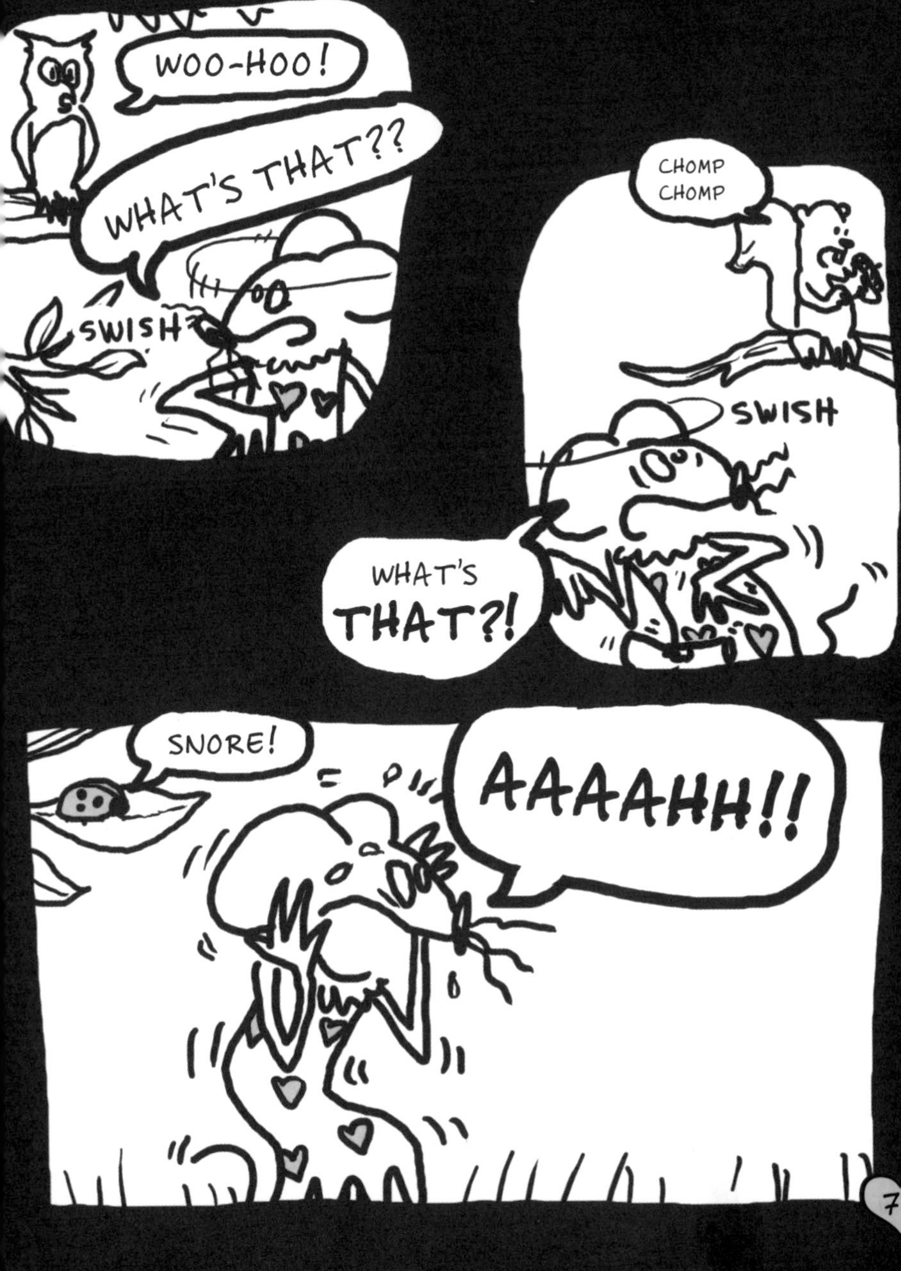
WOO-HOO!
WHAT'S THAT??
SWISH
CHOMP CHOMP
SWISH
WHAT'S THAT?!
SNORE!
AAAAHH!!

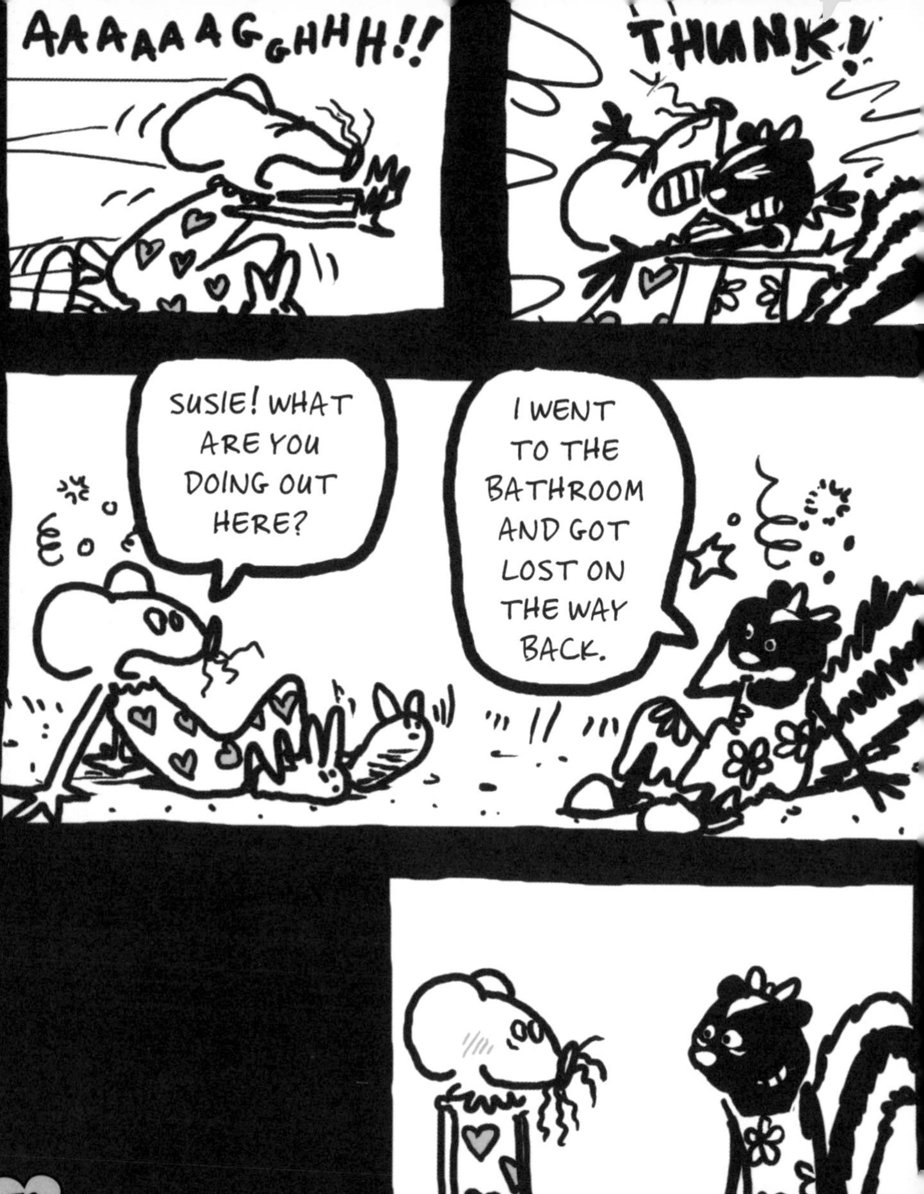
AAAAAAGGHHHH!!
THUNK!
SUSIE! WHAT ARE YOU DOING OUT HERE?
I WENT TO THE BATHROOM AND GOT LOST ON THE WAY BACK.

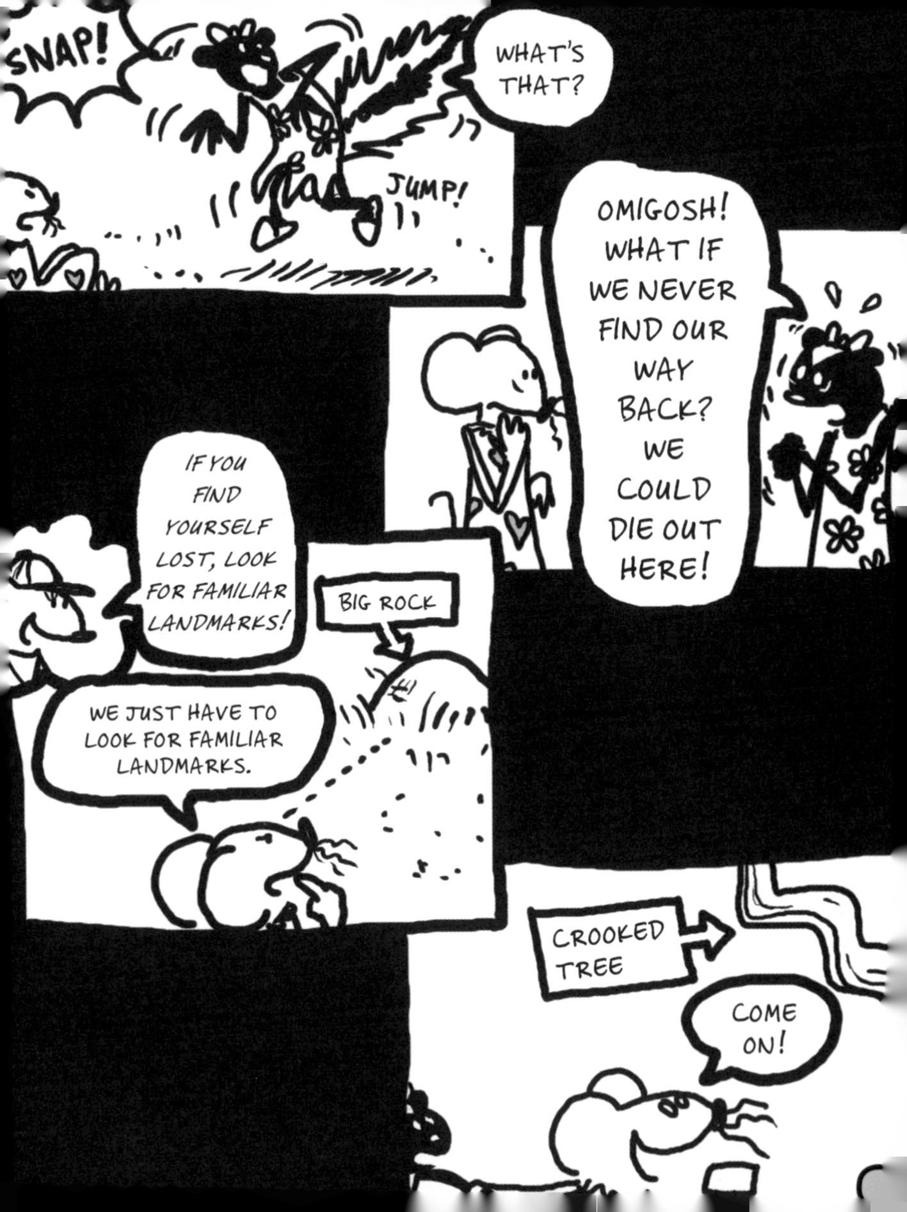
SNAP!
JUMP!
WHAT'S THAT?
OMIGOSH! WHAT IF WE NEVER FIND OUR WAY BACK? WE COULD DIE OUT HERE!
IF YOU FIND YOURSELF LOST, LOOK FOR FAMILIAR LANDMARKS!
BIG ROCK
WE JUST HAVE TO LOOK FOR FAMILIAR LANDMARKS.
CROOKED TREE
COME ON!

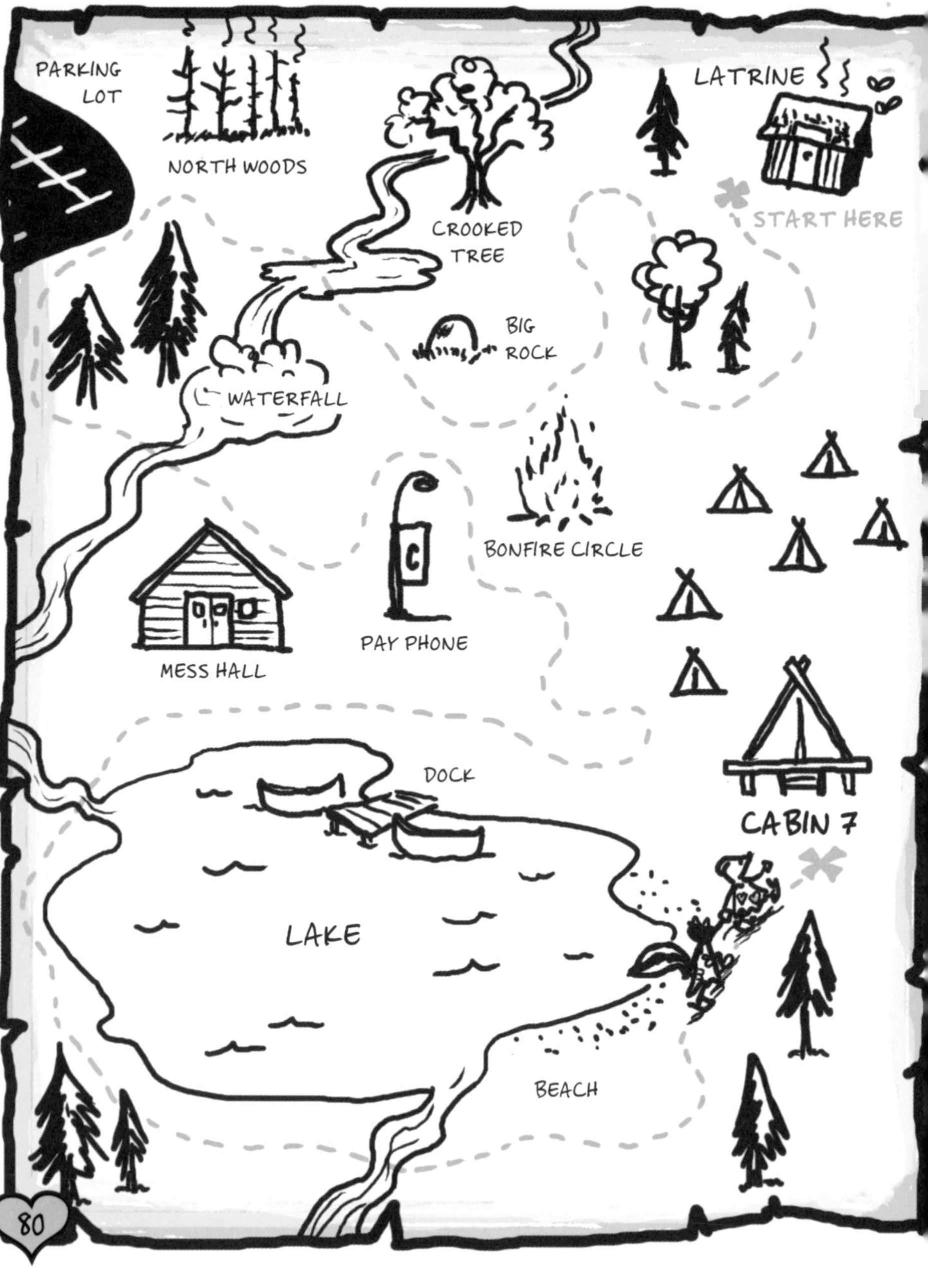
PARKING LOT
NORTH WOODS
CROOKED TREE
LATRINE
START HERE
BIG ROCK
WATERFALL
BONFIRE CIRCLE
PAY PHONE
MESS HALL
DOCK
CABIN 7
LAKE
BEACH

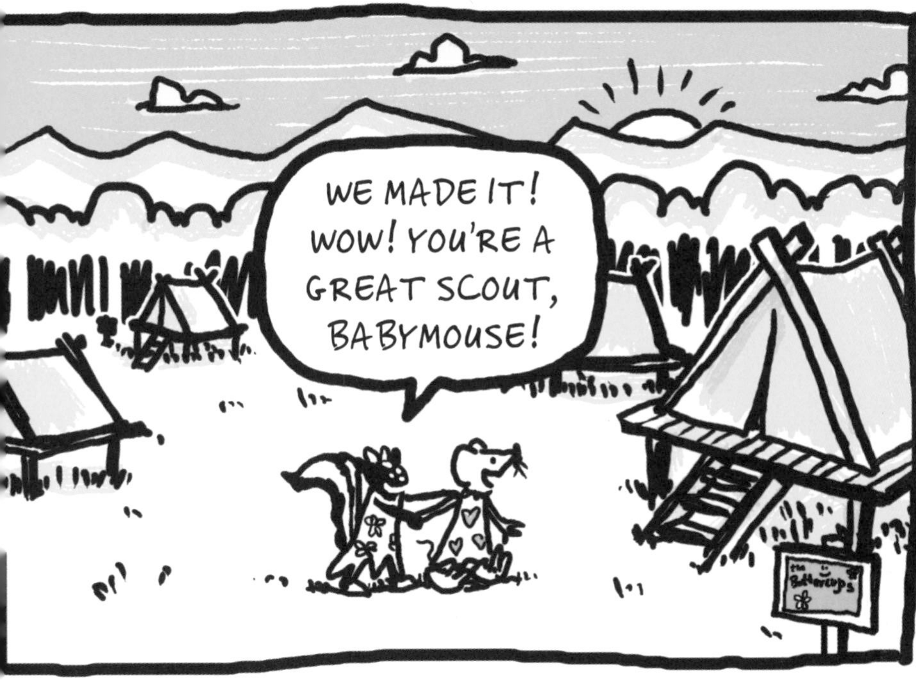
WE MADE IT! WOW! YOU'RE A GREAT SCOUT, BABYMOUSE!

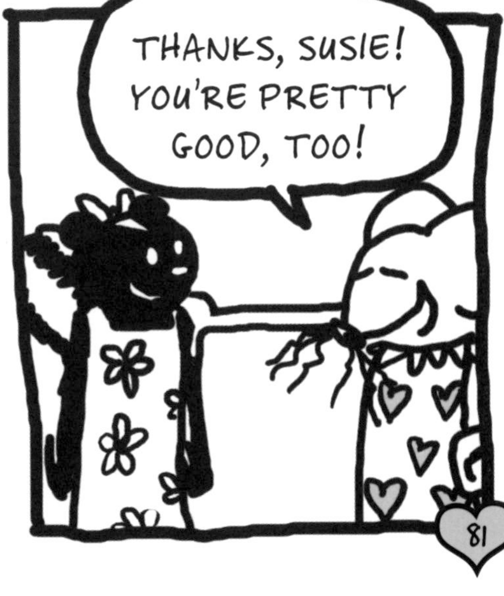
THANKS, SUSIE! YOU'RE PRETTY GOOD, TOO!

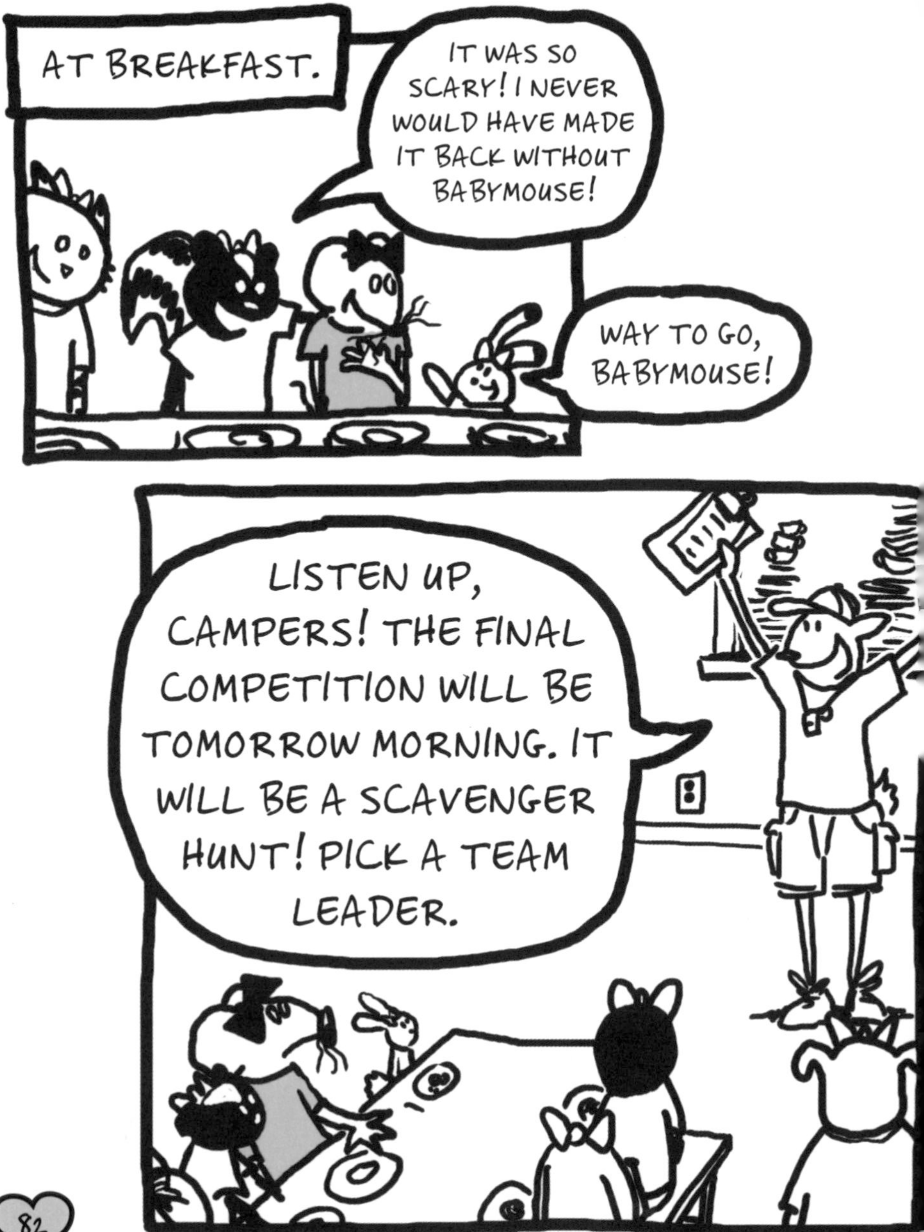
AT BREAKFAST.
IT WAS SO SCARY! I NEVER WOULD HAVE MADE IT BACK WITHOUT BABYMOUSE!
WAY TO GO, BABYMOUSE!
LISTEN UP, CAMPERS! THE FINAL COMPETITION WILL BE TOMORROW MORNING. IT WILL BE A SCAVENGER HUNT! PICK A TEAM LEADER.

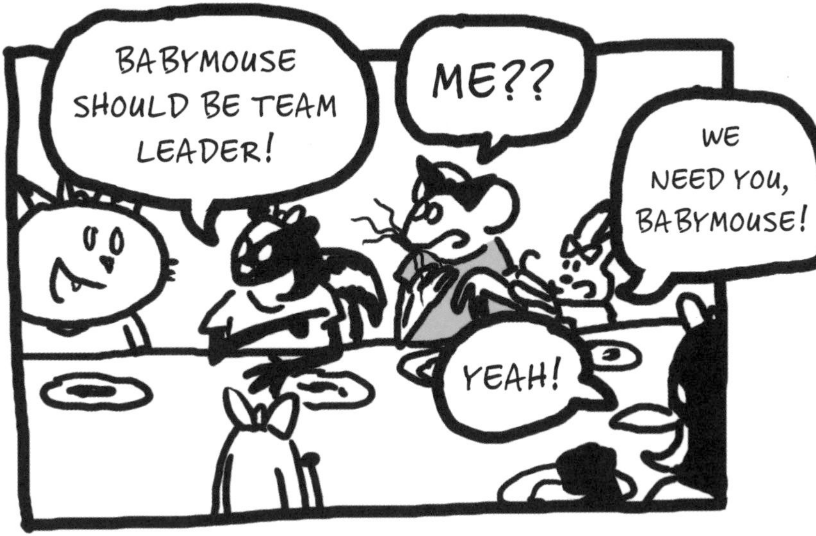
BABYMOUSE SHOULD BE TEAM LEADER!
ME??
WE NEED YOU, BABYMOUSE!
YEAH!

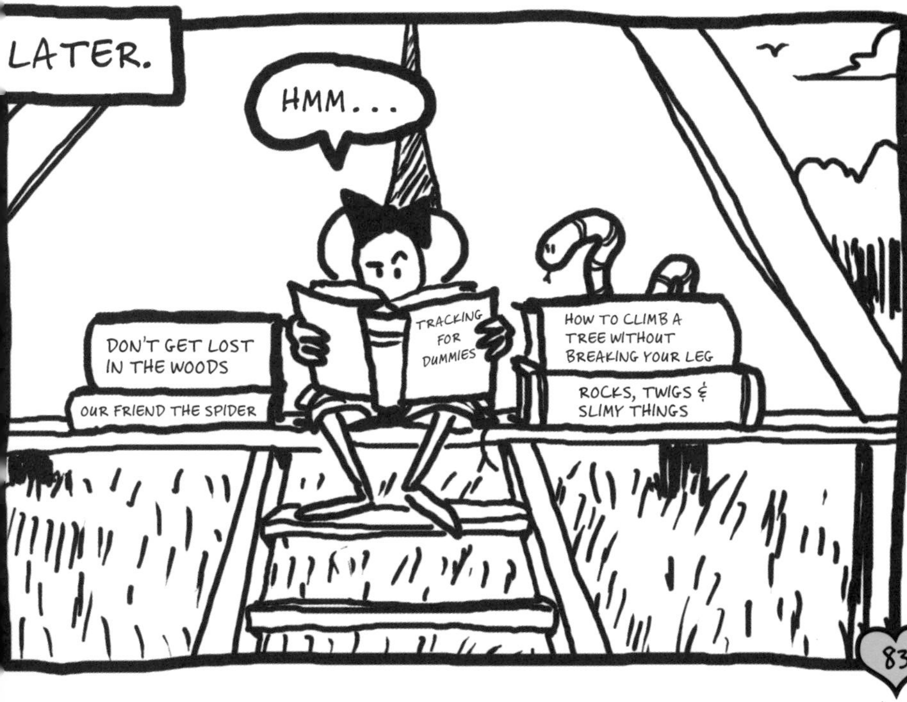
LATER.
HMM...
DON'T GET LOST IN THE WOODS
OUR FRIEND THE SPIDER
TRACKING FOR DUMMIES
HOW TO CLIMB A TREE WITHOUT BREAKING YOUR LEG
ROCKS, TWIGS & SLIMY THINGS

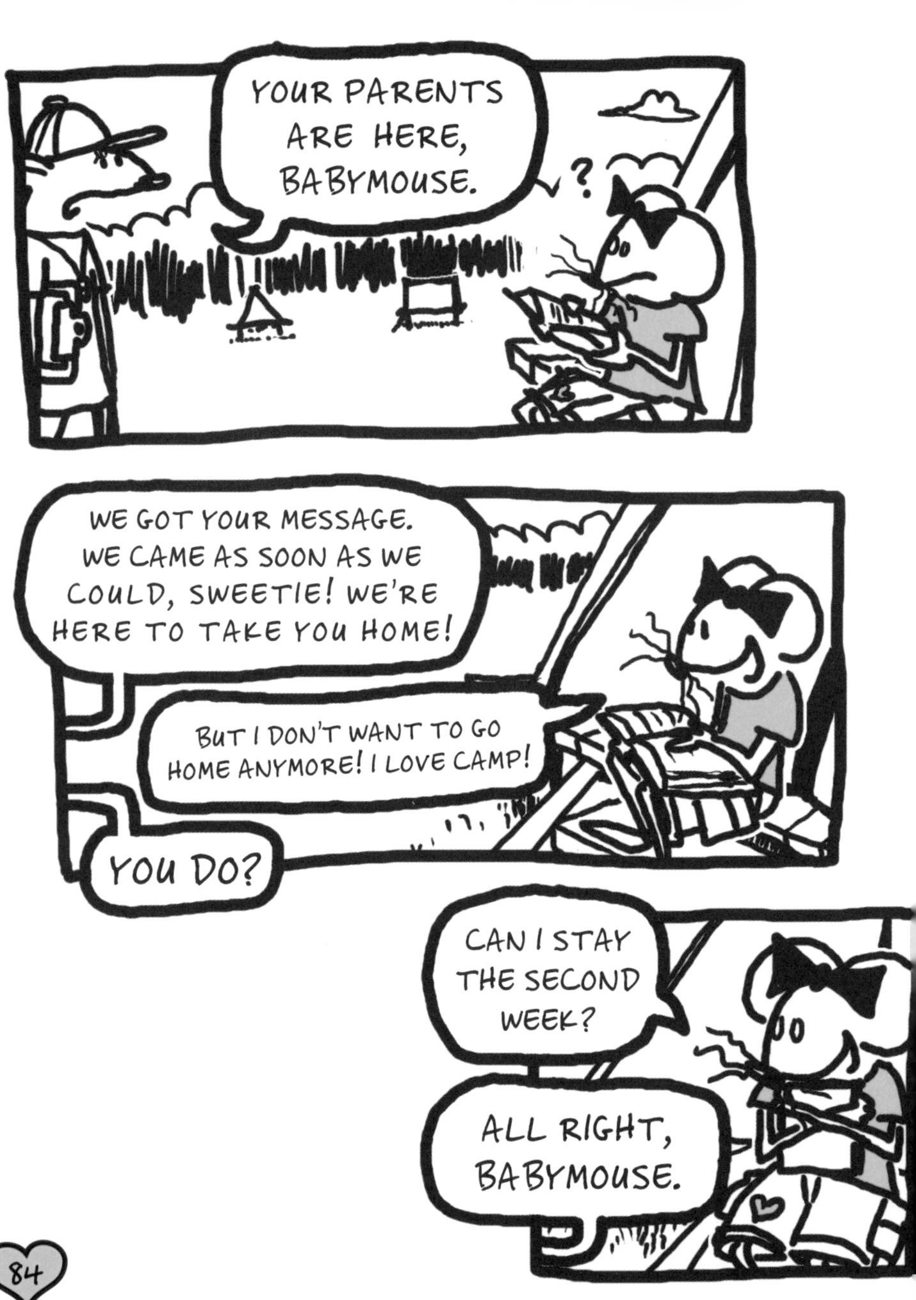
YOUR PARENTS ARE HERE, BABYMOUSE.
?
WE GOT YOUR MESSAGE. WE CAME AS SOON AS WE COULD, SWEETIE! WE'RE HERE TO TAKE YOU HOME!
BUT I DON'T WANT TO GO HOME ANYMORE! I LOVE CAMP!
YOU DO?
CAN I STAY THE SECOND WEEK?
ALL RIGHT, BABYMOUSE.

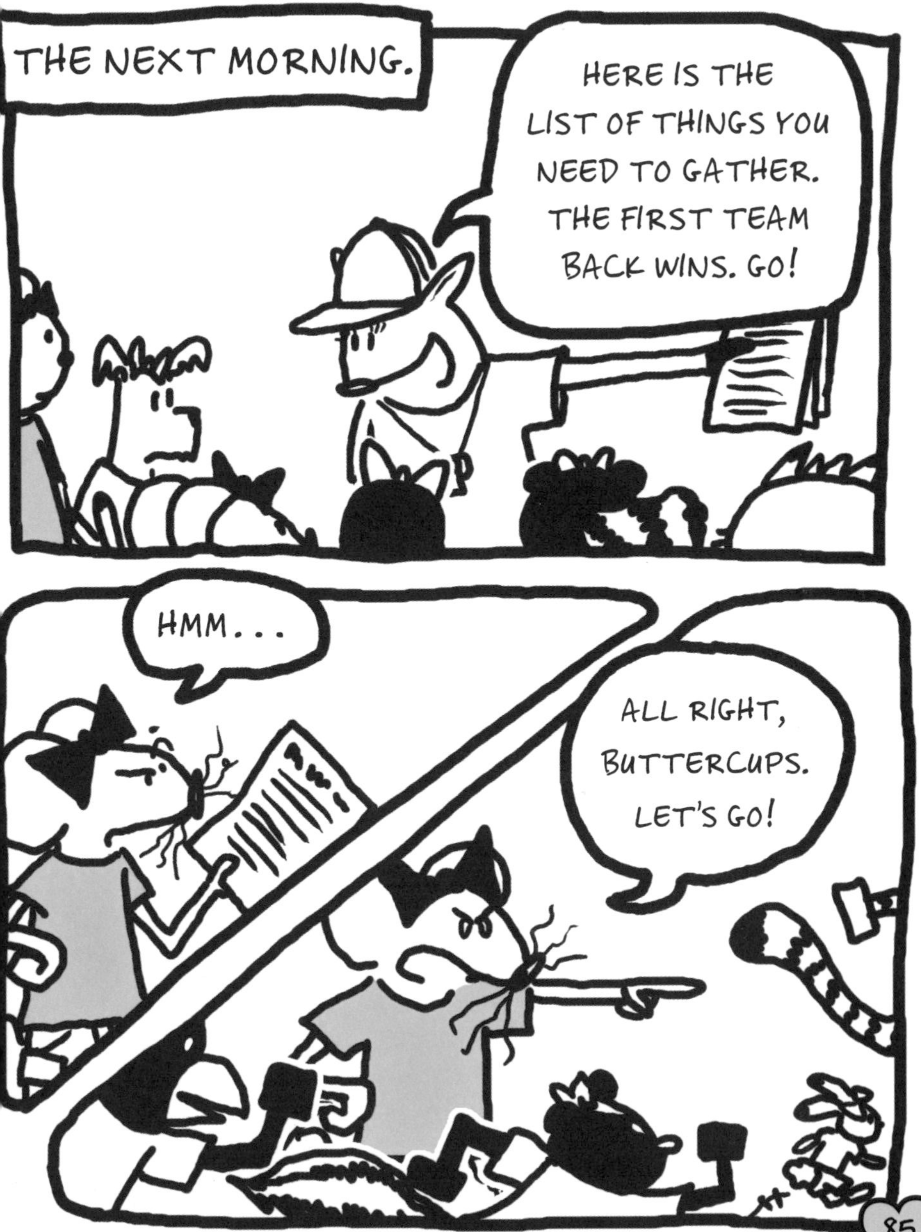
THE NEXT MORNING.
HERE IS THE LIST OF THINGS YOU NEED TO GATHER. THE FIRST TEAM BACK WINS. GO!
HMM...
ALL RIGHT, BUTTERCUPS. LET'S GO!

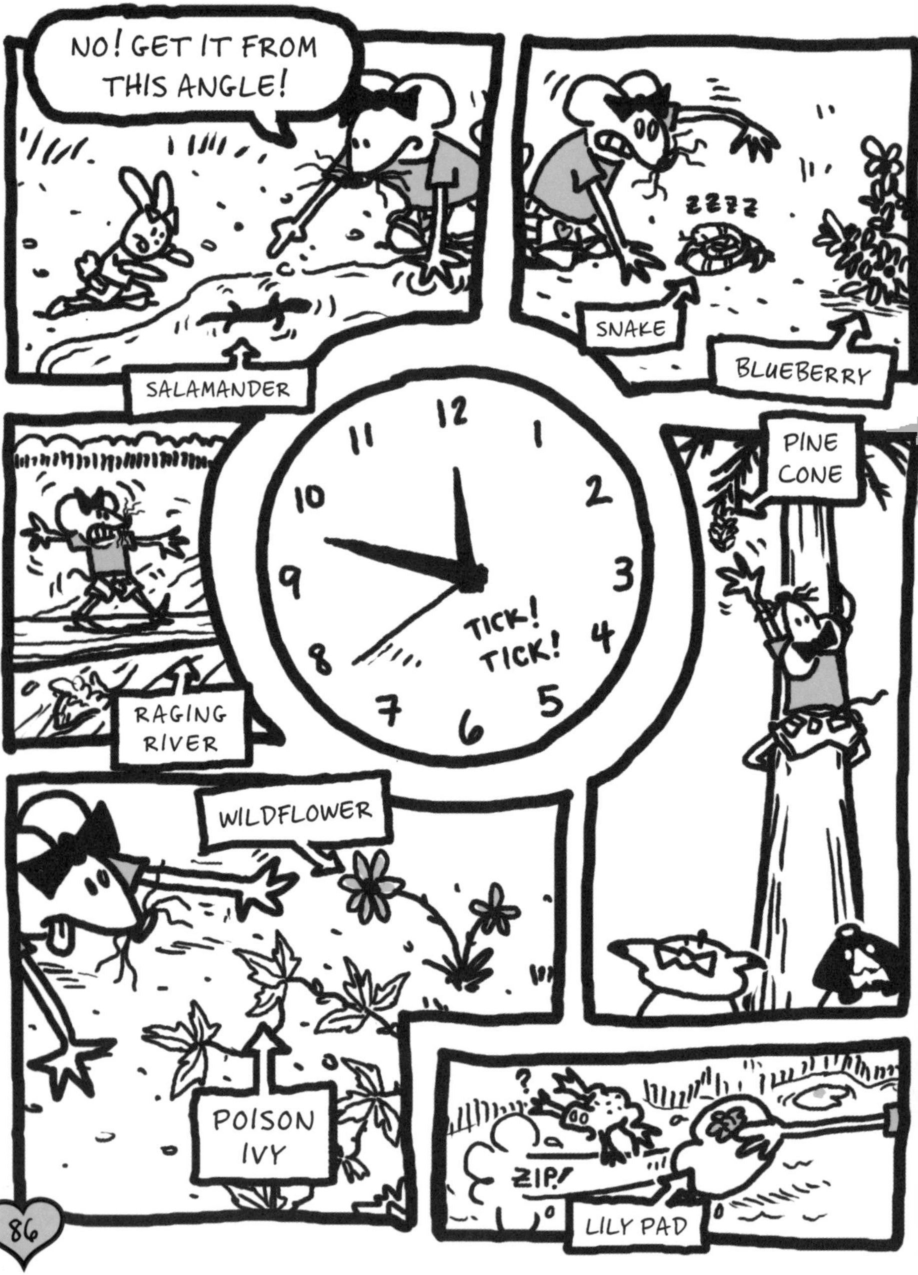
NO! GET IT FROM THIS ANGLE!
SALAMANDER
ZZZZ
SNAKE
BLUEBERRY
RAGING RIVER
PINE CONE
TICK! TICK!
WILDFLOWER
POISON IVY
?
ZIP!
LILY PAD

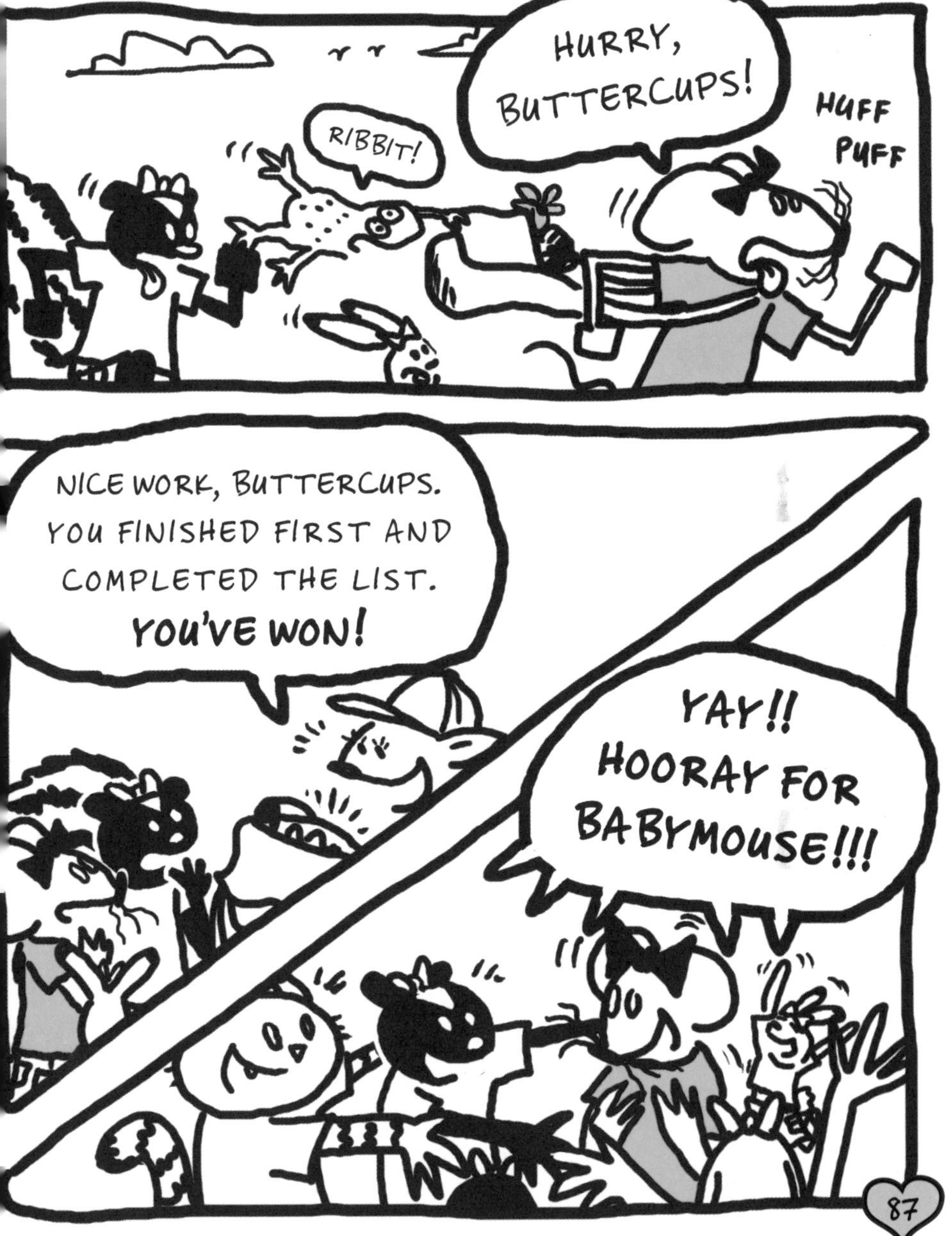
HURRY, BUTTERCUPS!
RIBBIT!
HUFF PUFF
NICE WORK, BUTTERCUPS. YOU FINISHED FIRST AND COMPLETED THE LIST. YOU'VE WON!
YAY!! HOORAY FOR BABYMOUSE!!!

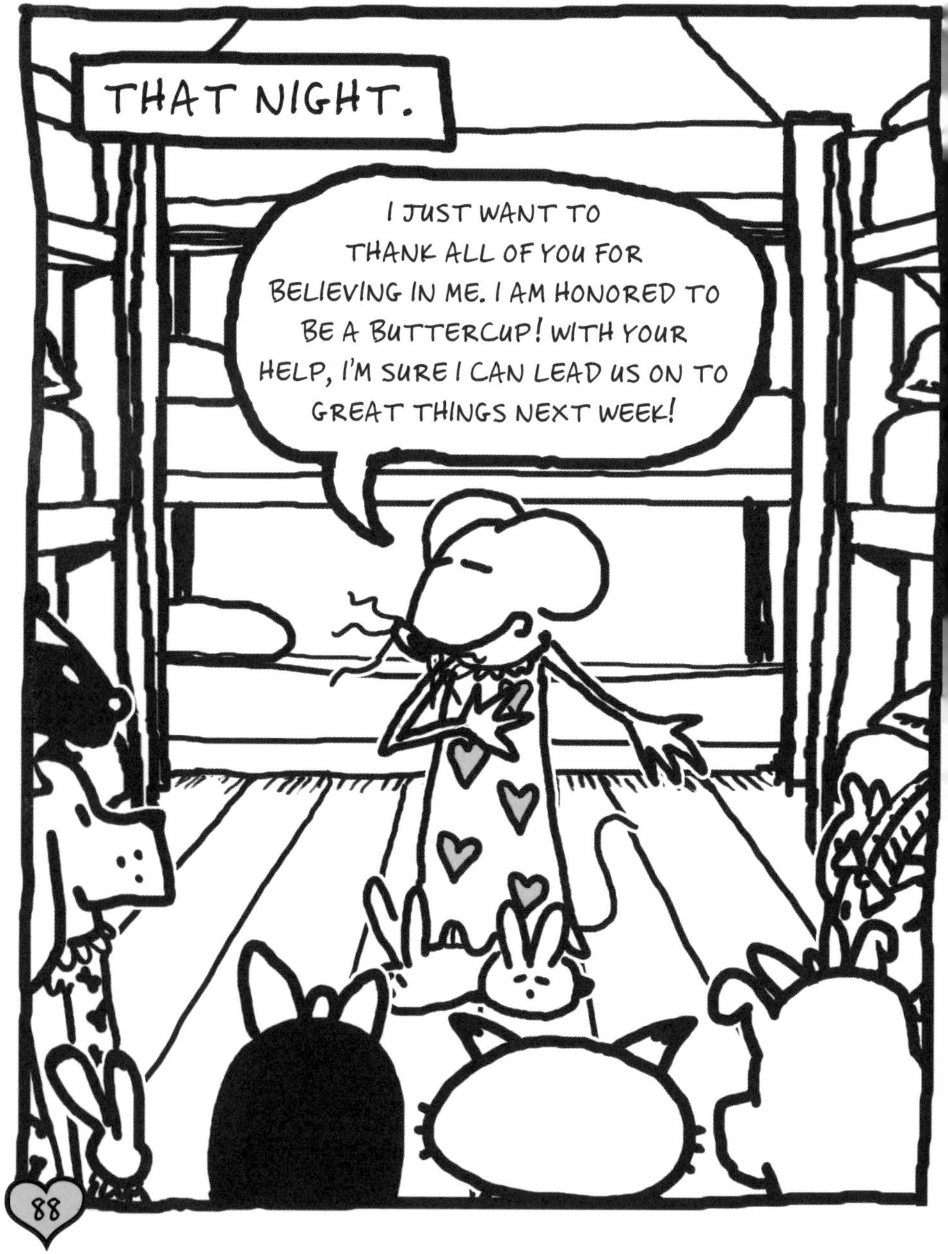
THAT NIGHT.
I JUST WANT TO THANK ALL OF YOU FOR BELIEVING IN ME. I AM HONORED TO BE A BUTTERCUP! WITH YOUR HELP, I'M SURE I CAN LEAD US ON TO GREAT THINGS NEXT WEEK!

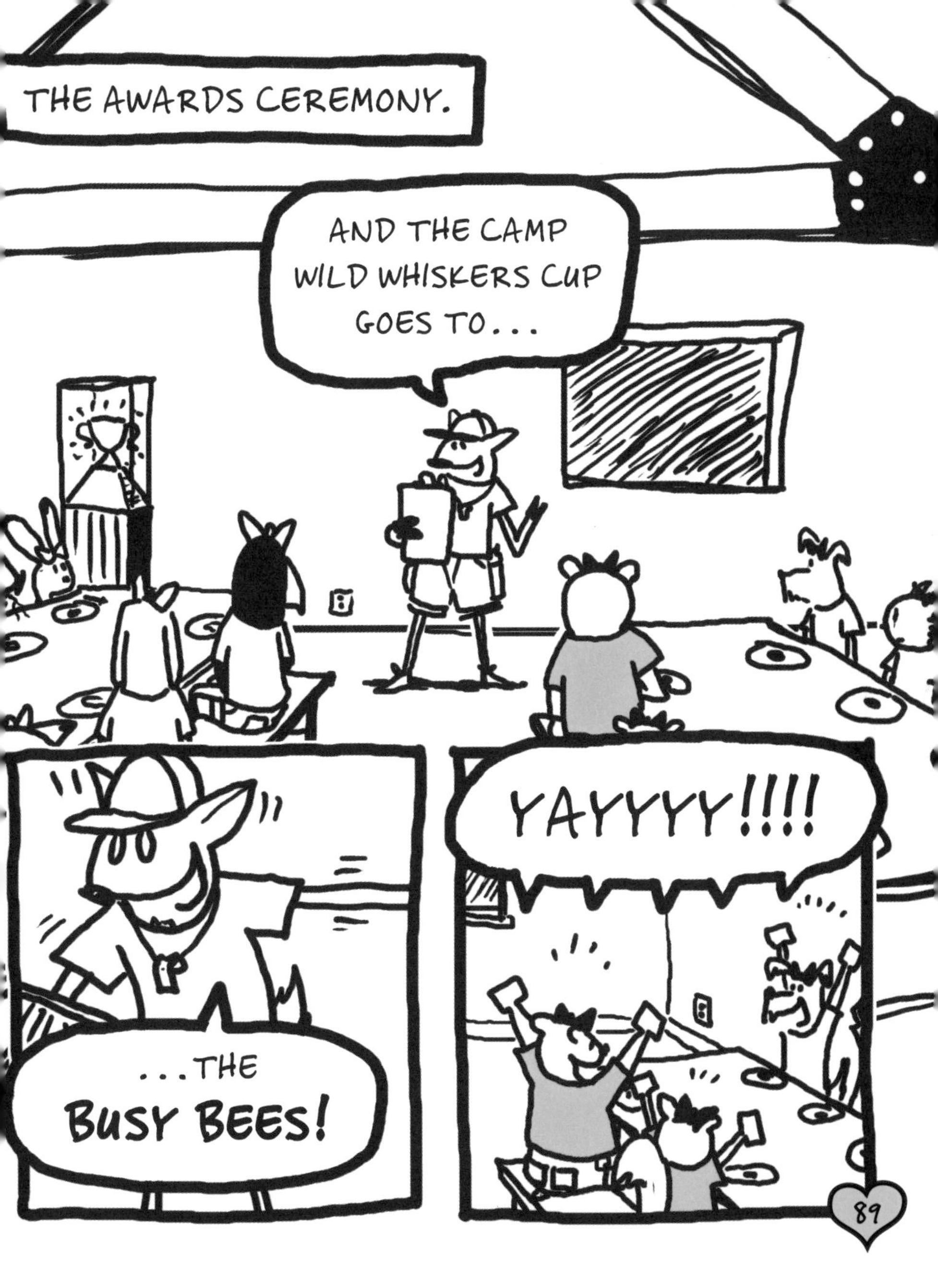
THE AWARDS CEREMONY.
AND THE CAMP WILD WHISKERS CUP GOES TO...
...THE BUSY BEES!
YAYYYY!!!!

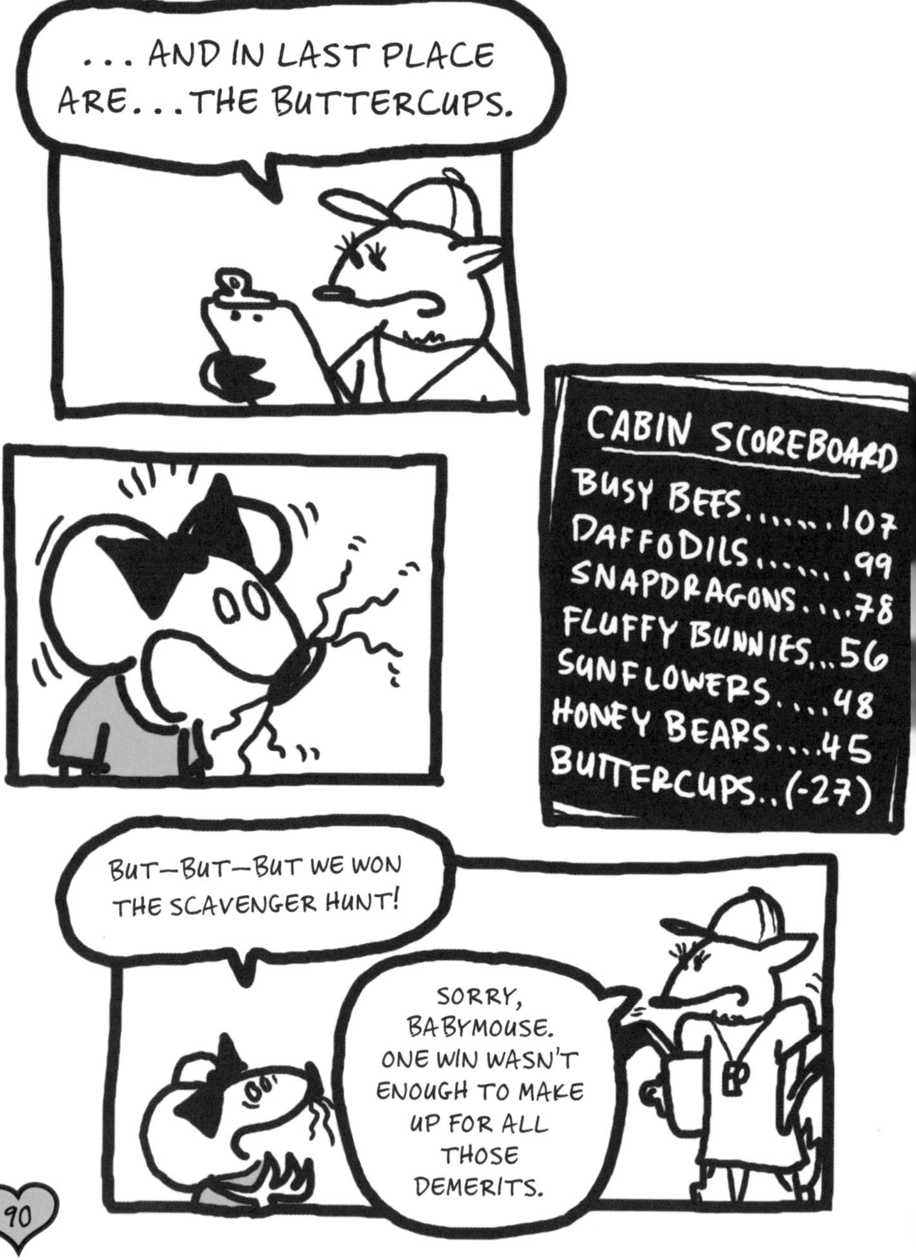
. . . AND IN LAST PLACE ARE. . . THE BUTTERCUPS.
CABIN SCOREBOARD
BUSY BEES.......107
DAFFODILS.......99
SNAPDRAGONS....78
FLUFFY BUNNIES...56
SUNFLOWERS....48
HONEY BEARS....45
BUTTERCUPS..(-27)
BUT—BUT—BUT WE WON THE SCAVENGER HUNT!
SORRY, BABYMOUSE. ONE WIN WASN'T ENOUGH TO MAKE UP FOR ALL THOSE DEMERITS.

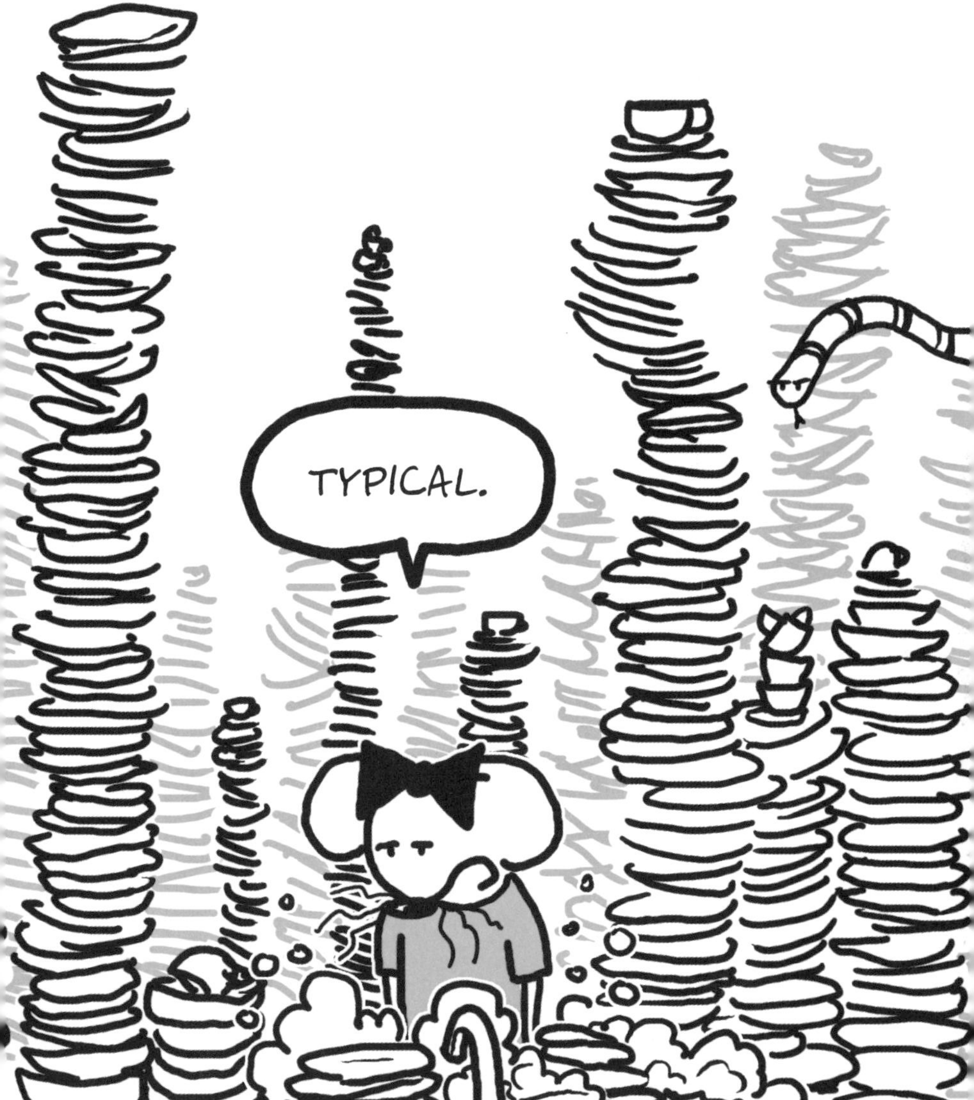
TYPICAL.

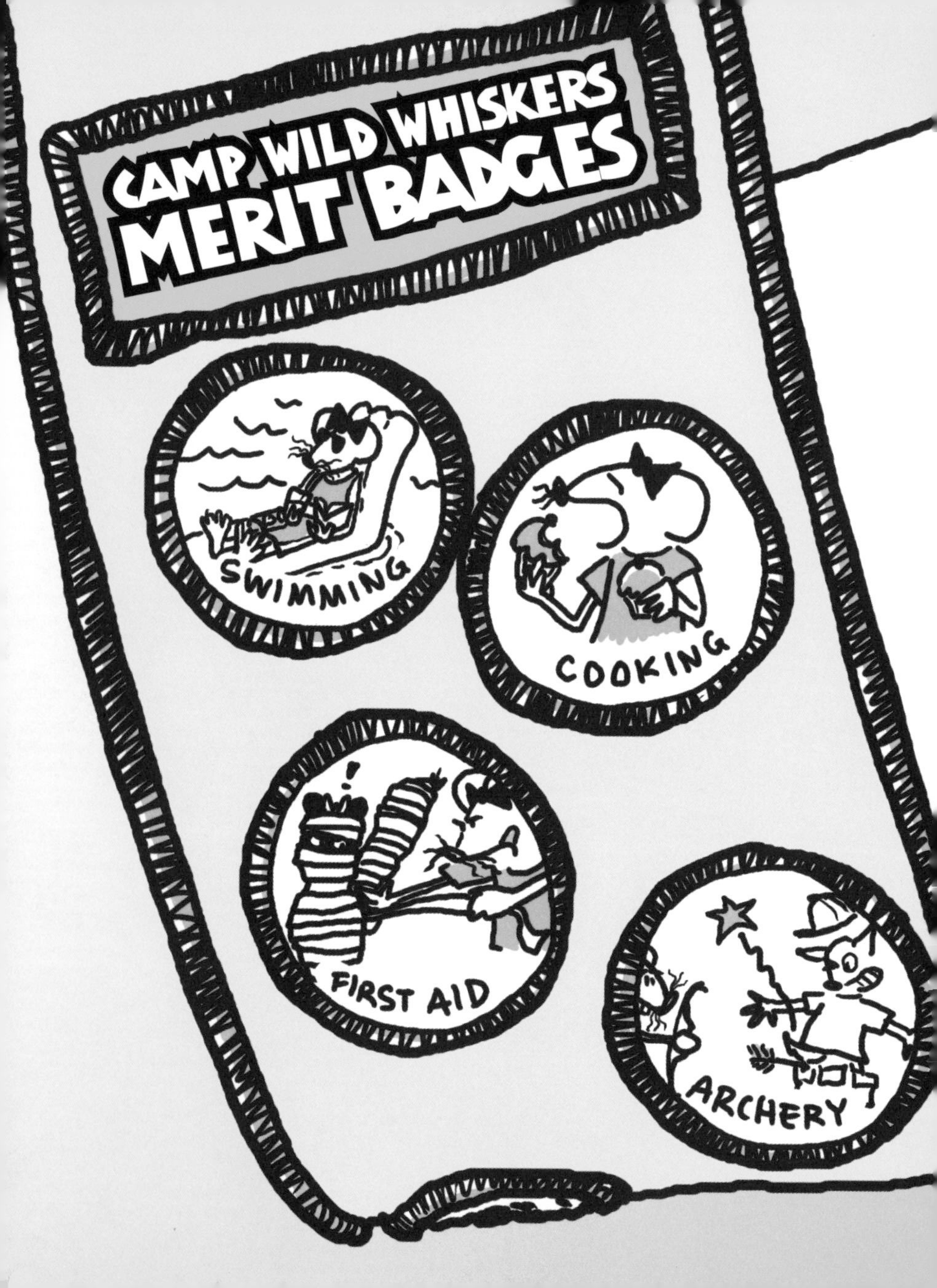
CAMP WILD WHISKERS
MERIT BADGES
SWIMMING
COOKING
FIRST AID
ARCHERY

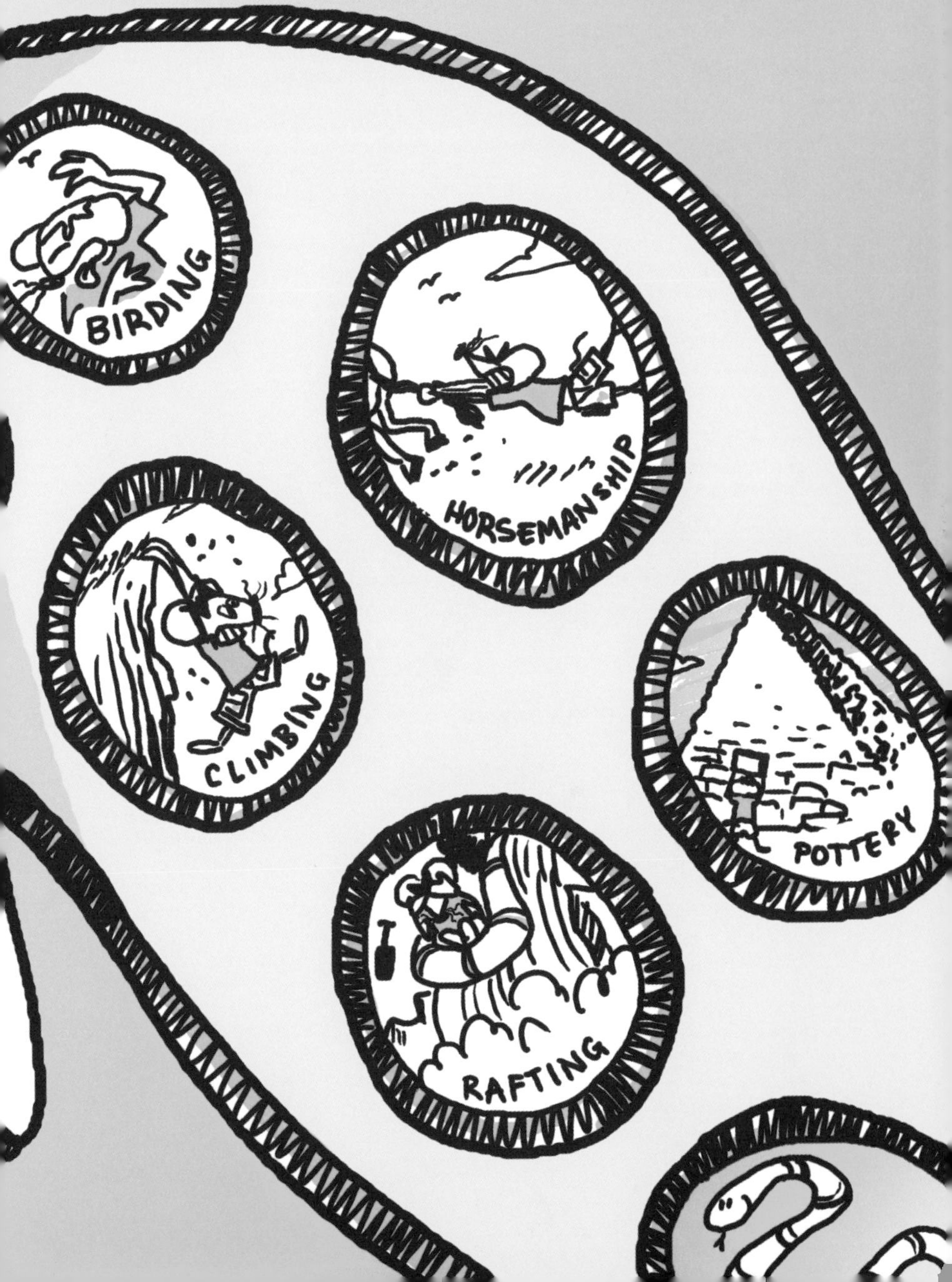
BIRDING
HORSEMANSHIP
CLIMBING
POTTERY
RAFTING

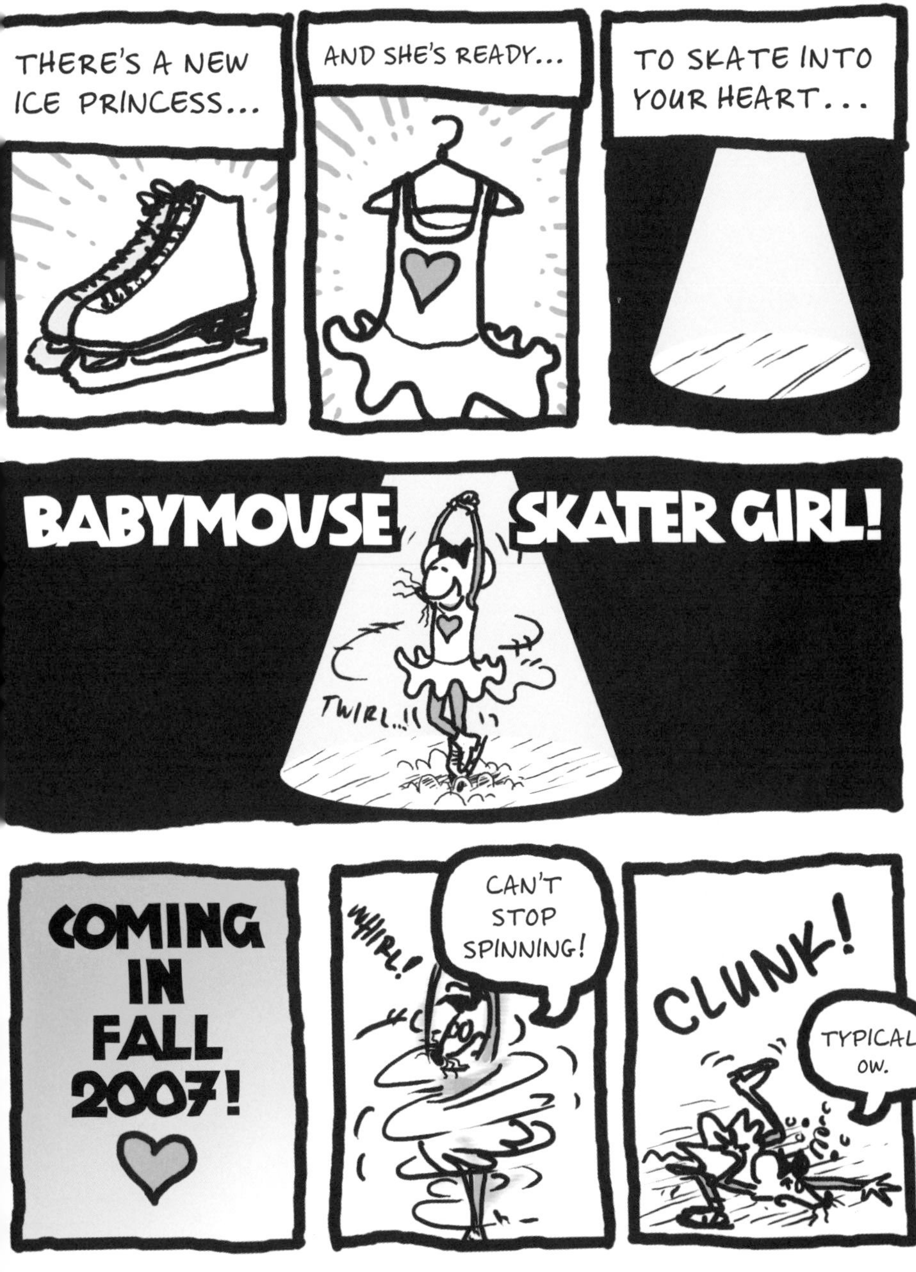
THERE'S A NEW ICE PRINCESS...
AND SHE'S READY...
TO SKATE INTO YOUR HEART...
BABYMOUSE SKATER GIRL!
TWIRL..!!
COMING IN FALL 2007!
WHIRL!
CAN'T STOP SPINNING!
CLUNK!
TYPICAL. OW.